Carla grabbed Harriet's arm. "What was that?" she whispered.

"I don't know." Harriet went back to the connecting door. She twisted and pulled on the knob. "It's locked." she said.

"Are you sure it isn't just stuck?"

Harriet pushed, pulled, twisted and rattled, but the knob didn't budge. She turned around and noticed two doors at the back of the kitchen. The one in the left-hand wall led to a screened porch. She went onto the porch, crossed and tried its door.

"Locked," she reported.

The door in the right wall opened onto a dark stairway that led downward. She shut it again quickly.

"I'm not going down there. We're going to find another way out of here that doesn't involve a dark, damp stairwell into the unknown."

Carla took a thin spatula from the dish rack and went back to the door between the kitchen and the sewing room. She slid the flexible blade between the door and the jamb. It clicked as the blade hit metal.

"Someone's turned the deadbolt," she said, her eyes round.

"Don't panic." Harriet looked around for other possible ways out. She turned a full circle, noting the high clerestory windows. Her eyes came back to the door Carla was standing at.

"Oh, jeez," she said. A thin curl of smoke was seeping under the door. "Get away from the door."

ALSO BY ARLENE SACHITANO

Quilt As Desired

Chip and Die

Widowmaker (2009)

QUILTER'S KNOT

A Harriet Truman/Loose Threads Mystery

BY

ARLENE SACHITANO

Zumaya Enigma

2008

Austin TX

QUILTER'S KNOT

© 2008 by Arlene Sachitano

ISBN 978-1-934841-10-5

Cover art and design by April Martinez

Zumaya Enigma is the mystery and suspense imprint of Zumaya Publications LLC, Austin TX. Look for us online at http://www.zumayapublications.com

This book is dedicated to the late
Doreen Morris

Acknowledgments

I would like to thank the following people for their input, support and information while I was writing this book. First and foremost, my family: husband Jack, sister Donna, children Karen and Malakai, Annie and Alex, David and Tanya and Ken, Nikki and Kellen. Special thanks to my sister-in-law and brother in-law, Beth and Hank Bohne for everything from hosting me in their home to providing medical information to rambling around the country marketing my book. Thanks to my nephews Brett, Nathan, Jason and Chad, who have remained true believers.

In addition, I'd like to thank my critique group, Katy and Luann, as well as my local Sisters in Crime chapter. I would also like to thank Dr. Doug Lyle, who shares his knowledge of forensics freely with his fellow Sisters in Crime. The Portland Police Bureau's central precinct has been very helpful in providing information, particularly Sgt. Brian Schmautz, Sgt. George Weatheroy and Detective James Lawrence. Once again, thanks to Susan and Susan, my close friends and confidantes, who have to put up with my unwelcome absences at coffee when I'm writing and my endless rambling about my characters when I'm present. Many thanks go to in-laws Bob and Brenda for their unwavering support and down-home Texas cooking.

Last but never least, thanks to Liz at Zumaya, without whom none of this would happen.

Chapter One

"Tell me again why we have to go to a workshop with Lauren," Harriet Truman said. "She blames me for her last quilt being ruined. And she's the one who's been copying TV cartoons for her images. You'd think she'd be thanking me for pointing it out—if I *had* pointed it out, which you may remember I didn't. Bertrand probably did her a favor when he destroyed her Kathy the Kurious Kitty knock-off. Now she won't be sued for plagiarism." She brushed her hair away from her face.

"Now, honey," Mavis Willis said and set her teacup down on the piecrust table in the sitting area of Harriet's long-arm quilting studio. "Lauren knows you didn't ruin her quilt. And she is trying to mend her ways. She was already in a two-year series in creative fiber design she's finishing this year. She's even signed up for the guild certification program. Her best work will be scrutinized by judges in London.

"We need to support that. Besides, it'll be fun, and heaven knows we could use a little fun. And most of the Loose Threads are going."

The Loose Threads was the quilting group Harriet's Aunt Beth had belonged to forever and that Harriet had joined upon her return to Foggy Point, Washington.

"I'm not signing up for two years of anything," Harriet said and punched the stop button on her long-arm quilting machine. "Besides, if Kathy the Kurious Kitty was the best she could come up with after a year of training, I'm not impressed with her school."

1

"Oh, honey," Mavis protested. "She made that cat quilt two years or more ago, before she started her schooling. She spent a lot of money making patterns before she knew better—she was hoping she could sell the patterns and get her money back. That's why she was so sensitive about her quilt. She knew what it was.

"And in any case, the school doesn't let students show their classwork outside the program until they graduate."

Harriet ran her hand over the stitching she'd just completed and decided it would do. She crossed the room and flung herself into the leather wingback chair opposite her older friend.

"And, honey, the great part is," Mavis continued, "you don't need to sign up for a two-year program. The center has a set of week-long workshops they do a couple of times a year. They'll be bringing in teachers from all over the country. That's what we're going to. It'll be fun. You'll see."

"Do I have to send my work to London? Harriet asked.

"Of course not. That's just for the two-year program, and then only if you want that certificate."

"What kind of classes do they have?"

Mavis poured hot water from an electric pot sitting on the table over the used tea bag in her floral china teacup.

"They have all sorts." She pulled a folder from the canvas tote that held her current hand-stitching project. "Let's see here." She adjusted the tilt of her bifocals. "You could take hand piecing classes. There are several people teaching that. Marla Stevens is coming from Indiana to teach dye techniques."

"Don't you think it's a little soon for me to be taking time off from the business?" Harriet asked. "I mean, it's only been two months since I took over, and during those two months, Aiden's mom was murdered and my studio was trashed and I was held at gunpoint—let's not forget that part. I'm just now getting a normal routine going. I hate to upset the apple cart."

Mavis folded back the cuff of her faded green-and-brown plaid flannel shirt. "That's all true, but with the Loose Threads going to the workshop, your workload will be reduced, and your aunt Beth is willing to come out of retirement and stitch anything that has to be done. I asked her. The Wal-Mart in Port Angeles has tablecloths on sale, so Beth and I went yesterday to get pastel cloths for the guild's mother-daughter tea. We were talking about the workshop, and she said since she's just back from her cruise and still getting settled into her new place, she was only going to come to the open house part. I asked her if she would be willing to cover any emergency stitching that needed doing, and she said of course she would, so there you have it. You're free to come."

Harriet wasn't sure she'd ever get used to having what felt like everyone in town not only knowing her business but planning her life. After having been raised by parents who only occasionally noticed she existed, she sometimes felt smothered by the attention of her aunt Beth, whom she'd lived with off and on during her childhood, and the Loose Threads. The fact that Foggy Point was a small town didn't help. With fewer than 10,000 people, it was also geographically isolated, exactly the feature that had caused Victorian sea captain and reputed pirate Cornelius Fogg to choose the area for his home base.

Located between Port Angeles and Sequim, Foggy Point itself was shaped like the head and front claw of a tyrannosaurus rex, which provided multiple lagoons and coves perfect for hiding the tall sailing ships that had plied the waters of the Strait of Juan de Fuca laden with treasure more than a century earlier. Just one road connected it to the highway, which meant winter storms often left the community cut off from the rest of the state. So, the local citizenry kept its collective nose firmly planted in each other's business.

"But Aunt Beth has only been retired for a couple of weeks. And she's not even unpacked."

Aunt Beth had given Harriet the large Victorian home that housed her long-arm quilting business, Quilt As Desired, along with said business, two months earlier when Beth had decided on the advice of her doctor to retire and enjoy life. She had purchased a small cottage on the strait side of Foggy Point then promptly left for a month-long cruise of Europe.

"You can talk to Beth yourself, but she agrees it would be good for you to get out and have some fun. Besides, you might meet potential customers. Look at it as a business trip."

Harriet knew she didn't need to talk to her aunt. Mavis was one of Beth's oldest and dearest friends. If Mavis said Aunt Beth was willing, it was true.

She held out her hand for the brochure. "Let me look," she said.

The next hour passed in a blur of class descriptions and tea, but in the end, and with help from Mavis, Harriet had chosen a selection of workshop activities that would fill up her week of attendance. She set the registration form on her desk.

"I'll fax this in the morning," she said.

"Make sure to say you want to be with the other Loose Threads on the line where they ask for housing preferences, and note that they're at the quilting school," Mavis began gathering up her stitching and stowed it in her bag. "The school is for arts and crafts, not just quilting, so there will be other workshops going on at the same time. You could end up bunking with the painters or potters if you don't specify." She buttoned her shirt, which had belonged to her husband and doubled as her jacket, gathered her bag and purse and headed for the door. "I have to run. Look who's here."

Aiden Jalbert held the door as she stepped out.

Harriet tried unsuccessfully to change the fluttering in her stomach to anger. Aiden had no-showed for a dinner date three weeks before, and she hadn't heard from him since.

She reminded herself there was no reason she *should* have heard from him, given she had told him herself she was too old to date him. He was, after all, ten years her junior. Yet in spite of her logical self talk, her heart soared at the sight of him.

Strands of straight black hair fell over his forehead. He flicked a lock off his face, and she could see the dark circles under his odd white-blue eyes.

"Can I come in?" he asked and hesitated.

"Suit yourself," she said and continued straightening papers on her desk.

He collapsed his tall frame into the leather chair and closed his eyes. "Feels good to sit," he groaned, and her anger fled.

"Would you like a cup of tea?"

"What I'd like is to curl up with you and sleep for about a week," he said without opening his eyes. "Since that's not likely, I'll take the tea."

She crossed the room and checked the electric kettle; there was

4

enough water for one cup.

"You're darn right it's not likely."

"There's a good reason I didn't show up for dinner."

"You don't owe me any explanations. Jorge told me you'd called, and he fixed me a chile relleno with a new sauce he's working on and he ate dinner with me and it was fine."

"I would have called you myself, but I was in the middle of something."

"Look, it's okay. I understand—things come up." She pulled a ceramic mug from a shelf on the wall behind the wingback chair. "Lots of things, apparently, since that was three weeks ago." She put a teabag in the cup and poured water over it.

"Do you read the newspaper?" Aiden asked and straightened in his chair.

"Are you trying to change the subject?"

"I'll take that as a no." He took the mug of steaming tea. "Because if you did read the paper or watch the local news, you'd know there's been an epidemic of tainted pet food. We've got cats and dogs both going into kidney failure. All of us have been working round the clock, and we've still lost eight dogs and four cats."

Harriet could see the toll that loss had taken etched into the lines on his face. "I don't know what to say."

"I'm sorry," he said. "I shouldn't be ragging on you. I should have found a minute to call. There's no reason you *should* know what's going on at the vet clinic."

"I knew DeAnn's dog had been in the hospital, but I didn't realize you had so many others."

"We have no way of predicting how bad this is going to get. I don't think we're out of the woods yet, but we've had a little slowdown this week. It's probably temporary, but Dr. Johnson decided to go ahead and send me and one of the assistants to Angel Harbor to do a spay-neuter clinic he agreed to months ago."

"You've got to be kidding," Harriet said and sat down again.

"Why would I kid about a spay-neuter clinic?"

"It's just that the Loose Threads are going to a quilting workshop in Angel Harbor next week."

"Geez, doesn't anyone in Foggy Point work? Besides you and me, of course."

Aiden hadn't been living in town much longer than Harriet had, having spent several years in Africa doing vet work. Most of the members of the Loose Threads were a mystery to him.

"Well, Robin and DeAnn are stay-at-home moms. Connie and Mavis are retired, you knew that." She counted her quilt group friends on her fingers. "Sarah has some kind of job at a company that runs assisted-living facilities in the area. Her uncle owns the business, and Aunt Beth said Sarah's mom made her brother hire Sarah because she kept getting fired from other places because of her charm. I'm guessing he's happy to have her take as much vacation as she wants. The sad part is, she has her masters in sociology. She probably could do a good job if she could get over herself."

"What about Lauren?" he asked. "She must do something besides trying to sell unoriginal quilt patterns."

"As a matter of fact, she's apparently some kind of freelance designer in the high-tech industry. I think Aunt Beth said she designs microchips or something like that. She's self-employed, so she can take off whenever she doesn't have a pressing contract."

"Who would have guessed." He took a sip of tea and grinned. "Things are suddenly looking up. You're a Thread, aren't you?"

"I guess I am. In any case, I'm going."

"Will you let me take you out to dinner to make up for our missed date?"

"I'm just now signing up. I haven't talked to anyone but Mavis. I don't know how structured our evenings will be."

Aiden made a sad face.

"If it's possible, yes, I'll try again, if only to avoid having to watch a grown man cry."

Chapter Two

"Are you sure you don't mind working again so soon?" Harriet asked Aunt Beth the next morning as the two women sat in the sunny yellow kitchen. Harriet's fuzzy gray cat Fred wove between Aunt Beth's ankles under the table.

"It's no trouble. I had a full month to rest while I was on my European cruise." She wheeled her arm around. "My shoulder feels great, and besides, I think most of the Loose Threads are going to the workshop so no one will be breathing down my neck waiting for anything. And it'll give you a chance to network with other quilters from our area."

"Mavis said you'd say that. I guess I'll fax my registration in, then. This late maybe they won't have room for me, so it won't even matter."

The two women got up and passed through the door that connected the kitchen to the studio. Harriet picked up the registration form from her desk and pulled a fax cover sheet from the shelf behind the desk.

"Oh, I think they'll make room," Beth assured her. "They're already paying the teacher to appear, so the more people they cram into the class the more money they make."

"That sounds kind of harsh," Harriet said with a smile at her tell-it-like-it-is aunt.

"Wait until you get assigned a bed in the sleeping room that's ten flights of stairs up and is really an attic to the attic."

Harriet pulled her papers back from the fax machine.

Aunt Beth laughed. "I'm exaggerating. They only over-booked

us once and they got such an uproar they had to refund people's money, so they never did it again."

Harriet put the papers back into the fax machine and hit the send button.

"I'm still not sure I should be leaving," she said. "I'm just barely used to being back in Foggy Point. My mail still has yellow forwarding stickers on it." She paced the length of the workroom.

"Would you settle down? You aren't moving to the other side of the moon, you're just going to a workshop in Angel Harbor. It's only a two-hour drive from here and you're only going for a week."

"Two hours and a ferry ride," Harriet began unhooking the tension clips and loosening the roller from a yellow-and-white Sunbonnet Sue quilt on the long-arm machine. Aunt Beth had christened this particular machine "Mabel" when she'd purchased it as a replacement for "Gladys," her previous machine. Mabel's guide handles and stitching head reminded Harriet of the horned milk cows her boarding school in France had kept.

Aunt Beth had remodeled the parlor of her house to accommodate Gladys when she'd first started the long-arm quilting business more than ten years ago, and fortunately, she'd made the room large enough it had no trouble accepting Mabel's larger frame. The twelve-foot-long table could hold a king-sized quilt with no trouble, and its fifty-two-inch width gave Harriet lots of room to work any pattern her customers could imagine.

She finished unpinning the current project from the frame, spread it on her large cutting table and ran her hand over the surface, looking for threads that needed clipping. She had checked for threads on the back as she'd unrolled it from the machine, but she always checked both sides a second time on the flat table before folding up a quilt and returning it to its bag, just to be sure.

"Well, I'm going down to Pins and Needles," Beth announced. "Margaret is sending Carla to the workshop, and I want to buy the girl a sewing bag."

Margaret was the owner of Pins and Needles, Foggy Point's quilting store. She had hired Carla after she'd been laid off from her job at the Vitamin Factory, a business that had been owned and operated by Aiden's mother until her untimely death a few weeks prior. Harriet, too, had noticed the young single mother carried her sewing supplies in a grocery sack.

"Here, let me make a donation," she said, going back into the kitchen and rummaging in the coat closet, emerging with a black nylon duffel bag. "I got a new overnight bag when I went to Tacoma with Robin and DeAnn last week. Carla will need something to put her clothes in, too. This one…" She held up the bag. "…has a few more trips left in it."

"That's very kind of you," Beth said, "I did raise you well, didn't I?" Beth took the bag, picked up her purse and jacket and went out the door.

"Well, Fred, all I can say is it's a good thing Aunt Beth can't read minds, 'cause she wouldn't think I was so nice if she knew what I was thinking about Lauren. That woman's nuts if you ask me. And I still don't see why we have to go reward her for bad behavior."

Fred meowed once and went to the connecting door.

"It's not lunch time yet," Harriet told her furry friend and went back to start on the next project on her to-be-stitched shelf.

Chapter Three

Harriet got up early on Monday morning. She showered and washed her hair before she came downstairs.

"Okay, Fred," she said when she reached the kitchen, "Aunt Beth will come and check on you this afternoon. Your automatic feeder is full, but don't eat it all in one sitting. Your water bowl is fresh, and Auntie will refresh it every day." Fred wove between her legs, wiping his face on her slippers. "And I'll leave my slippers by the door and you have my permission to have your way with them."

"Who are you talking to?" Mavis asked as she came in. Her customary plaid flannel shirt had been replaced by a long, loose jacket in a rust-and-green batik fabric that accentuated the touches of auburn that still streaked her otherwise gray-white hair, worn with wide-legged black pants. "The studio was open, so I let myself in," she added.

"I was just reviewing Fred's instructions with him." Harriet double-checked the stove burners and turned the overhead light off.

"Robin's in the drive with the car running. Do you need help with your bags?"

"No, I'm not bringing much. Should I be?"

"Not the first time," Mavis said and led the way to Robin's blue mini-van.

In spite of her misgivings, Harriet enjoyed the trip to Angel Harbor. The drive through the cool dark forest always seemed magical. She found herself relaxing.

The women got out of the car on the big green-and-white ferry that carried them to Whidby Island. Harriet scanned the shiny water for signs of fins. She'd seen the orcas that swam the waters of the sound when she was little, but was still waiting to see them as an adult. She wanted to see if they were still as awe-inspiring or if her own diminutive size had been a factor.

"I don't know about you, but I've seen enough killers to last me a lifetime," Robin McLeod said as she, DeAnn and Sarah joined Harriet at the rail and learned what she was looking for. The group was still mourning the murder of their long-time member, Avanell Jalbert.

"Amen to that," DeAnn agreed. "I think this week away will be very healing for all of us."

"I've heard this week will be very hard," Sarah Ness griped. "My friend Lillian took the workshop last year, and she said the teachers are very demanding."

"Great," said Harriet, "Something to look forward to."

The various members of the Loose Threads never failed to give her a look at all sides of any situation that came up. No matter what happened, Robin would exude the calm she gained through her daily meditation and yoga sessions. Sarah, the group narcissist, could be counted on to explain why anything that went on was really being done to her, for her or because of her. Mavis and, by proxy, Aunt Beth would have words of wisdom for her, and as long as Connie was along, she knew she would be well-hugged. Lauren would keep her humble, with her harsh opinions on everything. She didn't know DeAnn very well but hoped to remedy that this week, as they would be roommates. She had to admit, there were advantages to having moved back to Foggy Point, even if the price was giving up her anonymity.

"We better go back to the car," Robin said. "The ferry's going to be docking soon."

"Do you think Carla's going to survive riding with Sarah?" DeAnn asked her traveling companions once they were back in the car.

"She'll definitely know more about the life and times of Sarah Ness then anyone ought to," Mavis chuckled.

The Angel Harbor Folk Art Center consisted of three large pavilions hidden in a stand of old growth forest five miles south of the community of Angel Harbor. The pavilions were large round buildings surrounded by a series of smaller outbuildings. Robin pulled her mini-van into the visitors parking area in front of Building B, the Fiber Arts Center.

"Let's go get our room assignments and keys," she said and got out of the car.

Harriet followed the other Loose Threads as they picked up their class schedules, room keys and meal tickets and returned to the car. Robin drove them down a narrow lane through the cool dark forest, parking in front of a cedar-shingled building that looked more like a grounded Tree House than a cottage.

"Wow," she said as she got out of the car and had to tilt her head to see the top floors of the place she would call home for the next week.

"They've really done a nice job of blending their buildings into the woods," DeAnn explained. "Our dorm is actually called The Tree House." She breathed deeply of the damp, fragrant forest. "I love spending time here. It's so peaceful I could stay forever."

Inside, Harriet carried her overnight bag up a series of stairs that narrowed with each flight she ascended. She had checked the box on her registration that said she was able to climb stairs and realized now they were serious when they'd asked.

The rooms were paneled in rough cedar plank and were furnished with two single beds, two desks, night stands and lamps and a row of pegs under the window that looked out into the woods and divided the room into two identical halves. Their bathroom was down the hall, but at least they didn't have to share it with anyone else. A vase of dried wild flowers sat on a small wooden stand near the door.

"How does it look?" Mavis asked when Harriet came back down the stairs.

"It looks cozy—I think the comforters are real goose down. You'd think they would have artistically handcrafted bed quilts."

Mavis looked away.

"What?" Harriet asked.

"What Mavis doesn't want to tell you is that the first floor

12

rooms *are* filled with unique handcrafted items," Robin said. "The decorator hasn't gone upstairs yet."

"They probably don't tour prospective guests beyond the first floor," DeAnn said as she came down the stairs. "If the dried weed decoration in our room is any indication, these folks aren't rolling in money. Either that, or they pour their money into their art."

"What she's trying to say is, they're stingy with the heat and most meals are some kind of soup," Lauren informed them. "And be careful when you sit on the sofa in front of the fireplace. Its springs are killer."

Count on Lauren to hit the low points, Harriet thought.

"Come on, ladies, we should go on down to the fiber arts pavilion—new student orientation will start in…" Mavis glanced at her watch. "…fifteen minutes, and if she has to lecture Carla and Harriet on punctuality it will be that much longer until we get our tea."

The women gathered their purses and sweaters and left the Tree House.

"Who is *she*, and does she lecture a lot?" Harriet whispered to DeAnn as they walked along the wooded path that led to their destination.

"*She* is Selestina Bainbridge, the head of the fiber arts department and owner of the whole shebang," DeAnn replied, and waved her arms to indicate the woods around them. "Legend has it she inherited it from her husband who died years ago in the arms of his lover at the no-tell motel out by the highway. Apparently, he was sent to meet his maker by the lover's unforgiving spouse."

"So she doesn't have any issues, right?" Harriet said with a laugh.

DeAnn just rolled her eyes skyward.

Chapter Four

℘lease come in and take a seat," said a short, wiry woman with dull blonde hair that was just starting to go gray. The woman wore faded blue jeans and a camp-style shirt that appeared to have been made from mottled-blue hand-dyed sheeting. She paced nervously to the back of a pie-shaped room that was set up with a podium at the point of the pie and concentric rows of chairs radiating out from there; a cloth-covered table held several thermal carafes, a tray of cookies and neat rows of mugs, spoons and napkins at the wide end of the room.

"First-time visitors, please sit in the front rows," the woman barked as she walked back up to the front of the room. She adjusted the microphone that was attached to the podium and tapped on its surface. It responded with the amplified hollow sound microphones the world over make when bludgeoned.

"They *have* done this before, right?" Harriet asked Mavis.

"Don't you worry, honey," the older woman replied. "Patience is a nervous thing. She's Selestina's right hand, but she acts like every class or program they do is the first and their very existence depends on its success."

Harriet, Carla and the other first-timers took their places at the front of the room, while Mavis, DeAnn and Robin sat at the rear. Without introduction, a tall, thin woman who turned out to be Selestina appeared at the podium and started the orientation, beginning with her personal fiber art history, which included schooling then faculty positions at several prestigious folk art schools, and ended with her founding the current school.

She then laid out a set of restrictions and regulations that would have made the Marine Corps proud. She ended with the announcement that all first-time students were to meet with her in this room in precisely thirty minutes for an inspection of their tools and supplies.

They were dismissed, and Harriet found the other Loose Threads standing around Connie Escorcia at the food table.

"Where did you come from?" she asked.

"I got here just as you were coming down for orientation. I've already heard that old battleax try to scare the bejeezes out of her new students, I didn't need to hear it again. I'd complain to the management if it wasn't her." Connie picked a chocolate chip cookie from a tray on the table and took a bite. Her Latin exuberance and soft heart had made her Foggy Point Grade School's favorite first grade teacher before her retirement. She believed a firm but gentle hand was the best way to tame young hooligans. "Did she have any announcements I need to know about?" she asked when she'd swallowed.

"She told us the ceramics students would be having an exhibition tomorrow night in Building A. We're welcome to attend and encouraged to make a donation for the privilege," DeAnn said.

"You mean our tuition wasn't enough of a donation?" Harriet asked.

"Shouldn't you and Carla be getting your bags?" Sarah prompted. "Selestina doesn't like to waste her time."

Carla jumped up and headed for the door.

"Wait up," Harriet called, and followed the younger woman out.

They made the trip back to the Tree House and returned with their supplies with moments to spare. They carried their bags up to a row of tables that had replaced the podium.

"Listen up, ladies," Patience Jacobsen said. "Take a place along the table. Place your stack of fabric on your left and then line up your thread to the right of the stack. Put your scissors and rotary cutter in front of you and lay your six-and-a-half-by-eighteen rulers and your six-and-a-half-inch square to the right."

This was starting to sound a little weird. Carla had taken the place to Harriet's right. Harriet sneaked a glance in her direction.

Her face was chalky white, and she nervously twisted a stringy lock of hair.

"Don't worry," Connie said. She put her hands on Carla's bony shoulders. "Selestina's bark is worse than her bite, and she isn't going to risk losing a paying customer. Just let her paw through your stuff, promise you'll change the blade in your cutter, even if it's new, and then we can go back to the Tree House and have a good cup of tea."

Carla forced a crooked smile to her lips, and Connie retreated to the back of the room.

To say the ensuing orientation was a blood bath would be an understatement. The first student, a pear-shaped woman whose bright-red lipstick was in stark contrast to her faded pink cotton house dress, had dared to bring old-fashioned polyester sewing thread, the kind that comes on a gold plastic spool and has been sold in every five-and-dime in America for decades. Harriet knew that sewing cotton fabric with polyester thread is an invitation for the quilt to fall apart before its time. Polyester is stronger than cotton and works like a saw against the softer fiber given the everyday motion of a functional quilt.

It was also true that beginners needed to learn about high quality cotton thread, but Selestina apparently felt she needed to emphasize the point by sweeping the spools off the table and throwing them across the room in the general direction of the garbage can.

The second student had pre-washed her fabrics. It was an acceptable technique and at times even a preferred method when quilting. Washing ensured that all the sizing chemicals—the compound that keeps fabric smooth and flat when it's rolled onto the bolt—are washed out and any dye not fully set is removed. If the fabric is going to shrink, it will happen with this first washing before it's been cut and stitched.

However, high-quality cottons purchased from a reputable fabric store are unlikely to either shrink or bleed, so the debate about the value of pre-washing raged on.

In the case of the second student, pre-washing had revealed that one of her three pieces of fabric was of much lower quality than the rest. Low-quality material shrinks to the point of distortion, and no amount of ironing will cause it to look smooth and square once the sizing is gone. Low-quality cotton will never result in a prize-winning project.

All of which Selestina pointed out at length.

"I understand why I shouldn't make a show quilt or even a quilt I'm giving as a present out of discount store fabric, but why can't I practice on it?" the skinny blond woman whined.

"Inferior fabric will lead to inferior technique," Selestina proclaimed.

Patience quietly picked up the offending fabric and carried it to the back of the room. Harriet didn't see if it went into the garbage or not, but the woman cried out then covered her mouth with her hand.

Now Selestina stood in front of Harriet. The teacher's gauzy black unconstructed jacket had small violet flowers embroidered along its cuffs and hem. She wore the jacket over a tailored black wool skirt and white blouse. She took a step closer.

Bring it on, Harriet thought.

Because of her parents' constant travels, Harriet had been the perpetual new kid at schools around the world, and as a result had faced more than her share of bullies.

Selestina looked at Harriet's fabric and tools then took a long look at her; she stared right back. Selestina fingered Harriet's rotary cutter and put it down. Harriet knew her fabric was top quality and her tools and supplies first rate. She also knew Selestina had recognized that Harriet wasn't going to be a student she could intimidate.

Perhaps it was due to their confrontation, or maybe Selestina would have blown up at the next person no matter what else had happened. In any case, Carla was firmly in her sights.

"Young woman, you cannot possibly believe that printed fabric is appropriate for beginning machine quilting."

Carla's eyes got large.

"And what is this?" Selestina continued, her voice rising. She picked up the well-used ruler Margaret, the owner of Pins and Needles, Foggy Point's quilt store and Carla's employer, had provided for her. "You can't even read half the numbers. You will replace it before your first class."

She picked up two of Carla's thread spools. They were German, and the brand had to be one of the top quilting threads sold. Harriet was curious how Selestina would be able to find fault with them. She never found out. A hand reached out and grabbed the thread from Selestina.

"That's enough," DeAnn Gault said firmly. "Nothing in the catalog says her fabric has to be plain, and even so, any qualified teacher would know that both sides of the fabric can be used and would just have her turn her print over," She flapped Carla's folded print fabric over, revealing its plain back.

Carla looked at her shoes. "It's okay, DeAnn," she mumbled.

DeAnn turned to her. "No, it's not okay. She doesn't get to talk to you that way. You paid good money to learn how to quilt, not to be belittled because you don't know how yet." She turned back to Selestina. "I can't stop you from abusing your students, but I don't have to watch you do it. I'm leaving, and I will have a full refund or you will be hearing from my lawyer." She whirled around to face the shocked group of quilters at the back of the room. "If you guys are smart, you'll leave, too, instead of subjecting yourselves to the abusive ramblings of this windbag."

She headed for the back of the room. When she reached it, she hesitated. "By the way, she has a piece of coarse sandpaper in her left pocket that she slips under the fabric before she tests your cutter. That's why brand-new blades make ragged cuts."

The room fell silent, the only motion the reflexive clutching of Selestina's hand in her left pocket. Patience walked along the table, quietly helping the students return their supplies to their bags. She motioned for them to leave then gestured to the ones at the back of the room that they should follow suit.

✂ ✂ ✂

"Well, that was weird," Sarah said when they were all outside and headed back to the Tree House. "Even for this place, and that's saying something."

"I didn't mean to cause trouble," Carla said, the distress plain on her face.

"Now, honey, you didn't do anything wrong," Connie reassured her.

"Selestina's always like that, but I don't know what got into

DeAnn," Robin said. "She had the usual orientation dressing down last year, but nothing the rest of us haven't gotten."

"Maybe she couldn't stand seeing someone..." Harriet paused. She had been going to say *someone so helpless*, but caught herself. "...so new to quilting," she corrected with a glance at Carla, "attacked in such an unfair manner."

"Seemed like something more than that," Mavis said. "Is she having troubles at home?"

This last was directed at Robin. DeAnn and Robin were friends, but Harriet knew that if she were DeAnn she'd find Robin's hard-bodied perfection a bit of a deterrent to spilling her problems.

"I don't know. She hasn't said anything. I think things are fine."

"Let's go make some tea and see how DeAnn's doing," Connie suggested. "Maybe the walk back gave her time to cool down and reconsider. She'll realize she doesn't have to see Selestina if she doesn't want to, and the school does have good teachers."

"What did I miss?" Lauren asked as she joined the group just as they reached the door. Her straight honey-colored hair was caught into a single long braid.

"You've got to be kidding," she said a few minutes later, when they were all seated in the Tree House common room, tea mugs in hand. A large riverstone fireplace defined the social area of the dormitory. Two worn leather sofas sat at right angles to the hearth toward the center of the room, with a large round oak coffee table in between and a high-backed twig rocking chair between the sofas and the fireplace.

As the Loose Threads' unofficial second in command, Mavis had recounted the orientation session.

"She stormed out? Just like that?"

"Just like that," Sarah said. "And how about the sandpaper reveal? I never noticed her doing that. Did anyone else?"

"Her sleight-of-hand must rival Houdini's," Mavis said. "My boys tried to sneak everything from candy bars to car keys past my watchful eyes. I thought I could spot anything, but she's good." Mavis had raised five sons, and although they had grown into fine young adults, people in Foggy Point still referred to the Willis boys' antics as the standard for mischief-making.

19

A sharp rap sounded on the Tree House door, followed by the sound of the door opening.

"Is anyone here?" called Patience Jacobsen.

"We're in the common room," Sarah called as she stood up to greet the new arrival. Sarah had an annoying way of attaching herself to any authority figure she met. It was as if she believed her proximity to them would confer some kind of specialness on her. She couldn't take a class or participate in an activity without trying to make the leader her new best friend. It didn't seem to matter if the teacher deserved her worship or not.

Patience came in from the entry hall and stood in the middle of the seating area.

"Is DeAnn here?" she asked. "I've come to smooth her ruffled feathers."

"If that's your attitude, you aren't going to get very far," Lauren told her. "I think everyone here would agree that DeAnn defending Carla from Selestina's attack is a little more serious than 'ruffled feathers.'"

"I didn't mean to minimize DeAnn's distress," Patience said. "I just wanted to see if I could help her understand that Selestina was not attacking the new students—"

"Carla and that woman who had her thread thrown across the room would disagree with that," Lauren snapped. "How would you feel if it was *your* fabric that went into the dumpster? Don't you think that would feel like an attack?" She stood up and got in the woman's face.

"Sit down, Lauren," Mavis ordered. "Let's just all take a deep breath." Mavis had been around Robin too long—deep breathing was Robin's answer to everything.

Connie went into the kitchenette, picked up the teakettle and returned. "Does anyone need a refill?"

Robin held up her mug, and Connie crossed to fill it, causing Lauren and Patience to separate. Lauren stalked into the kitchenette.

"What can I do to make this better?" Patience asked, the distress plain in her voice.

"Take a flying leap," Lauren said in a stage whisper.

"I think we all just need some time to calm down," Mavis said.

"Some of us are a little more excitable than the rest."

"If you want to do something, maybe you could convince your boss to eliminate the public humiliation session," Harriet suggested. "I can tell you, it doesn't make me want to spend the rest of the week here."

"Sit down." Robin indicated a place on the sofa she was seated on. Patience crossed the room and sat. "I know Selestina has been running this school very successfully for a lot of years, and I know she has very high standards, but she didn't use to be mean. I came years ago, and now I've come for the last three short sessions, and I have to tell you, Patience, she's crossed the line. If she keeps up this approach, she's going to lose more than just *our* tuition."

"You're not *all* leaving, are you?" Patience asked. She had pulled a wadded-up tissue from her jeans pocket and began rolling the edge between her thumb and forefinger, causing small white shreds to fall on the rug at her feet.

"I don't know," Robin replied honestly. "We were just talking about things when you got here."

Harriet got up. "I'll go check on DeAnn," she said.

If they called for a vote right now there was no question, she would be the first one on the bus home. She didn't need to learn how to hand stitch bad enough to deal with this drama all week.

She climbed the stairs and called out to DeAnn from the last landing. She wasn't sure what she was warning her for—it was unlikely the woman was sobbing on her bed. But you never knew about these things, and Harriet wasn't familiar enough with her roommate to know if she might be prone to throwing things when she was angry.

She needn't have worried; when she stepped into the room, it was empty.

"DeAnn?" she called again. She went back into the hallway and to the bathroom. The door was open, and the room was empty. "DeAnn?" There was still no answer.

She went back into their shared room. This time she noticed what she hadn't seen before—a folded piece of pale-blue paper rested against the pillow of her twin bed.

Harriet sat on the bed and quickly read the note. She looked around the room and confirmed what the note had explained. DeAnn was gone.

21

Chapter Five

She's gone," Harriet said as she returned to the common room. She held up the note. "This was on my bed. It says she got a ride into Angel Harbor and will catch a ride home with Aunt Beth."

Beth was coming that evening to see the the long-session students' fiber exhibition. In addition to actual technique classes, the folk art school taught students how to solicit and fulfill commissioned works, how to book gallery showings and how to hang an exhibition of their work. Lauren's class was doing the latter this week.

"That was quick," Lauren commented. "We weren't that far behind her. I wonder if she had this all planned."

"Don't be ridiculous," Robin told her.

Lauren glared at her, but kept quiet.

"Here's what I think we should do," Mavis said. "We don't have any more meetings today and classes don't start until tomorrow, so we eat dinner, we go to Lauren's exhibit, get a good night's sleep and then see how we feel about it in the morning."

"That will give us a chance to talk to Beth about it, too," Robin added.

As one of the founding members of the Loose Threads quilting group, Beth's opinion would carry weight even if she hadn't been present for the original incident.

The rest of the group agreed.

"We'll let you know what we decide in the morning," Mavis told Patience.

"That's fair enough." Patience carried her teacup to the kitchenette and went to the door. "I hope you won't let one unfortunate experience color your opinion of our very fine school," she said and left.

"Anyone want to go for a walk?" Harriet asked when Patience was gone. "It's too early for dinner, and I don't think I can sit and stitch right now."

"I'll go with you," Robin said. Mavis and Connie declined.

"I'm going to check on my display," Lauren announced. "Selestina is inspecting our hanging in an hour and a half, and from what I've heard, I won't feel like joining you for dinner afterward, so I guess I'll just see you at the show."

"I'll bring you something you can eat after," Connie offered.

"Thank you," Lauren said as she went out the door.

"There's a loop trail around the perimeter of the school," Robin said. "It goes by a little duck pond down below the painting pavilion."

Harriet put on her gray hooded sweatshirt, and Robin pulled on a hip-length yellow jacket whose bottom edge curved up at her hips. The jacket was the same obscure athletic brand as her black yoga pants and pale blue form-fitted top and was a fabric that was undoubtedly the latest in technical sportswear.

In the months since she'd returned to Foggy Point, Harriet had learned that Robin was a popular yoga teacher; she'd also avoided having to take a class with her.

✂ ✂ ✂

The two women strolled through the woods in silence, each lost in her own thoughts. They had just come into the clearing that contained the painting pavilion when they spotted three men ahead of them. Two were dressed in jeans and denim shirts. The third was taller and thinner and wore tan wide-wale corduroy slacks and a dark-brown sweater vest over a pale-blue oxford shirt.

"The boundary stake should be somewhere around the base of that taller pine tree." He pointed to the center tree in a cluster of pines then, when he turned back to the path, discovered Harriet and Robin. "Hello," he said. "I hope you're enjoying the grounds."

When they didn't respond, the man stepped toward Harriet with his hand outstretched.

"I'm Tom Bainbridge. My mother owns this place."

Harriet shook his hand and found it warm and firm. "I'm no one of consequence," she said.

"I find that very hard to believe," Tom protested with a smile. He leaned back and looked her up and down. Harriet blushed. "A quilter, I'd guess. Am I right?"

"What gave it away? Am I covered in thread clippings?" She brushed at her pants.

"No." He laughed. "With quilters, it's all about what's *missing*. Potters' hands tend to be chapped and red. The painters usually wear their art. Even when they clean up, there are telltale paint signs—you know, under their fingernails, specks in their hair."

"We could have been photographers," Robin pointed out.

The man spread his hands in front of him. "Not possible," he said. "No photographer could walk through those woods and into this beautiful meadow without clicking off at least a dozen pictures."

"Okay, you got us." Harriet conceded.

"If only that were true," he said, a bit wistfully.

"Hey, don't look at me," Robin said. "I'm married."

He spread his hands wider. "A beautiful meadow, perfect weather and two beautiful women—a man can dream, can't he?"

"Do you want us to identify each tax lot or do you just want the outer perimeter?" one of the denim-clad workers asked Tom Bainbridge, interrupting his flirtation.

"I'm going to need the individual tax lots. I should be able to infer the outer boundaries from those, right?"

The man nodded and turned back to his partner, who was stomping the ground around the pine tree.

"I better go help find that stake before he tramples the whole meadow. If you're looking for the duck pond, keep on this path and it will come up on your left after you get past the pavilion." He bowed slightly from his waist. "And, ladies, it's been my pleasure."

"He's a charmer," Harriet said when he was out of earshot.

"Not quite as striking as a certain vet we know."

"But a bit more age appropriate," Harriet noted, and began walking again. "I wonder why he's surveying the property."

"The real question is why is he breaking out the individual tax

24

lots? That's the kind of thing you do when you're planning a residential development."

"Have you heard any rumors to that effect?"

"No, but then, I'm not sure that's the kind of thing they would broadcast. And maybe they're just trying to assess the value for future planning."

"You mean like when the evil son gets the mother declared incompetent then sells her life's work out from under her?"

Robin stopped and turned to look at her. "Let's have a little faith in our fellow man here. Maybe he wants to be sure her insurance is adequate or her tax assessment is accurate." She set off again.

"Well, he seemed a little slick, if you ask me."

A brown mallard duck with six fuzzy ducklings waddled across the path ahead of the two quilters. Harriet pulled a crumbled cellophane packet of crackers from her sweatshirt pocket, the leftovers from last Wednesday's soup and salad lunch at the Sandwich Board, one of Foggy Point's lunchtime hot spots. She sprinkled the crackers over the water, pausing to watch the ducks splash into the pond after them.

Then, they continued on the path in silence, entering the dark woods on the opposite side of the meadow and returning to the Tree House.

Chapter Six

The Loose Threads reassembled in the common room and walked in pairs to a cedar-sided building tucked in the trees just beyond their dormitory.

"In spite of what Lauren said, the food here is good," Mavis advised as she climbed the steps onto the porch of the dining room.

"Lauren may have overstated the situation, but they do serve economical meals," Robin added and pulled the door open.

The room they entered was a large rectangle filled with long plank tables and benches. Double doors on the opposite wall presumably led to the kitchen. The side walls were hung with primitive art. Harriet took a deep breath. Whatever was cooking smelled delicious.

Clusters of people sat along the length of two tables; a third table stood empty.

"There *is* a method to their madness," Mavis said as she led them to the empty table. "There's no seating chart, but this one, as indicated by the quilted runner, is designated as the fiber arts table."

Harriet looked at the other two tables and noticed the top of one was covered with butcher paper decorated with graffiti. The other was topped with black-and-white photos under glass.

"Clever," she said. "I'm not sure how I feel about the segregation, though."

"Patience explained it to me the first time I came here," Mavis explained. "In order to not overwhelm the kitchen, they stagger the activities in each pavilion so only a third of the people arrive at any one time."

"I never knew that," Robin said.

"Just part of the well-oiled machine that is the school," Sarah said and sat down.

A middle-aged woman with a long gray braid that fell to her waist came through the double doors carrying a tray laden with bowls of steaming soup.

"You can help yourself to drinks on the sideboard," the woman said as she began setting the bowls on the table. "The bread just came out of the oven. I'll have it out here in a few minutes," she added over her shoulder as she walked back through the double doors.

"Thanks," Harriet said as she sat down with the glass of ice water she'd just poured at the large oak buffet. The soup was Italian, with chunks of sausage, bowtie pasta and zucchini in a tomato-basil broth. It was hardly the watery gruel she'd expected after Lauren's comments.

When the quilters were finished eating, the woman with the braid brought a wrapped bundle.

"Here's a little sandwich for Lauren," she said and handed it to Connie. "She'll need her strength."

A slender blond man in a khaki work uniform began clearing the table as Harriet and her friends headed for the door.

"There's a new restroom behind the cookhouse," he said in a soft voice without looking up. "Follow the porch around to the back."

✂ ✂ ✂

"This is convenient," Mavis said as they waited for Sarah to come out of the bathroom. "Before, we had to go back to our rooms after meals."

"Seems like they add something new every time we come here," Connie noted.

Robin pulled a round plastic brush from her purse and began brushing her hair. "Maybe if they weren't building all the time, they could afford to feed us something besides soup."

"I liked the soup," Harriet protested, and started down the path as Sarah emerged.

The three classroom pavilions at the Angel Harbor Folk Art Center were of similar construction: large pie-shaped spaces around a central supply room hub, with two large rooms on one side that extended all the way to the exterior windows. The rest of the rooms were bordered by a wide hallway that curved around the building, providing ample wall space for hanging student's work.

"Wasn't your aunt Beth supposed to meet us here?" Sarah asked Harriet as they reached the stairs to the porch that surrounded the fiber arts pavilion.

Harriet looked around and, not seeing her aunt, glanced down at her watch. "She was, but we're early. I told her to meet us at seven, and it's only quarter till. Feel free to go in. I'll wait for her." She glanced hopefully at the door, but Sarah didn't move.

"We'll all wait. I wouldn't want it to be said I'm not a team player," Sarah announced.

"We'd never want that," Aunt Beth said as she walked up behind her. "But since I'm here, you'll have to find another opportunity to display your team spirit."

Robin looked at Harriet and rolled her eyes skyward. "Let's go see what our buddy Lauren has been up to all these months."

Sarah began commenting on the first exhibit the group came to. The assignment must have involved granite, since all six quilts looked like some variation of a granite countertop, the veining created with dense stitching. The backgrounds looked like hand-dyed muslin and varied from rose-gray to almost black.

"Clearly, some students understood the task better than others," Sarah pronounced.

"Let's go the other direction around the hall," Harriet whispered to Carla.

The younger woman smiled briefly and followed Harriet as she strolled in the opposite direction. When Harriet paused in front of a display of hand quilting, she realized Robin had joined them.

"I couldn't take Sarah's commentary," she explained.

"Hey, you don't have to explain it to me." Robin leaned close to a small sampler that had been stitched with a variety of thread weights. "I never thought about using such a heavy thread to do the actual quilting. It looks like three or four strands of embroidery floss. I've used it to do embellishment, but not for the actual quilting."

"I wish we could see the back side."

"It's the same as the front," Carla said, surprising her. She wasn't sure she'd heard the woman utter a dozen words since they'd left Foggy Point.

Carla glanced up when no one said anything. Her cheeks turned pink, and she stared at her feet. "It tells what they did on this card," she said, and pointed at a white printed page that was mounted on a piece of mat board and hung at the end of the display. "They were supposed to make the back side look exactly like the front side."

"I wonder where Lauren's exhibit is," Robin said.

"Probably wherever she's standing," Harriet said, and looked down the curve of the exhibit hall.

"I just want to get there before Sarah. I've been witness to enough train wrecks for one day."

"Let's walk until we spot her. Then we can go back and look at the rest of the stuff at our leisure," Harriet suggested. The other two agreed, and they continued down the hall, searching for Lauren.

"Isn't that the janitor from the dining room?" Harriet pointed at the slender man in the khaki uniform, who was now standing beside Lauren.

"Looks like it," Robin replied. "I wonder what they're talking so intently about."

The three quilters approached, and the janitor turned and left.

"I hope I didn't scare him away," Harriet joked.

"Why would you think that?" Lauren said. "He's just a janitor. Someone spilled a drink and he was cleaning it up."

"Is this yours?" Robin asked and pointed to the piece behind her. "It's wonderful."

Lauren's quilt was simple yet compelling. The background was tones of brown that ranged from beige to almost black. The stitching was cream-colored, and it looked like she had used a thread that was slightly heavier than most people used in functional quilts.

In the quilting world, there were two broad categories of work: functional quilts and art quilts. Functional quilts are just what the name implies; they can be used as bed covers, lap robes, table toppers or for any other task where a warm cover is useful. They're usually made from fabric and thread that can stand up to being washed and dried.

Art quilts, on the other hand, while incorporating traditional techniques also include materials and threads that may be more fragile. Dyes or fabric paints that are water soluble might be used; glues, metallic fabrics and threads, and pretty much anything else the artist can conceive of and attach to their work can be employed. Art quilts often take the form of wall hangings, but in exhibits, art quilts go hand-in-hand with other stitched constructions, such as fabric bowls or vases, boxes and even fabric dolls or quilted garments.

Lauren's work was a medium-sized wall hanging. The primary stitching was in evenly spaced lines around a lopsided figure-eight shape that was just left of center—it reminded Harriet of the grain lines in a piece of wood. She'd stitched a sheer fabric that might have been silk in irregular shapes over the grain lines, and then stitched a darker thread along one edge of the sheer pieces so the silk appeared to float above the brown background. The result looked like a magnified segment of tree trunk, complete with peeling bark. Harriet glanced at the two exhibits on either side of Lauren's and realized that trees were the theme of their grouping.

The other students in Lauren's group had taken an opposite approach and attempted to create groups of trees seen from a distance. The one on the left attempted to portray palm trees. The artist had created three-dimensional palm fronds using a woolly thread. It reminded Harriet of a crewel embroidery kit Aunt Beth had given her when she was thirteen. The fingers of the fronds had given her fits and probably contributed to her dislike of this piece.

The wall hanging on the other side was a bird's-eye view of pine-covered hills. It was competently done, if unremarkable. Lauren's was clearly a level above the rest of the entries in her group.

"She's outdone herself," Robin whispered from behind them.

Lauren was busy talking to a distinguished-looking older gentleman with a white goatee, who was pointing at her work. Mavis, Sarah, Connie and Aunt Beth came around the curve in the hall; Harriet waved to her aunt, and they came over to Lauren's display.

"Wow!" said Connie. "No more cartoon kitties, huh?"

"Looks like school has been good for our Lauren," Mavis agreed, and leaned in for a closer look.

The man smiled and gave a small nod to them as he walked off.

"Who was that?" Robin asked.

"He owns a gallery in Anacortes. He asked if I'd be interested in a commission to make a piece similar to this one for his entry alcove." Lauren's eyes were bright, and her cheeks were flushed with color.

"That's great!" Connie said, and pulled her into a hug. "Congratulations."

"Yeah, congratulations," Mavis echoed.

"Good job," Robin said.

Harriet looked at Aunt Beth, who was uncharacteristically silent. She had a solemn look on her face. Harriet raised her eyebrow in question. Beth shook her head once in a gesture Harriet knew meant "Keep your mouth shut and I'll tell you later."

The Loose Threads marveled over Lauren's work for another five minutes before they broke back into their separate groups and continued on their routes past the rest of the displays. The women regrouped a half-hour later by the exit door. Mavis led the way across the porch and down the stairs. When they reached the path back to their Tree House, she stopped.

"Okay, Beth, spill."

Harriet looked from Mavis to her aunt.

"She's at it again," Beth said simply. "It's true it's a lot more sophisticated, and probably took a lot more time to copy, but that is not an original piece of art."

"Whoa, are you sure?" Harriet asked.

"That can't be right," Robin protested. "I remember her talking about dyeing the fabric."

"She spent a lot of time picking the thread," Carla added in a louder than normal voice. She immediately looked down at her shoes as if she'd spoken out of turn.

"I'm not saying she didn't work hard on the piece. I'm saying I've seen it before," Beth said. "It's true she used a different border and binding, but I swear, the dyed fabric, the stitching lines—I remember the distorted figure eight. I might even have a picture of it. It was at a Fiber Guild exhibition in London when I was on my cruise."

"Well, I guess we know a leopard never changes its spots," Sarah said.

"Thank you for that little insight," Connie said and walked off toward the Tree House.

"I saw what I saw," Beth said and followed.

Sarah brushed past Carla, pushing her a little harder than was necessary. Harriet started to follow her, but Carla grabbed her arm.

"It's okay, really."

"It's not okay. She doesn't get to treat you like that."

"She's the one who won't be changing her spots any time soon," Carla said with surprising insight. She looked directly at Harriet for the first time. "She wasn't the center of attention, but she's afraid to do anything to get the attention back in front of Miz Mavis or Miz Beth. So, I did what my mama taught me and turned the other cheek."

And thus, Harriet thought, another generation of victims was trained at their mother's knee. As far as Carla had come, she still had a long way to go. But, at least she was trying, unlike Sarah.

"Let's go," she said. "If we're lucky, Sarah will have gone up to her room already." She turned and went up the path.

"What do you think everyone will do about going or staying?" Carla asked.

"I'm guessing we'll stay. We've all already paid. Aunt Beth will take DeAnn home and sort out what happened."

"Whew, I was afraid we would be going home. It's really nice sleeping in a bed."

Harriet stopped. "What do you mean? Don't you normally sleep in a bed?"

"Nothing. I didn't mean anything," Carla's head was down, her eyes avoiding Harriet's.

"Come on, Carla, where are you sleeping in Foggy Point?" Harriet put her hand on the younger woman's shoulder. "Don't clam up on me now."

Tears began to gently slide down Carla's thin cheeks. "We're living in a car."

"You are raising a baby in a *car*? What car?" She realized this was a dumb question as soon as it was out of her mouth. What difference did it make what car? The fact Carla hadn't owned a car two months ago was irrelevant.

"When the vitamin factory closed for a month after Miz Avanell died, I only had my part-time job at the fabric store, and I couldn't pay my rent. Then, when the factory started back up they only had day jobs, and Margaret said when Sally leaves in July she can give me full-time hours and a little for benefits, too, but I can't do that if I go back to the factory. It's okay, really. My friend Willy loaned me a van to live in, and Wendy goes to free daycare at the Methodist church, so she gets to run around all day."

"You cannot live in a van even for a few months," Harriet stated.

"Please, you can't tell anyone." Carla looked up, wiping at her tears with the back of her hand. "I'll figure something out. Promise you won't say anything."

"I can't promise that, Carla. You need help."

"Please, let me be part of the group this week without feeling like everyone's stray puppy. I know I'm here because Margaret paid for it, but she said it would make me a better employee so it was job training." She turned back to the trail and started to walk again. "I just want to be normal."

Harriet slowed, giving Carla time to enter the Tree House and pull herself together. As she approached the porch, she heard a familiar voice from the trail behind her.

"Les, if you have something to tell me, say it. If you don't, we'll have to have this little reunion later. I've got work to do."

She glanced back. Lauren stepped onto the porch as someone moved back down the path.

"Who was that?" Harriet asked.

"No one. And it would be none of your business if I *were* talking to someone." Lauren pulled the door open and went in. Harriet followed her, turning left into the common area while Lauren went straight up the stairs.

"Remind me again why I'm here," she said as she flopped onto the worn leather sofa. Mavis, Aunt Beth and Connie were seated in easy chairs around the river-rock fireplace. "And by the way, are we staying?"

"Yes, *mija*, we're staying," Connie told her. "DeAnn wasn't out of line with putting a stop to Selestina's behavior, but leaving is a little extreme. We've all spent a lot of money and made a lot of arrangements to be here. I don't think we should throw it all away."

"It's not like we didn't know about Selestina's behavior before we signed up," Mavis pointed out. "Robin's right—she is worse than she used to be, but she's always been over the top. DeAnn knew that."

"More important than all that," Aunt Beth said, and lowered her voice until it was barely above a whisper, "you need to find out more about Lauren's exhibition piece. She swore she was doing original work. I asked her about it last week, and she was pretty convincing, but I know what I saw and it was that exact piece." She stood and picked up her handbag. "I've got to go. I still have to meet up with DeAnn. I'll figure out a way to send a copy of that picture to you guys."

Harriet walked her aunt to the door. Then, she went to the kitchenette and poured hot water from over a peppermint tea bag she put in a pottery mug. She carried it into the common room and sat down again.

"Something strange happened when I was coming in tonight," she told Mavis and Connie. She related her encounter with Lauren, including Lauren's insistence she hadn't been talking to anyone.

"Honey, that doesn't necessarily mean anything. In spite of Selestina's behavior, this isn't a jail," Mavis said. "Maybe Lauren has a boyfriend. Maybe she's met someone in Angel Harbor. She's been taking classes for a while now."

"I've got my first class with Selestina tomorrow." Harriet took a drink of her fragrant tea. "I could feign ignorance and ask her about the European exhibit Aunt Beth saw. It wouldn't be much of a charade, since I *don't* know anything about it."

"I'll see if I can get anything more out of Lauren," Connie said. "We're taking a machine embroidery class together tomorrow."

"You'll be in hand quilting tomorrow morning, won't you, honey?" Mavis asked Harriet.

"I'll be hand quilting all day tomorrow—Carla, too."

34

"Don't worry," Mavis assured her. "Selestina likes to intimidate people in the orientation session, but she really is an expert in her field, and a good teacher to boot."

"Well, it can only go uphill from here. What will you be taking?"

"Tomorrow..." Mavis read from the schedule lying in her lap. "...I will be dyeing."

"Let's hope not," Connie teased with a smile.

Chapter Seven

The next morning dawned clear and cool, and the Loose Threads walked briskly through the dark woods from the Tree House to the fiber arts pavilion. The women had opted for toast and tea in the Tree House; no one had wanted to chance an encounter with Selestina or Patience before they'd fortified themselves.

Harriet pulled the sleeves of her gray hooded sweatshirt over her hands. She glanced at Carla; the younger woman was dressed in new-looking blue jeans and a gray hoodie with the hem of a red T-shirt hanging out below. Harriet glanced at her own jeans and slightly-too-long red T-shirt and realized they had the same personal shopper. She was definitely going to buy some new clothes when she got home, and not at Wal-Mart, either.

"Okay, everyone, shall we meet back here at eleven-thirty and walk to the dining hall together?" Mavis asked.

Lauren declined, saying her class had arranged for a local delicatessen to bring sandwiches in. Harriet could understand that, if you were here once a month for a period of months, you could get tired of soup, even if it was really good soup. Everyone else, however, agreed to the plan, and the group broke up to find their various classrooms.

Sarah and Robin turned left to go to their class in fusible techniques. Lauren went on to the right, but Connie stayed with Harriet and Carla.

"Here we are, chiquitas," she said when the trio reached the stitching classroom. "Good luck,"

Patience Jacobsen was waiting inside the door when Harriet and Carla entered. The classroom held a dozen two-person tables with chairs arranged in two rows with an aisle down the middle. Several students were already there, unpacking notebooks, scissors, needles and thread from their bags. At the front was a single table. A flannel curtain hung behind the table, and several examples of hand quilting were pinned to its surface. The side walls displayed a variety of hand quilted pieces in various sizes, colors and materials. Harriet and Carla went over for a closer view.

"Look how small and even the stitches are," Carla said, and for once didn't follow her comment with a downward glance or a face-burning blush.

"Yeah, and the fabric looks like it might be silk or something similar." Harriet turned over the corner of the wall hanging. A label read *Selestina Bainbridge, Silk on Silk, October 9, 1993*. She read it to Carla then patted the quilt back into place. "That is some really fine stitching."

Three more students had entered and taken places at tables. The only table left where Carla and Harriet could sit together was in the front, to the left of the teacher's table. Carla looked around like a caged animal.

"Come on," Harriet said and nudged her forward. "We'll be able to see better up here."

Carla looked doubtful but went to the front table, setting her sewing bag on the side away from the teacher.

Patience took roll and had the students introduce themselves. She described what they would be doing in class that day, told them where the restrooms were and asked if anyone had questions. No one did, so she walked down the aisle, went around the curtain and disappeared. She reappeared five minutes later with Selestina in tow.

"The entire art of handcrafting multi-layer constructions, frequently for the purpose of making bed covers, is referred to as *quilting* by the lay population," Selestina began. "Among skilled craftsmen, however, quilting is understood to refer to stitching with thread through a top cloth, a stuffing or batting and a back cloth to create a single joined unit. Quilting in its purest form is always performed by hand." She went on to explain the role of quilting throughout history, including the quilted garments seen in medieval times and the padded cloth armor utilized by the Japanese samurai. After an hour, Harriet had to bite the inside of her cheek to stay awake.

Selestina finally concluded her introductory lecture at ten minutes before eleven. Patience stood up and, in a well-choreographed move, unfurled a lap-sized sample. She held it up and carried it slowly down the center aisle. A simple feather pattern had been stitched on cream-colored muslin.

"When a quilt is made using a single, continuous piece of fabric on the top and another single piece of fabric for its backing, we call it a *whole cloth quilt*. Quilts of this type have been popular in England for hundreds of years," Selestina explained. "In America, however, fabric was scarce until industry developed and fabric mills were built."

Harriet was afraid Patience's arms were going to break before Selestina got them through the Industrial Revolution and up to modern times, but she finally finished; and Patience spread the quilt over the front table.

Selestina glanced at a delicate silver watch that encircled her wrist. "We will now take a break for lunch. You will return at one p.m. sharp," she said. Without another word, she turned and disappeared around the curtain.

"Oh, my gosh," Carla moaned. "My head hurts."

"My tail is going numb from sitting in one position for so long." Harriet stood up and went to the head table. She pulled the curtain aside and looked behind it. As she did, Patience came through a closed door concealed there.

"Can I help you?" she asked. She was carrying a tray that had a wooden hoop, a thimble, a pincushion with needles sticking out of it and a small rack with several spools of thread on it.

Harriet had the good grace to blush. "I just wondered what was behind the curtain," she said and let it fall back into place. "You know, like in the *Wizard of Oz*."

"All the classrooms open into a common center area that's divided into offices and storage space," Patience explained. "It allows teachers to move efficiently from one classroom to the other, as well."

"How efficient," Harriet said.

"If you'll excuse me," Patience said, and Harriet realized she was blocking her path to the front table. She returned to the table where Carla waited.

"Let's go find the others," she said.

Connie was waiting on the steps.

"I thought your group was having lunch brought in," Harriet said.

"It turned out the long-term students in the class made that arrangement, not the actual dyeing class. They made sure we knew we weren't part of their club."

Harriet put her arm around Connie's shoulders. "We still love you, right, Carla?"

"Yeah, Señora Escorcia, we'll eat lunch with you," Carla said with a half-smile. Connie had taught her first graders basic Spanish vocabulary, including the proper form of address for a married woman. Carla's use of the term revealed her past history as one of "Connie's kids," as her former students liked to call themselves.

Lunch was the expected soup. This one was a white chili made with chicken breast, cannellini beans, rotel tomatoes and green chilies. It was seasoned with cumin and oregano and topped with jack cheese and lime juice.

"I'm telling you," Connie said as she pushed back from the table and her empty bowl, "I talked to Lauren for over an hour. I asked her if she was inspired by another quilt. She was insulted, and I finally just told her about the piece Beth saw. She insists her piece was completely original. She even showed me the chunk of bark she used as inspiration. She has it in a plastic sandwich bag in her sewing box."

"Don't stop there," Mavis urged. "How did it look?"

"Mostly, like a piece of tree bark. I have to say her dyeing was a good match to the color."

"Figures." Mavis looked down at her dye-stained fingers. "She's spent all this time copying other people's work, and she'll be the one who turns out to have all kinds of talent."

"The stitching pattern didn't match, though," Connie pointed out. "The tree bark didn't have the figure-eight pattern that was so distinct in Lauren's piece."

"Okay, I guess she can stay in the group, then," Mavis said and smiled. She glanced at the wall clock in the dining room. "Come on, we need to get back."

"Hopefully, we'll get to do something this afternoon," Harriet said to Carla.

Chapter Eight

𝒫atience was waiting just inside the door to the class-room when Harriet and Carla entered. She handed each of them a stapled handout.

"Please take out your hoop, quilting needle, thread, scissors and thimble and put everything else under your table. Do not touch the fabric sandwich you will find at your workspace."

Harriet and Carla looked at each other. Carla's face had a determined set to it, but Harriet just rolled her eyes and led the way back to their workstation, where they found the layered muslin fabric and batting Patience had referred to as a "sandwich."

"This looks promising," Harriet said in a hushed tone. "I'm not sure why I'm whispering, though," she added with a laugh.

"It's because that scarecrow at the door is so intimidating," said a short plump woman at the table behind theirs. She was dressed from head to toe in pale-blue denim covered in machine embroidered motifs of puppies and kittens.

The woman glanced nervously back toward the door, checking to be sure she hadn't been heard. "I came here to learn how to stitch, not to be treated like a misbehaving schoolgirl."

"It's a small price to pay for being able to learn from one of the top experts in the field," said the other woman at her table. Harriet hadn't noticed before lunch, but the second woman was wearing a dark skirt and white blouse that were very reminiscent of Selestina's. "Her work hangs in galleries and museums all over Europe."

Carla's eyes widened. Harriet could see she was impressed.

41

"Trust me," she whispered. "There's nothing magic about having her work in Europe. They obviously have a longer preserved-textile history than we do in America, but their contemporary work is done by people just like us."

The disbelief was plain on Carla's face.

"Okay, so it's done by people like we will be when we finish taking all our classes," Harriet said and grinned. She could see Carla was still skeptical. "I went to boarding school in London and Paris and a bunch of other places, and trust me—they all put their socks on one foot at a time, just like us."

"Please, take your seats," Patience instructed them.

The room fell silent as everyone sat. Patience walked down the aisle, glancing at each table as she passed. She stopped at the second table on the right side of the aisle, picked up a ruler and marking pen from the surface and dropped them into the sewing bag underneath. There was a slight rustle as several other students removed items and stowed them in their sewing bags.

Patience took one last sweeping glance around the room and, satisfied that only the listed items were on each table, swept behind the curtain.

Selestina appeared within moments.

"Hand quilting is an art," she began. "Although in recent centuries it has taken a back seat to elaborate piecing and embellishment techniques, hand quilting is very able to stand on its own. Down through the ages, many beautiful works of art have been created that are no more than careful stitching on a blank piece of cloth. Please hoop the fabric sandwich that is on your table."

Quilting hoops consist of two concentric rings with one fitting closely inside the other, like embroidery hoops. They are commonly made of wood, but can also be made of plastic or combinations of metal and plastic. The purpose of a hoop is to hold the quilt sandwich smooth and to better enable a stitcher to accomplish her task. The larger of the two rings is centered on the area of the quilt sandwich to be worked, the smaller is placed underneath and then the two rings are pushed together, one inside the other, trapping the quilt and pulling it taut.

Harriet quickly snapped the fabric sandwich into place in her wooden hoop then helped Carla center her fabric and set her hoop.

Patience paced up and down the aisle, checking to see that all the students had accomplished the task. When she reached the back of the room, she gave a slight nod and Selestina began speaking again.

Selestina picked an elaborately decorated silver thimble from the tray on her table.

"There are many styles of thimble available in today's marketplace. They can be made of metal, plastic, leather, or…" She held up her silver thimble. "…finely wrought from silver. Which you choose will be based on your own preference. The most important features are fit and function. It must protect you from needle pricks, and it must fit snugly enough that it won't fall off your finger as you move your hand up and down." She slid the little metal cup onto the tip of her second finger.

Patience gestured to the class. "Gather round the front table," she ordered.

The students rose and did as instructed. Harriet and Carla only needed to step around their table, since they were already at the front of the room, so they were looking directly at Selestina when her hand began to shake. She tried to get up, only to fall back into her chair. She clutched her right hand over her chest.

Harriet was just in time to catch her as she started to slide to the floor. With her arms under Selestina's armpits, she kicked the chair out of the way and lowered the older woman to the floor.

"Call nine-one-one," she yelled.

The class stood rooted where they stood.

"Where's your phone?" Carla answered.

"In the front pocket of my bag."

Carla pulled out the phone and dialed. In a clear firm voice, she relayed necessary information to the operator.

"Give me that quilt," Harriet ordered, but the woman in denim had already started pulling the sample quilt from the display board.

"No," Selestina moaned.

To her credit, the woman didn't stop. She tossed the quilt to Harriet; she covered Selestina, who was beginning to shiver. Patience folded up her jacket and started to put it under Selestina's head.

"Not under the head," the woman in embroidered denim said

as she approached. "Here." She pushed Patience out of the way, put the folded jacked under Selestina's feet and tucked the quilt around her. "She's going into shock," she announced. She grasped the teacher's wrist with professional-looking expertise between her thumb and fingers and glanced at her watch.

Harriet could hear sirens. "Come on, come on," she whispered to herself. She wasn't sure what was wrong with Selestina, but the woman's skin was covered with a sheen of moisture, and she continued to shake. Her breathing was rapid, and a small trickle of spit slid from the corner of her mouth.

Everyone jumped when the door slammed open and the paramedics rushed in. Harriet stepped aside and guided Patience away from Selestina.

"Let them do their work," she said.

Two young men in blue jumpsuits and a red-haired woman with pale freckles and crow's feet surrounded Selestina. The redhead spoke to the denim-clad lady, who identified herself as Dr. Jan Hayes.

The young men started IV fluids as a pair of firemen came in pushing a gurney. Dr. Hayes loosened Selestina's skirt and blouse, borrowed a stethoscope and listened to her chest. Harriet could tell by the expression on the doctor's face she didn't like what she heard.

"Let's go ahead and transport her," she said and stepped back while the three paramedics collapsed the gurney next to Selestina and lifted her on to it, raising it back up in one fluid motion. Dr. Hayes trotted alongside as they wheeled out the door and disappeared.

Harriet and Carla were putting their tools back in their bags when Patience returned.

"What are you doing?" she demanded, looking around the room. Everyone was in the process of gathering their things. "Class will continue," she said, her chin held high in defiance. "I'm sure Selestina would want class to continue." But her chin quivered, and her face was unnaturally white.

"Maybe we could take a little break," Harriet suggested, hoping they weren't about to see a repeat performance of the one that had just played out. She went around her table and gently grasped

44

Patience's arm. "Why don't you sit for a minute, gather yourself? Isn't it about time for the scheduled coffee break? Carla here could get you something to drink.

"Okay, folks, let's go on ahead to coffee," she added to the students, who were standing or sitting at their work tables. "Class will resume when we get back."

Carla stood up and nodded. "What can I bring you?" she asked. "Tea? Coffee?"

"A bit of tea would be nice," Patience said, and sat in the chair Harriet had eased her toward.

Carla returned a few minutes later with a steaming cup of peppermint tea and a chocolate cake donut clasped in a paper napkin.

"Good job," Harriet said quietly. The corner of Carla's mouth twitched up slightly in what might have been a smile.

Patience sipped the tea, and the color started to return to her cheeks. She took a big bite of the donut. When she had finished chewing, she wiped her mouth and set the pastry on the table.

"Thank you," she said. "I think we can proceed. I know Selestina will expect me to continue with class until she returns." She said it as if her boss had stepped out to the ladies room and would be coming right back. Harriet was pretty sure Selestina wasn't returning for the foreseeable future; but they were all here, and not having class wasn't going to do anything for anyone.

"I just heard what happened." Mavis came up the aisle to the front table. She looked at Patience. "Can I do anything to help?"

Patience stood up. "No, thank you. I'll just put Selestina's tools away and get my sewing bag." She put Selestina's thimble and scissors back on the tray, picked it up and disappeared behind the curtain.

"Are *you* okay?" Mavis asked Harriet. "And you?" She grasped Carla's hand.

"We're fine," Harriet assured her. "I'm not sure the same can be said for Selestina."

Chapter Nine

I heard a woman in the restroom say Selestina had collapsed and was taken away in an ambulance," Mavis said.

"That's pretty much what happened," Harriet told her. "Everything seemed fine when she started her lecture then all of a sudden, down she went."

"She got real pale," Carla added.

"Well, you never know. Maybe she has a bad heart. When Lucille Graham had her attack last summer, she was at church. We stood up to sing a hymn and down she went like a sack of potatoes."

Mavis glanced at her watch. "Looks like things are under control here, so I guess I'll get back to dyeing. I'm not sure when we'll finish. We've only got a little more to go on today's samples.

"We'll meet you back at the Tree House," Harriet said. "It won't surprise me if we run over, given today's disruption."

Mavis left, and Patience reappeared with a quilting bag that looked like it had been hand-made, using a lavender pre-quilted fabric and with wooden dowels for handles. She pulled out a large wooden hoop that already held a muslin fabric sandwich.

"Success in hand quilting is all about your wrist motion," she began.

She proceeded to demonstrate how to insert a threaded needle into the hooped fabric and, with a gentle rocking motion and correct thimble placement, create a small, neat quilt stitch. She soon had the class practicing their own stitching, and proved to be a competent teacher.

The room was silent except for her words of encouragement as the students strained to master their new skill. Harriet looked over at Carla, who was biting her lower lip as she concentrated on her work. She had completed half of the first feather they had drawn on their fabric. Her stitches were small and very even, and her needle moved up and down in the rhythmic motion Patience had demonstrated.

Harriet looked at her own work. Her stitches were uneven, and she'd only completed the first two curves of her feather. She readjusted her hand position, trying to imitate Carla's movement. Her needle jumped out of the fabric, and as she grabbed for it, her thimble fell off onto the floor. As she reached for it, a hand touched her shoulder.

"Here," Patience said, and dropped the escaped thimble into her palm. "All right everyone. The last technique we need to learn is the quilter's knot. Gather around the front table please."

The class assembled, and she showed them how to make the invisible knot used to start a new thread when hand quilting. She created a small knot by threading a needle, holding the tail end of thread parallel to the needle and coiling the body thread three times around it. Then she pinched the coils of thread against the needle with one hand and pulled the needle through the coils with the other hand. The result was a small neat knot at the very end of the thread.

To start stitching, she dipped the needle into and then out of the quilt top then gently tugged the quilter's knot through the top layer of fabric.

"Remember to stop while there is still enough thread on your needle, so you can pull the remainder between the two layers of fabric and bring the thread to the surface again away from your last stitch." She demonstrated as she spoke. "Then, you simply clip off the excess thread and you'll have buried the thread below the surface. Pull the thread a little before you cut it, and it will retract back through the surface."

She pulled on her fabric, and to everyone's amazement, they could no longer see the thread.

"A well-executed knot will be strong, yet no one will know it's there—a sufficiently buried end thread will not return to the surface. Return to your stations, stop wherever you are and make a quilter's knot. Take a few stitches then bury your thread."

Carla sat down and, on her first try, buried her knot without a trace. Harriet's knot disappeared, but when she ran her finger over the spot where it had been she could feel a lump. She sat back with a sigh. As the owner of Quilt As Desired, she was paid for her skill as a machine quilter, and fortunately, that was a technique she did very well. Besides, if she really needed something hand quilted, she apparently could call on Carla.

"Oh, my goodness," Patience said. "Where has the time gone? Thank you all for bearing with us today. I'm sure Selestina will be back teaching before we know it." She turned to go then stopped and turned back. "Don't forget there will be a pottery exhibition in Building A starting at six-thirty."

Harriet put her hooped piece on the table and started clearing her space. Carla made a few more tiny stitches then buried her thread. She held her work in front of her and looked at her perfect feather.

"Look at that," Harriet said, leaning closer to look at the even stitching. "You may have found your true calling here. Good work."

Carla's face turned so red, Harriet was afraid she was going to have to call the paramedics. "Thank you," she mumbled.

"Let's go see what the others have been up to," Harriet suggested.

Chapter Ten

$\mathcal{Y}$our young man has been looking for you," Mavis said as Harriet and Carla came into the kitchenette. Harriet looked around to see who she was talking to.

"Don't look at me," Sarah said, and put her hands up as if to block an attack. "Besides, he's older than me so he would never be my *young* man."

Harriet rounded on her, but before she could speak, Mavis thrust a piece of paper into her hand. "Here, he left you a note and his number. You'll have to use the house phone. I tried my cell phone when I got back to see if Beth has turned up any information about the quilt Lauren copied, and there was no reception."

"Has Beth found out anything?" Harriet asked.

"I haven't called yet. I didn't want to make a toll call on the Art Center phone without asking. I'll go up to the office after dinner. Now, I'm going to go put my feet up. You call Aiden."

Harriet looked at the message. "If you want to join me for the pottery exhibition and then dinner afterward," it said, "leave me a message and say what time and where you want to meet. I'll be in surgery until 6."

"Does he want us to make charity quilts for the pets?" Sarah asked. "We used to make them for the clinic all the time before Dr. Earp retired." Her tone indicated it was unthinkable Aiden would be calling Harriet for any other reason.

The internal debate Harriet had been having with herself ended.

"He wants me to meet him for dinner," she said, and felt like a schoolgirl answering a rival's taunts.

"Whatever," Sarah said, and stormed out.

Harriet picked up the house phone and dialed the number Aiden had written in the note. She was surprised when a woman answered, but left her message anyway—six-thirty, in front of Pavilion A.

She looked at the ceramic wall clock that hung on the wall above the small sink. She had almost an hour and a half before she had to meet Aiden. That should allow for a quick nap and a shower.

A thirty-minute power nap was all the rest she allowed herself. She laid out her clothing options on DeAnn's vacant bed and wished once again she hadn't put off clothes shopping. Truthfully, she didn't regret not going shopping—she regretted the fact that clothing hadn't magically appeared in her closet.

She finally decided that nothing with a hood was appropriate, which left a moss-green sweatshirt that zipped up the front she could wear with black jeans and a white T-shirt. She stopped by Robin's room for approval, having long since realized the older members of the Loose Threads were likely to tell her anything looked good on her, while Sarah and Lauren would assure her that nothing really worked with her figure and hair.

Robin told her she looked fine and spritzed her with an aromatherapy spray allegedly guaranteed to give her confidence. Harriet was pretty sure the only thing it was guaranteed to do was attract mosquitoes, but she thanked her and left for Pavilion A.

She ended up standing on the steps to Pavilion A a full ten minutes early. She was still standing there forty minutes later when she spotted the Loose Threads coming through the woods. She scrambled up the steps and into the entrance of the ceramics building.

The hallway to the right was lined with display pedestals, each holding a large pottery bowl of some kind. Niches had been cut into the wall every three or four feet, creating a series of lighted display shelves for smaller pieces—in this case, assorted vases. She pretended to study the exhibits until her friends stepped into the hall then dived through the nearest open doorway.

She shut the door quietly and turned around. Tom Bainbridge sat at a table with a man in a charcoal-gray suit, white shirt and a yellow club tie. The guy had that muscle-bound look that said he spent more time in the gym than around a conference table, but who was she to judge?

When Tom saw Harriet he scooped the papers they had been looking at into a pile and handed them to the other man as he got to his feet. "Can you give me a ball park figure by Friday?"

"Sure. I can probably give you an estimate before Friday." The other man slid the papers into his black leather briefcase, stood up and shook Tom's hand and left.

"I'm so sorry," Harriet said with an involuntary glance around her feet, searching for a hole to crawl into. "I was trying to find the main part of the exhibition."

"Oh. You just continue on around the hallway, and you can't miss it. It's in the first big room with windows." He swung his arm in an arc, in the general direction she'd just come from. "I suspect you already knew that, however, since all our buildings are round and you pretty much can't miss if you follow the hall."

"I'm sorry," she stammered. "I thought I could cut through a classroom and get there more directly." Her face was flaming hot.

"Let's try this again. Who are you hiding from?" Tom sat on the edge of his table.

"Is it that obvious?"

"It's been my experience that people don't usually close a door with that much care unless they are trying to avoid detection. So, tell me, do you have an angry stalker? Or maybe a quilting rival?"

Harriet pulled out the nearest chair and sat down.

"I'm afraid it's nothing that exciting. It is embarrassing, though, which is why I'm hiding from my friends."

Tom dragged over a chair and sat down opposite her, taking her hand.

"It can't be that bad," he said "You can tell Uncle Tommy. Come on, you'll feel better."

"I'm not sure how publicly confessing my social ineptness is going to make me feel better."

"Try it and see," he urged with a wolfish grin.

"You're right, this evening can't get any worse." She proceeded to tell him about being stood up, and how her rational mind knew Aiden had probably gotten stuck in surgery, but that her irrational mind didn't want to be seen by Sarah or Lauren, both of whom knew she was supposed to be meeting Aiden and both of whom would not be able to resist making a comment.

"See? Don't you feel better?"

"No, I feel foolish, and I feel awful for dumping my silly problems on you when your mother is in the hospital. How is she doing, by the way?"

"I think the jury is still out on that. Her cardiologist isn't sure what's going on with her heart. Apart, that is, from her being seventy-five years old and still working at a demanding business. She was awake and insisted I come take care of business. Her doctor is hoping to know more tomorrow when they get some of her test results back."

"I'm sorry," Harriet said.

"I've tried to get her to slow down a little, maybe hire another assistant, but she insists she and Patience can handle things."

"Maybe she'll listen to you now."

"I doubt it, but one can hope. Now, back to your problem. Why don't you let me show you the exhibit? I'm sure your friends won't say anything in front of me. And then maybe you could join me for a late dinner."

"I'd love to have a tour of the exhibit, but I should call Aiden after that and see if he finished at the clinic. He's probably starving if he's been in surgery all this time."

"Fair enough," he said. "I'll take whatever time I can with the lovely lady." He smiled his rakish smile at her. She had to admit he was charming. "Now, let me show you a real shortcut," he said and led her to the opposite side of the room and through a door that opened into the central supply room. He turned left as he guided her across a circular space and through another door into the large windowed room that held the main exhibit.

"This first section features work by a group of advanced students who worked with experimental glazes," he said and pointed to an array of four-inch tiles artfully arranged on a pale green wall. They ranged from finely textured pastel colors to ones that looked like pieces of wet stone. "These bowls," he said, and gestured toward a dozen bowls on a tabletop, each of which sat on a color-coordinated hand-woven mat, "are from a throwing technique class. Notice how thin they are—the more skilled the potter, the thinner the wall of the bowl."

"These are amazing," Harriet said. "How do—"

Before she could finish, Tom pulled her around a free-standing display wall, turning her away from the crowd and putting his arm around her shoulders. The momentum jostled her into the back of a tall man who was looking at a free-form piece on a wooden pedestal.

"Excuse me," Harriet apologized.

And turned to find herself looking into the ice-blue eyes of Aiden Jalbert.

"I'm sorry," Tom explained, "your friends were coming around the corner."

"I assumed you were too busy to call," Aiden said. "I can see I was right."

"Why aren't you in surgery?" Harriet demanded.

The muscle in Aiden's jaw tensed.

"Have you seen enough? I'm hungry," said a tall, slender blonde with a pixie haircut and gold pirate hoop earrings. She had a little girl's voice and was wearing black-and-white striped tights and a strip of leather that might have been a skirt. She looped her arm through Aiden's and pulled him toward the door. He turned as he went and looked back at Harriet, the hurt plain on his face.

"I'm guessing that was your date?" Tom said.

Harriet nodded. She stood rooted in place, looking at the door.

"Come on," Tom said, and pulled her through yet another door into the center room. "Let's go get something to eat."

The shock of seeing Aiden with the blonde prevented her from protesting. By the time she could speak, she was already outside, following him down a wooded path that led to a gravel parking lot.

"I think I want to go back to the Tree House," she said.

"Do you really think facing your friends back there and trying to explain what happened is going to be easier on an empty stomach?" he asked. "Besides, wouldn't you rather come home late from a date with a mysterious stranger and keep them guessing?"

"When you put it that way, how can I refuse?"

"That's what I thought." He opened the passenger door of a black Ford Explorer.

He pulled out of the parking lot and followed the access road off the school property. When they reached the crossroad, he turned toward Angel Harbor.

"What kind of food do you feel like?" he asked as they approached the downtown area.

"I'm not really hungry," Harriet said in a flat tone. A small voice in her head was telling her she should have known better than to trust a man again. Her husband Steve had lied to her. Look where that had gotten him. He was dead. She'd sworn she was never going to trust a man again, hadn't she?

"Italian? Wow, that's just what I was thinking," Tom said as he pulled to the curb.

When he'd parked, he got out and came around and opened Harriet's door. "Come on, help me out here. If I have to undo your seatbelt I'm going to feel like I'm with my grandmother instead of out on a hot date."

She finally smiled.

"What? Was that a smile I saw?" Tom asked hopefully.

Harriet laughed. "I'm sorry. I'm acting like a sulky teenager, and you're being nothing but charming."

"Hey, I'll take what I can get. It's not every day a beautiful woman breaks into my business meetings, and a damsel in distress, at that. I'll guarantee that things will seem better by the time dinner is over."

"I feel better already," Harriet said and wanted to believe it.

Tom led her into the restaurant.

"Hey," said a dark-haired man with a white cloth apron tied around his waist.

"Hey, Giovanni. Got a quiet corner where we can drown our sorrows in pasta?"

"Right this way," he said with a not-too-subtle wink at Tom.

"I suppose you come here all the time." Harriet realized she'd probably be the topic of tomorrow's gossip. At least she didn't know anyone in Angel Harbor.

"I might have been here a time or two."

"Please tell me you don't take all your first dates here."

"Okay, I won't. Tell you, that is." His eyes danced as he tried not to laugh.

Harriet sighed. This was turning into a nightmare. "Maybe this wasn't such a good idea after all." She started to get up.

"Fine," he said. "The truth is, I don't date." Harriet's discomfort turn to horror. "I'm not married or anything," he added quickly.

She sat back down, letting her relief show on her face. She wasn't about to complicate her life by dating someone who was already entangled.

"I *was* married," he continued, "but I've been divorced for two years."

She was beginning to like him in spite of herself.

"If it wouldn't be too presumptuous, may I order for both of us?"

She agreed, and he proceeded to order an antipasto plate and salads made of delicate Italian greens and a light vinaigrette dressing. He added a main course of sea scallops poached in garlic butter with angel hair pasta tossed with capers, sun-dried tomatoes and olive oil. Their meal was accompanied by crusty Italian bread they dipped in extra-virgin olive oil.

"Okay, it was worth it," Harriet declared when they were finished.

"Dessert?"

"After that, I couldn't eat another bite. And as nice as this has been, I really should get back. I do have class in the morning."

"I can't talk you into playing hooky?" he teased with a roguish smile.

"No. Besides, I have to face my friends, and I'd rather do that tonight and get it over with."

"What kind of friends are these that you have to hide from them and then dread telling them a legitimate problem?"

"It's not my friends I'm dodging. In any group, you have to take the good with the bad, and there are a couple of people in ours who are…a bit of a challenge."

She reached for the bill, but Tom was quicker.

"Hey, I asked you out, so I get to pay. Besides, what kind of knight in shining armor would I be if I made the damsel pay?"

55

"Okay, but I get to pay next time. If there is a next time, that is."

"I like the sound of that. You've got a deal."

She excused herself and went to the restroom while he paid. The ladies room had an old-fashioned multi-paned window covered by cafe curtains in a fabric with the red, green and white of the Italian flag. She glanced out through the space between the curtain and the valance.

The alley was lit with the yellow glare from a lamp at the back of the building. She was about to turn away when she saw two people enter the alley, passing through the bright circle of light cast by the lamp then stopping at a dark door in the building opposite the restaurant. The first person reached in and turned on a light that illuminated the stairway that ascended from the small entry.

The two people were clearly visible in the light. The second person was Lauren. The one leading the way was the janitor they'd seen talking to her the night before. He was carrying an armload of papers and file folders as he held the door and let Lauren inside.

Chapter Eleven

Harriet was thankful Tom dropped her in the parking lot to the Tree House and let her walk to the door unescorted. She hoped the Loose Threads had turned in early, but as she entered she heard voices coming from the common area.

"Don't even think of sneaking upstairs without making a full report," Mavis ordered from her perch on one of the leather sofas.

Harriet surrendered to the unavoidable and went in where they were seated.

"Sit down," Connie said. "I'll make you some tea." She got up and put the kettle on to boil.

As expected, Lauren was absent, and Harriet was glad to see that Sarah was also.

"Sarah is helping Patience prep materials for her class tomorrow," Mavis explained, as if reading her mind. "Carla is taking advantage of the clawfoot tub and the lavender bath salts in the downstairs bathroom. So, talk. What happened, and what was Aiden doing with that blond bimbo?"

Harriet crossed the room and picked up a pillow from the couch. She carried it to the twig rocking chair and put it against the back then sat down. She knew she wasn't fooling anyone with her stalling tactics, but she needed to gather her thoughts.

"Start at the beginning," Connie suggested, and set a steaming cup of Constant Comment on the hearth within reach.

Harriet recounted the note, her call back and Aiden's failure to show up. She ended with her bumping into him at the pottery exhibit. She left out the part where she'd hidden from them.

57

"If he no-showed, where have you been and why weren't you at the pottery show?" Mavis demanded.

She explained how she had met Tom while looking at the pottery and that he'd asked her to dinner, since Aiden was obviously otherwise occupied.

"He's cute," Robin said.

Mavis glared at her.

"We ran into him on our walk the other day," Robin added in self-defense.

"Shouldn't he be at the hospital with his mother?" Connie asked.

"He said she wanted him to come make sure the school was surviving in her absence. I didn't think I should refuse his invitation, given the circumstances."

"Don't even try to make us believe you went out with him out of sympathy," Mavis said. "You went with that fellow because you were hurt when you saw Aiden with another woman. There could be a completely innocent explanation."

"And what would that be?"

"Maybe he didn't get your message."

"Of course. He didn't get my message, and instead of calling or asking someone if that were the case, he asks the blond bombshell to go in my place. Is that how you figure it?" She got up and strode across the room.

"I'm sure there's a perfectly innocent reason for that," Mavis insisted.

"Yeah, but you can't think of one, can you? Well, I couldn't either, so, yes, you got me. I had an opportunity to go to dinner with a handsome, available man, and given the alternative of coming back here and telling all of you I'd been stood up, I took it."

Connie got the kettle and topped off Mavis's and Robin's cups then took it back to the kitchenette. Robin busied herself with her hand stitching.

"On an unrelated subject," Harriet continued. "When I was in the ladies room at the restaurant, I looked out the window, and you'll never guess who I saw."

"Don't keep us in suspense, honey," Mavis said.

"Lauren and the janitor from the other night. And they went

through a door that opened onto some stairs that looked like they went up to apartments over the storefront."

"That's weird," Robin said. "I wonder what she was doing with him."

"I don't know, but he was carrying an armload of papers. They looked like files or something."

"She said she was going back to the classroom to dye some thread for tomorrow's class," Connie said. "Are you sure it was Lauren?"

"She walked right under the streetlight, and so did he."

"Maybe she has a boyfriend," Mavis offered. "It *is* allowed. And you did see her with someone last night."

"Yeah, but I can't imagine her being evolved enough to date a janitor. Besides, their body language didn't look like they were a couple."

"You're right," Mavis acknowledged, "it is interesting."

"So, what class is everyone taking tomorrow?" Robin asked, ending speculation about Lauren's love life.

Harriet and Carla would be together again, this time taking a two-day class working on pieced patterns that used elongated triangles to create the illusion of curved shapes. Lauren and Connie would continue their advanced machine embroidery and Mavis her dyeing. Robin and Sarah were going to be doing bobbin work. With that established, everyone decided to call it a night.

Chapter Twelve

Clouds greeted the Loose Threads as they stepped off the Tree House porch and headed for the dining cabin. Harriet pulled the hood of her gray sweatshirt over her shower-damp hair. Carla gave her a sheepish glance and drew her hood up over her own dark hair, pulling the strings to close it around her face. They all made room as a small group of pottery students descended the steps and turned down the path toward building A.

Inside, the oak sideboard was set up with insulated carafes of coffee, hot water and hot cocoa. A large pitcher of orange juice surrounded by clean glasses sat to one side of the hot drinks. Sarah grabbed it and poured a glass. She held it up to the light as if it were a fine wine she was evaluating.

"This is probably that frozen kind that comes in a can," she said to no one in particular as she sat down at the long table.

The cook's braid was pinned up in a thick coil on top of her head this morning, giving her a Scandinavian look. She carried a tray laden with bowls of steaming oatmeal to the table and started setting one at each place.

"I squeezed the juice this morning while you were still getting your beauty sleep," she said without looking up from her task. "I've got the peels in the compost pile out back if you need proof."

"I'm sure that won't be necessary," Mavis soothed her, and glared at Sarah.

"The oatmeal looks delicious," Connie added. "And were those raisins and dates I saw on the sideboard?"

The cook glared a long moment at Sarah's back—Sarah refused to turn and face her—before she turned to Connie.

"Yes, you'll find raisins, dates, brown and white sugar, honey, butter and cream on the tray over there. And maple syrup in the brown pitcher. Help yourself."

Harriet carried her bowl to the condiment tray and sprinkled a handful of raisins and a spoon of brown sugar onto it. Lauren appeared and joined her at the sideboard.

"You have to fix this," she demanded.

"Fix what?" Harriet asked.

"You have to prove I did my quilt first. You owe me."

Ever since a show quilt Lauren had placed high hopes for a win on had ended up shredded by a murderer, the woman kept insisting the loss was Harriet's fault and demanding reparation. Harriet had finally accepted it was pointless to argue otherwise.

"How am I supposed to do that?" She tried to remain calm.

"You're so clever—figure it out," Lauren spat, then spun around and stormed out of the building.

Harriet carried her bowl back to the long table and sat down. "Remind me again why I 'owe' her?" she asked.

"Because she's Lauren," Robin replied, busy with her own bowl of cereal.

Carla waited until Harriet had finished eating.

"Are you going to do it?" she asked without looking up.

"For the record," Harriet snapped, "I don't owe that woman anything."

The chatter stopped abruptly. Harriet looked at her friends.

"What?"

"No one's saying you owe her anything," Mavis agreed. "But..."

"But don't you want to know who copied who?" Connie finished.

Carla finally looked up, watching Harriet's reaction.

"Personally, I don't care," Sarah said and got up, leaving her dirty dishes on the table. "I'm going back to the Tree House. I left my thread case in my room."

"Don't forget to take your dishes to the kitchen," Connie said, as Sarah started to leave.

Sarah sighed and rolled her eyes skyward, but she picked up

her bowl, spoon and glass and carried them into the other room. They could hear her thanking the cook for breakfast before she came out. Harriet hoped it sounded more sincere to the recipient than it did to her.

"May I leave now?" Sarah said to Connie, the sarcasm dripping from her voice.

Connie stood and looked at Sarah's place at the table.

"You may," she said. Her thirty years of taming Foggy Point's young gave her a commanding presence, and Sarah wasn't immune. She turned and left without saying another word.

Connie sat back down. "Now, about Lauren's quilt…"

"I'm not sure what you think I can do," Harriet protested.

"I'm sure you'll think of something," Connie said.

"Why don't we all give it some thought while we're in class, and then we can put our heads together at lunch and see if we can come up with a plan," Mavis urged. She got up and carried her dishes to the kitchen. The rest of the Loose Threads followed suit then stepped out onto the porch.

Mavis and Connie took the path around the dining hall to the bathrooms. Robin started for the parking lot to look in her car for scissors that weren't where they should be in her bag. Harriet was following Carla along the trail to the fiber arts pavilion when someone pulled her from the path.

Carla looked back, gave her a crooked smile and hurried away. Harriet spun around and found herself face to face with Aiden.

"Hi," he said.

She pulled out of his grasp and pushed his arms away as he reached for her.

"Leave me alone," she snapped and strode toward the path.

"Leave you alone? Why on earth would I do that? You've got some explaining to do."

"*What?*" She whirled back around. "*I* have explaining to do?" Her voice was rising, and she could feel her face heating. "*You're* the one who left me hanging when you got a better offer."

"What are you talking about? I didn't leave you. You never called me back. That's why I came by this morning. I wanted to find out why." He pulled a purple hat from his back pocket. "That, and I wanted to give you this."

He put it on her head. She pulled it off and looked at it. ANGEL HARBOR SPAY AND NEUTER CLINIC, it read.

"This was the only purple one. It made me think of you." He tapped the brim of the hat. "One of a kind."

"Dr. Jalbert," a voice called from the woods.

Aiden turned toward the sound as the blonde from the previous night emerged at a jog on a path off to the right.

"There's been a fire on one of the boats down at the harbor," she said in a breathless voice. "Two dogs and three cats were injured; the call just came over the radio." She displayed the portable unit, as if they needed to see it to believe her story.

"We're not finished here," Aiden informed Harriet as he started after the blonde. "We're going to talk."

Harriet opened her mouth to reply, but he was already gone.

A steady drizzle broke through the canopy of branches overhead. She looked at the purple hat then put it on her head as she went to her classroom.

Carla had saved a place for her at a two-person table. She'd placed a large cutting mat in the space between the two sewing machines and was bent over her bag pulling tools out and setting them to the left of her machine.

"Did I miss anything?" Harriet asked.

"The teacher told us to get out our basic sewing tools and to thread our machines with neutral thread if they needed it." She was twisting her fingers nervously; and she stared at them as if they were small rodents fighting and she had money on the outcome. "I threaded yours with off-white." She glanced up at Harriet before returning attention to her hands.

Harriet placed her hand on Carla's, stopping the motion.

"Thank you," she said. "Did she say anything else?"

Carla made as if to resume twisting her hands then dropped them from her lap and grabbed the two sides of the chair she was sitting on. "No."

Their teacher, Ray Louise Hanson, returned carrying a sheaf of graph paper and launched into her lecture on the usefulness of half-rectangle construction, a geometric design composed of two different fabrics dividing a rectangle diagonally from corner to corner. As she spoke, she handed several pieces of the grid paper to each student, and soon everyone was creating her own design based on the divided rectangle.

The class was soon immersed in their work, and before Harriet knew it, her paper was filled and it was lunchtime.

"Class will resume at one o'clock sharp," Ray Louise, a tiny woman with flame-red hair said. She turned and disappeared behind a three-quarter wall at the narrow end of the room that concealed the door to the central storeroom.

Carla stood up and started to leave. She turned back when she realized Harriet had not followed.

"Are you coming to lunch?" she asked without making eye contact.

"You go ahead, I'm going to try out a short cut."

Harriet fiddled with her scissors and rotary cutter on the cutting mat until everyone else was gone. When the coast was clear, she hurried up the aisle to the front of the room and stepped around the dividing wall and through the access door. She was prepared to use her short-cut story if anyone was in the central room, but it was deserted.

She turned slowly. The layout had seemed simple last night but now, on her own, it was confusing. The classrooms all led to the center, but some rooms had an enclosed space between them and the part of the storage area where she was. She could see no other choice than to start opening doors. The third one she tried led to the room she was looking for.

Selestina's office was small but efficient. A simple colonial-style maple desk sat in the center of the room. A matching credenza stood behind it and two wooden-backed maple guest chairs in front. A series of framed botanical prints hung on the wider wall. Selestina clearly didn't do any fiber work here.

Harriet stepped around the desk and tried the file drawers but found them locked. She froze at the sound of a door closing, but when no other noise followed, she continued her search, rifling the small stack of papers on the desktop. A quick look determined they were packing slips for recent materials deliveries. She took one last look around, but there was nothing related to the shipping of quilts to Europe or anywhere else, and nothing that could shed any light on a duplicate quilt that may or may not have been created at the

64

folk art center.

She listened for sounds of life in the storeroom and, when she heard none, stepped quickly across the space back into her classroom then on into the hallway and through the door. She only took a deep breath when she was back out on the trail to the dining hall.

✂ ✂ ✂

"Where have you been?" Lauren demanded the moment Harriet sat down at the fiber arts table. The cook brought a blue pottery bowl filled with posole and sat it in front of her. The fragrance of the spicy pork-and-hominy soup made Harriet's mouth water.

"Can I eat before we do this?" she asked.

"Fine," Lauren said.

"Where have you been?" Mavis asked when Lauren had returned to the opposite end of the table, where she'd been sitting with a group of students from the two-year program.

Harriet scooped a spoonful of soup into her mouth and followed it with a bite of crusty homemade French bread. The group got the message and let her eat in silence.

"Okay, so where were you and did you find proof that someone copied my work?" Lauren demanded, once more swooping down on Harriet after her lunch companions had left the dining hall.

"I didn't find anything that indicated Selestina copied your work. As your advisor, I assume she's the one who would see your design first. Since it would take some time to produce the copy, I can't think of anyone else who would have enough access to do it." Harriet put her spoon down. "I searched her office."

"That's my girl," Mavis said, sounding like the proud mother of a spelling bee winner.

Harriet looked at her. "I didn't find anything useful, though. Her desk only had a few packing slips on it, and her file cabinets were locked, so it was a big zero."

"I could have told you that," Lauren sneered. "I told you to find me proof. If it was that easy, I'd have my proof already."

"What, *you* searched her office?" Harriet asked, jumping to her feet. "If you're finding your own evidence, why are you guilt-tripping me? I'm through with your games—you can untangle your own mess." She stomped into the kitchen with her empty bowl.

65

Lauren followed her through the double doors as she was rinsing her bowl at the deep copper sink.

"Okay, I'm sorry," Lauren apologized. "I was just counting on you to come up with something. You don't know what it's like having everyone think they know something bad about you but really they don't."

Yeah, thought Harriet, I know what it's like. And what it's like when everyone actually knows something bad and doesn't tell you.

Her husband Steve had kept the fact he had a genetic condition that could kill him before he was forty from her, yet he somehow felt free to tell all their friends about it. Not one of them thought she needed to be bothered with the information, and when he died from a burst aorta, they couldn't understand why she didn't want their sympathy.

Harriet knew all about being an outsider.

"So, what did you find out," she asked without turning around.

Lauren slid onto one of the tall stools that circled a knife-scarred wood center island. "There was a stack of papers and files on her desk."

Harriet took a stool on the opposite side. "So?" she prompted.

"There wasn't anything useful. There was a receipt for a package that was mailed to England two months ago—it was for a quilt, but there was no detailed description so it was worthless."

"Let's let me be the judge of that. I want the papers. All of them."

"I'm telling you, there's nothing there."

"Look, do you want my help or not? If you don't, we're through here." Harriet started to get up.

"I don't have the papers."

"What? I thought you said you took them."

"Actually, I didn't say I had the papers." Lauren's shoulders slumped, and she let out a big sigh. "My brother took the files that were on Selestina's desk."

"Your brother?" Harriet said, louder than she'd intended.

"Shhh," Lauren said, and lowered her own voice to barely above a whisper." She leaned across the table. "Yes, my brother. He's the janitor here."

"Why are we whispering?" Harriet asked in a normal voice.

"Are you embarrassed because your brother is a janitor?"

"Shhh," Lauren said again. "Of course I don't mind if my brother's a janitor. It's way more complicated than that, not that it's any of your business."

"Fine."

"Look, just because you're finding out why I'm being accused of copying Selestina's work, it doesn't mean we are suddenly BFF's."

"BFF's?"

"My point exactly. My brother has the files at his apartment in town. He doesn't get off work until six. I'll have him bring them back to the Tree House after dinner."

Lauren stood up, and Harriet understood she was being dismissed. She was still sitting at the island when Mavis came through the doors.

"You're not bleeding," she said. "Does this mean we're still on the case?"

"*We* are not on the anything."

"You mean you're not the least bit interested in finding out who made her quilt first?"

"I didn't say I wasn't interested. I just don't think we should make a major production out of finding out. And might I remind you there's no proof Selestina was the one who produced the duplicate quilt?"

"My money's still on Selestina," Mavis said.

Robin leaned through the doors. "Come on, ladies, time to get back to class."

67

Chapter Thirteen

Carla and Harriet were at an ironing board at the back of their classroom starching their fabric rectangles to within an inch of their lives when their teacher interrupted.

"Class, would everyone return to their seats, please?"

The students looked at each other in puzzlement but did as she asked. When they were all seated, Ray Louise came around to the front of her table and sat on the edge.

"I'm afraid I have some sad news," she said. "I've just been informed Selestina Bainbridge has passed away."

"What happened?" a dark-haired woman at the back of the room asked.

"I thought she was awake and alert at the hospital," said a younger woman toward the front.

The teacher held her hands up. "We don't know anything yet. They were treating her for a heart arrhythmia, and she must have had a heart attack before they could control it. I'm not a doctor, so I can't really tell you any more than that—I just don't know. The important thing is that this tragic event will not impact your time here. Of course, there will be some staff changes for a few of the classes, but it was Selestina's wish that school continue. It was her legacy. She told her son Tom it was important to her that her students not be disappointed."

"Almost makes you feel sorry for her, doesn't it?" said Jan Hayes, the doctor, who was standing next the Harriet.

"Almost," Harriet conceded, remembering how vicious Selestina had been to Carla.

"Well, I can tell you one thing," Jan said.

"What's that?"

"If she had a heart attack, it was a kind I've never seen before."

"How so?"

"People often have pain in their left arm if they're suffering a heart attack. Although women often don't have classic symptoms, Selestina's were beyond atypical. She seemed to have numbness in both her arms. And there was something wrong with her pupils, too. You can mark my words. She had something else going on besides a simple heart attack."

"Having said that," Ray Louise continued, "we *will* cancel class for the rest of today. The teaching staff needs to meet to figure out how we will cover Selestina's work load for the rest of this week."

"Will we be able to stay here and continue working?" asked the dark-haired woman.

"No, we can't leave the room open without a staff member present, and we'll all be in the meeting. However, each of the dormitory buildings has a storeroom off the back porch. They should be unlocked, and if you look inside you should find card tables and chairs and power strips. You're are welcome to set tables up anywhere in your building as long as you don't disturb anyone else. If you didn't bring your own sewing machine, there are loaner machines available in the Folk Art Center office. The office is the smaller round building on the west side of Building A, which is the ceramics center." She paused and looked over the group to see if anyone else had a question. "Lastly, if you can find it in your heart to do so, please say a prayer for the soul of a fine, fine, woman— Selestina Bainbridge." Ray Louise left the room without another word.

A deafening clap of thunder broke the silence that had fallen over the room.

"I think that's our cue to leave," Harriet whispered to Carla. The two desk-mates quietly packed up their tools and headed for the door.

"Are you going to work any more on your rectangles?" Jan asked Harriet.

"I didn't bring my sewing machine, but I thought I might cut mine." She turned to Carla. "Are you going to do any more?"

69

Carla studied her toes. "I thought I would try to cut a few."

"Do you want to get together later and compare what we've done? You know, make sure they all look somewhat the same." Jan asked.

"Sure, I guess," Harriet looked at Carla, and the young woman nodded. "Would you like to come by our dorm later? We're staying in the Tree House."

Jan agreed, and they parted company at the classroom door.

✂ ✂ ✂

Mavis and Connie were already settled in the common room when Harriet and Carla arrived. Connie had a teapot and cups on a tray on the oak table between the sofas. She had wrapped a dishtowel around the pot to keep the contents warm until the rest of the group arrived.

Mavis was talking on the dormitory's cordless phone. She covered the mouthpiece with her right hand.

"Carla, honey," she said, "it's your sister. She says she needs to speak to you."

Carla took the phone and turned away from the group. Mavis put her hand on Harriet's back and guided her to the sofa.

"I presume you heard about Selestina?"

"Yeah, we heard. What did they tell your class?"

"Not much. They said Selestina died of a fatal heart arrhythmia."

"I don't think heart rhythm problems are unusual for women her age," Connie said. "A couple of ladies in my aerobics class take heart rhythm medications already."

"Yeah, but do they die from it?" Harriet asked.

Connie's face lost its animation as she thought about it. "No, I don't think so. I can't think of anyone I know who's died from a heart rhythm problem."

"Your record is still clean," Darcy Lewis said from the entryway. Darcy worked for the Foggy Point sheriff's office as a crime scene investigator. Foggy Point wasn't a big enough town to support one full-time CSI much less the three it had, but the state of Washington had made a deal with the county to host the unit that served the small towns in the northwestern part of the state. Foggy Point

70

wasn't a hotbed of crime; but the state politicians had discovered that if fingerprints were taken at every crime in every town, no matter how minor, the public felt safer and that meant votes for the incumbent regime. It didn't seem to matter to either side that the evidence collected at car prowls and simple burglaries didn't usually result in conviction. Even when it did, the perpetrator was out on the street in a matter of hours, if not minutes.

"Hi, Darcy," Mavis greeted the young woman. "What are you doing here? Did you decide to take a class after all?"

"I wish that was why I'm here. No, I'm here professionally. I'm on the state's poison task force, which means anytime someone dies from any type of poison anywhere in the state, I get to go there and collect samples."

"Selestina was poisoned?" Harriet asked, even though Darcy's presence made that obvious.

"Looks like it." Darcy took off her uniform jacket and draped it over the arm of the sofa. "And whoever did it almost got away with it."

"Sit, mija," Connie said, moving her sewing bag from the sofa to the floor to make space. "What happened?" She took a cup from the tray and started to unwrap a tea bag. "Can you stay long enough for a cup of tea?"

"As a matter of fact, I can." Darcy took the tea when it was ready and sat next to her. "I have to wait for the local investigator to arrive. I guess he's dealing with a mentally disturbed guy who attacked a clerk at the Angel Harbor Grocery Sack."

"Could we back up a second here?" Harriet interrupted. "We were told Selestina died from a heart problem."

"That's true. The reason I'm here is because someone thinks the heart problem was caused by poison. She had some rather atypical symptoms."

"So we've heard."

"We have?" Mavis asked; her left eyebrow rose.

"There's a doctor in our class. She was there when Selestina collapsed. She was just telling Carla and me that Selestina had unusual symptoms."

"And no one would have been the wiser," Darcy added, "if there hadn't been a pathology intern moonlighting in the ER when she came in. He recognized the symptoms right away, but unfortunately, he wasn't the first doctor to see her. She just hadn't gone up to ICU yet when he came in for the shift change. As I understand it, they already had a cardiologist seeing her in the ER. The pathologist was just doing a routine check of all the patients. If she'd been younger, maybe they could have saved her, but even then it would have been touch-and-go if it ends up being what they suspect."

"What *do* they suspect?" Harriet asked.

"Sorry, I've said too much already," Darcy said. "I'm sure there will be some kind of official statement after the test results are back." She tried to smile, but the gesture never fully materialized.

"This week sure hasn't turned out how I expected so far," Connie said and lifted the lid on the teapot. It was nearly empty.

"You stay where you are," Mavis told her. "I'll make this round."

Connie put her feet back up on the edge of the table as Mavis picked up the teapot and went for a refill.

✄ ✄ ✄

"What's wrong?" Mavis said as she came in. She set the pot on the counter and circled the island to where Carla stood, her packed duffel bag at her feet. She was surprised. She'd been so intent on Darcy's arrival and subsequent news, she hadn't noticed Carla had gone upstairs after her phone call. Tears were now running down the young woman's face, dripping from her nose and chin.

"Nothing," Carla said and scrubbed at her cheeks with the cuffs of her sweatshirt.

"Honey, if I'm not mistaken, people don't usually cry over nothing, and those don't look like happy tears."

"I'm fine," Carla insisted, trying for defiance but missing badly.

"I might not be able to fix what's wrong, but we won't know unless you tell me. I've learned that sometimes the telling can be a help, and with five boys, I've had a lot of practice listening."

Carla took a moment to compose herself as she pulled a stool away from the counter and sat on it. Mavis followed suit, placing her seat so her knees were touching Carla's.

"My sister has been taking care of Wendy." Carla hesitated,

and Mavis reached out and took her hand. "Wendy, she's my baby. Anyway, Cissy has been taking care of Wendy while I'm here, but she heard there was a new restaurant opening in Port Ludlow, and she called and got an interview for tomorrow. I have to go home and pick up Wendy from her." She looked around. "This was really fun," she said sadly and stood up. "I better go. Cissy said if I can get to the ferry that leaves in an hour and a half, her boyfriend is working construction in Port Townsend, and he can give me a ride back to Foggy Point."

"Just you hold on a minute. Let me see what I can do." Mavis patted the hand she held before she got up to fetch the phone.

Carla rubbed her sleeve over her face again. Mavis turned away as she spoke quietly into the receiver. After what must have seemed like an eternity to Carla, she hung up the phone and turned back around.

"Go unpack your bag," she said. "Then you can call your sister and tell her your friend Beth is going to pick up Wendy in the morning. Beth can keep her until one of you gets back."

Carla's eyes filled with tears again, but her shy smile had reappeared.

"Thank you, Miz Mavis."

The older woman smiled and handed her a tissue from a box on the counter.

"Now those are happy tears," she said. "Go tend to business, and then you can come down and have a nice warm cup of tea."

✂ ✂ ✂

"What took you so long?" Harriet asked when Mavis returned to the common room with the fresh pot of tea.

Before she answered, Mavis settled into her spot at the end of the sofa and picked up a plastic sandwich bag full of pre-cut triangular pieces of fabric in rich brown-toned batiks and an array of coordinating prints. She preferred to piece and quilt by hand with needle and thread instead of using a sewing machine. Harriet had to concede that hand work offered a portability and simplicity machine sewing didn't.

"Carla was having a little crisis, but we've got everything under control—for now, anyway. That little girl is truly living her life on the edge."

"Oh, you don't know the half of it," Harriet said.

"At least she has a job," Connie pointed out.

"That doesn't guarantee anything." Harriet refilled her teacup.

"Anybody want to tell me what's been going on here?" Darcy asked. "I send you gals off to have a relaxing week of quilting, and here we are." She swept her arms open to indicate the women sitting around the coffee table sipping tea.

No one spoke, and then they all started speaking at once.

"Hold on," Darcy said. "One at a time, please."

By the time Mavis, Connie and Harriet had finished recounting what had happened in the last two and a half days, starting with Lauren's exhibition and ending with Selestina's death, Robin and Lauren had joined the tea party.

"Have you figured out how to prove my piece is the original?" Lauren demanded of Harriet, breaking the silence that had fallen over the group.

"A woman's dead here, Lauren. Don't you think accusing her of ripping off your work is in poor taste, given the circumstance?"

"You're the one who said Selestina was the most likely person, not Lauren," Sarah pronounced as she swept in and plopped down on the couch between Mavis and Robin.

Harriet was trying to think of how to admit her lack of progress without setting off another outburst from Lauren when a tap on the door distracted the group and saved her.

"Hello? Anyone here?" Patience called from the entryway.

"We're in here," Connie called back. "We're just having a cup of tea. Would you like to join us?" She got up. "Here, you can have my spot." She picked up the once-again-depleted teapot for another refill.

Patience wore a gauzy skirt that appeared to be made up of several layers, each dyed a different shade of gray-black. She'd paired it with a black tunic-length ribbed turtleneck sweater that she'd belted at the waist with a wide black calfskin belt she had tied instead of buckled. She managed to look stylish in an arty sort of way and still honor Selestina with her mourning black.

"How are you doing," Mavis asked. "We're all so sorry for your loss."

74

"It *has* been quite a shock," Patience said. "Selestina was older of course, but I believe she was in good health."

"Are you sure you want us to finish out our week of classes?" Mavis asked. "Under the circumstances, I don't think anyone would expect a refund." By the look on both Sarah's and Lauren's faces, Harriet was pretty sure that wasn't a wholly accurate assumption.

"Thank you for that, but Selestina wanted the school to keep operating. She made plans for every eventuality. She was a bit compulsive that way. And this is her legacy, after all."

"Won't that be up to her son?" Harriet asked. "Or her other relatives?"

"Tom is her only child, and let's just say he's not all that interested in this place."

That's an understatement, Harriet thought. It looked to her like he'd been planning to sell it out from under his mother.

"Selestina knew Tom had his own interests and that those didn't include the folk art school. That's why she'd made other provisions. We were partners, you see." Patience curved her lips into a weak smile. "She's the front man, I guess you'd call it. I've always worked more behind the scenes." When she realized what she'd said, referring to Selestina in the present tense, she began to weep softly.

"I don't know how I'm supposed to go on without her," she blubbered. "I thought all our planning was just talk—you know, something to make her feel better, not something that was really going to happen. I can't run this place alone. This wasn't part of the plan." She covered her face with her hands, and tears leaked out between her fingers.

Connie went into the kitchenette for the tissue box. She pulled out three and brought them to Patience. Robin rubbed her hand on the teacher's bony back.

Patience blew her nose and sat up straighter, shaking off Robin's hand in the process. "I'm sorry," she said. "I didn't come here to make a scene. I came to make sure you were all right. And to be sure everyone knows school will go on as scheduled." She stood up. "Thank you for the tea. I've got two more houses to inform, so I better be on my way."

75

"That poor woman," Connie said when Patience was gone.

"I have to agree. I can't see her running the place, either," Harriet said. "Selestina seemed mean-spirited, but she also seemed to run a tight ship."

"Honey, let's not judge too quickly. We've only seen Patience in Selestina's shadow. She might be a great businesswoman in her own right. And kinder, too," Mavis suggested.

"Okay, so she's wonderful," Lauren said. "Can we get back to *my* catastrophe?"

"So, tell me again what the deal is," Darcy said. "Your piece looks like the teacher's piece and you're here learning from the teacher, so this is a problem why?"

"It's a problem because I didn't copy her work or anyone else's. Someone has to have copied mine."

"If you're learning a certain skill set from a teacher, isn't it likely that everyone who takes the class will end up with something that looks similar?"

"We're studying machine embroidery, and hand dyeing our fabric. Selestina gave us a theme, but beyond that we could do anything. My piece didn't look like any of the other students'. And Selestina certainly never gave us any indication she was working on her own piece."

"Couldn't she have made something similar without copying your work?" Darcy persisted.

Lauren stood up. "Come on. Since you can't seem to comprehend what I'm telling you, come look. You'll see what I mean. My piece is still hanging in the exhibit hall." She looked at the group seated around the table. "Anyone else want to come?"

Harriet and Robin got up.

"I don't need to join the drama," Sarah said. "I'm going to go read my teacher's book on the creative use of thread."

"Whatever!" Lauren shot a dark look at Sarah's back as she retreated up the stairs.

The women made a quick, silent trip through the woods to the fiber arts building.

"This way." Lauren led them around the display hall. "Arghhh!" she screamed.

Harriet, Robin and Darcy reached her and looked at the empty wall where her piece had hung the day before.

"Calm down," Darcy said. "Screaming isn't going to help anything."

"I'm sure there's a perfectly reasonable explanation," Harriet added. "Don't they send them to London to be evaluated at the textile guild? Maybe they took yours down so they could pack it for shipping."

"Okay, genius," Lauren snarled, fire in her eyes. "Why are all the others still here? Do you think they started in the middle of the exhibit? You do know they send everyone's work, right? They don't pick one person's work to send. They all go." She looked away in disgust then turned back. "Why are you defending them, anyway?"

Harriet held her hands up, palms out in placation. "Hey, leave me out of this."

"Why don't you go to the office and ask what happened?" Darcy suggested. "Come on, I'll go with you." She put her arm around Lauren's shoulders and turned her back toward the door then glanced back at Harriet and Robin and rolled her eyes skyward.

"Doesn't it seem a little strange that if only one piece has gone missing it would turn out to be Lauren's?" Harriet wondered aloud once they were gone.

"It's pretty convenient for Selestina. Or it would be if she wasn't beyond caring."

"That's the part that doesn't make sense." Harriet was quiet for a moment. "Maybe we're making this more complicated than it is. If Lauren has been her usual charming self in class, maybe she offended a classmate and *they* took her quilt in retaliation."

"Would her teacher know?"

"I'm not sure. I know she and Connie have been taking classes together, but the two-year students have some kind of advisor as well. Let's go see if any teachers are in the offices."

Harriet opened the next door they came to and led Robin into the honeycomb of offices and work spaces that made up the center of the building. In the third cubicle they went into they found three teachers sitting at a small table with coffee mugs and a plate of chocolate chip cookies in front of them.

Harriet explained only that her friend Lauren had been upset at lunch and was worried she'd offended some of her classmates. A large woman in baggy black corduroy pants and a purple felted vest over a red silk blouse leaned back in her chair.

"You either got some bad soup at lunch, or there are two Laurens here and we haven't met the second one." She looked over the top of her black-rimmed half-moon reading glasses. "The Lauren we know has raised offending classmates to an art form."

"Any classmate in particular?" Harriet asked.

The woman looked at the other two teachers before speaking. One shrugged and the other went back to reading her newspaper without comment.

"Lauren came to me with accusations that Selestina had copied her work." She shifted in her chair as if she suddenly couldn't get comfortable. "I'm her advisor now, but the students rotate through a series of teachers depending on which skill they are focusing on during any given term. The piece in question was made while she was taking class from Selestina. I had seen the piece as it developed, but I didn't pay close attention at that point. I knew I would see it before Selestina sent it to England for inspection."

Harriet's eyes widened.

"All the fiber arts department heads inspect work before it goes to be judged in England. So, I would have seen it, and I haven't."

"So, if Lauren's piece hasn't been sent off to be judged, where is it?" Harriet asked.

"I'm sure I have no idea. I wouldn't put it past her to have taken it down just for dramatic effect."

"No, that's not Lauren's style. She over-reacts, but she wouldn't create a crisis from whole cloth," Robin said.

"Are you sure?" Harriet asked. "She seems a little flighty to me."

"You've only seen her in stressful circumstances. She's not like this all the time. There has to be another explanation."

"Come on, let's go back to the Tree House."

Robin thanked the advisor for talking to them before following Harriet back to the hallway.

"I'm going to call Aunt Beth and see if she's found the picture of the European quilt yet. If she has, I'll have her fax it to the office. We've all seen Lauren's piece. If we see the other one we can get an idea of how similar they are. I can ask at the office about whether there's some innocent explanation for Lauren's quilt being gone. If Lauren was her usual charming self, she might not have gotten anywhere with them."

With that settled, they left the fiber arts building and returned to the Tree House. Darcy was in the kitchenette when they arrived.

Chapter Fourteen

Did you find out anything at the office?" Harriet asked.

"You mean besides how obnoxious Lauren can be when she's upset?"

Harriet laughed. "Yeah, besides that."

"No, not really. Lauren's attitude pretty much put an end to any information we might have gotten."

"I'm going to go call Aunt Beth and get her to fax us a copy of that picture."

"I'll walk that way with you," Darcy said. "I got cell reception out near the road. I'm going to check and see if my guy is anywhere close to getting here. Every minute that goes by means it's less likely we can collect a clean sample."

Aunt Beth had good news when Harriet called her. "I've found the picture I was telling you about," she said after they had exchanged greetings. "And speak up, I can hardly hear you."

Harriet turned her back to the woman sitting at the desk the phone was on. She raised her voice slightly.

"Good. Can you fax it to me?"

"Honey, I could, but that would be in black and white. I really think you need to see this in color. Ask and see if they have a Kinko's or something like that," she instructed. "I'll send it to your e-mail. Can you access your e-mail remotely?"

Harriet assured her computer-savvy aunt that she could.

"Do you have a phone book?" she asked the woman at the desk.

"I do, but if you're looking for a Kinko's there isn't one on the island. There *is* a UPS store that has computers and printers you can use by the hour." She looked up at Harriet and had the good grace to blush. "Sorry, your aunt talks sort of loud."

"How far is it to the UPS store," Harriet asked after she'd said her good-byes to Aunt Beth and hung up the telephone.

"It's about a mile and three quarters. Turn left out of the driveway then right at the first corner. Go straight up the hill on Harbor Drive. When the hill levels off, you'll see it on the right— you can't miss it."

She and Darcy were almost to the door when Patience emerged from an adjoining doorway. "Did I hear you ladies were headed to town?"

"I'm going to the UPS store to use the computer. My aunt is emailing me a picture," Harriet said. "Can I bring you something?"

Patience dabbed at her nose with a tissue. "If it wouldn't be too much trouble, could you bring me a bottle of aspirin from the pharmacy? I have a pounding headache, and I'm all out. I found a few packets in the first-aid kit…" She waved two small white packets. "…but these aren't coated. If I keep taking them my stomach will rebel. I'd really appreciate it."

"Sure, it's no problem."

Patience dug in her pocket and pulled out a crumpled five-dollar bill. "This should cover it," she said, and handed the bill to Harriet then left the office.

Harriet hoped Patience's runny nose was the result of crying sad tears or maybe an allergy rather than something contagious, since she'd had no choice but to take the proffered bill. She looked around for signs of a restroom and then spotted a pump bottle of hand sanitizer. She reached across the counter and helped herself to a good squirt. She wasn't going to leave with a cold if she could help it.

"It's getting kind of late to be walking, isn't it?" Darcy asked.

Harriet stepped out onto the porch. The sun was low in the sky.

"I think I can make it if I hurry. I really want to see the picture Aunt Beth has."

"If you get hung up, call me. If I don't answer, call the office and make them find me. That road is steep, and it's not well-lit."

Harriet hadn't even made it out of the driveway when rain started to fall as a fine mist. She took the purple hat out of her sweatshirt pocket and covered her hair. The mist was turning into a steady drizzle, and she was thinking about turning around when a white pickup pulled onto the shoulder, blocking her path.

"Going my way?" Aiden said as he leaned out the window and rested his chin on his bent arm.

Harriet ignored him and tried to walk around the truck, but he eased it forward, blocking her way again.

"Come on, you're going to catch your death of cold out here in the rain," he pleaded. "And you know me well enough to know I'm not going to leave until you get in."

She stood, pondering her options. She didn't have time to fool around.

"Don't make me come out there," Aiden said, a smile playing at the corners of his mouth.

"Fine." She pulled the purple hat off her head and shook the raindrops from it as she climbed in.

"Buckle up. I'm on my way to the No-tell Motel to have some fun."

She swatted him with the hat. "Brat!"

"I notice you're not getting out."

"I'm confident you aren't out trolling for women," she said and set her hat on the console between them. "What are you doing out and about at this time of day, anyway? I thought you were in surgery from dawn to dark."

"We were about to run out of anesthetic, and since I'm the newest, I had to drive to a clinic on the other end of the island. Besides, in case you haven't noticed, it *is* almost dark.

"And your school is donating quilts for the recovering patients to rest on, which I'm supposed to pick up when the teachers get out of their staff meeting. As soon as I deliver the drugs, I'm coming back here to do that, which is why I am at exactly this spot in the universe just when you need me most."

"Lucky me."

"Are you running away from school? You're traveling kind of light if you are."

"Very funny. Class was canceled this afternoon, and I am going into town to find a public computer."

"Are you one of those people who obsessively check their e-mail? You know the kind—they can't go twenty-four hours without checking, even if it means walking through a driving rainstorm to get to a computer. I never would have guessed."

"I am not obsessively checking my e-mail. It happens that my aunt is sending me some information that will help clear up a little problem we're having." Harriet quickly explained Lauren's belief that her work had been copied and the subsequent disappearance of that work.

"You're not one of those people who see trouble around every corner, are you? Do you have to have drama in your life constantly?"

"I don't see that my dramatic needs are any of your concern," she said, and turned to look at him.

"If I'm going to be your boyfriend, I need to know these things."

"You are not going to be my boyfriend. You stood me up."

"For the last time, I did not stand you up. You never called me back. I waited a reasonable amount of time, and then I went to the exhibit—alone, I might add."

"You didn't look very alone to me, and besides, I did call you back. I left a message with your assistant."

Aiden pulled to a stop in front of the UPS Store.

"I don't have an assistant. I'm the low vet on the totem pole. Notice how I'm the guy being sent to pick up supplies."

"Okay, call her what you want, I'm telling you, your phone was answered by a woman. I told her what time, and she assured me she'd give you my message."

"When did you call?"

Harriet thought for a moment. "It must have been around five."

"I was in surgery until almost six. My phone was in my jeans pocket in the locker room."

"Wasn't your locker locked?"

He leaned back and frowned at her.

"We're not exactly in inner-city Detroit here. I don't think the lockers at the pet shelter even have places to *put* locks. They're

83

more like kitchen cabinets."

"So anyone could have answered your phone."

"I suppose, but you said it was a woman. That narrows it a little. There is one woman vet, although her voice is pretty distinct, I think there are three female vet techs. After four, the receptionist is a high school girl, and I think there's at least one lady janitor. Take your pick.

"The point is, any one of them could have heard my phone ring, answered it and then forgotten to tell me. *The point is*," he repeated with emphasis, "that although I technically did stand you up, I didn't know I was standing you up because I never got the message."

"Okay, smart guy, that explains why you weren't at the show with me, but that doesn't explain the blond arm candy you were sporting."

"That's Doctor Johnson's assistant—and his granddaughter, I might add. She asked me to join her at the pottery show, and given her relationship to the boss, I didn't feel like I could say no. And why am I explaining myself to you? I didn't do anything wrong."

Harriet kept silent.

"I think this is the part where you say, 'Oh, Aiden, I'm so sorry I misjudged you…again,' and then we kiss and make up."

"That would be a lie. In my book, a guy who moves on with a blonde, boss's granddaughter or not, is not a guy to trust. And since we don't *have* a relationship, there's nothing to make up."

He sighed. "You are making this really difficult, and as much as I'd like to continue working on our relationship issues, I've got to get the drugs back to the clinic."

He jumped out of the truck and came around to Harriet's door before she could get out. He opened it and pulled her into a kiss before she could react—or at least before she could react the way she would have if she'd been able to think.

Instead, she wrapped her arms around him and felt the hard muscles of his back quiver under her touch. Her traitorous hands worked their way up his spine, and then her fingers tangled in his glorious black hair. He deepened the kiss and slid his hands down to her bottom and pulled her toward him. A part of Harriet wanted to know what was going to happen next, but a blue BMW started to pull into the parking spot next to Aiden's truck and they had to separate and move to the sidewalk to avoid being run over.

Two boys who looked like they were ten or eleven got out of the back seat and followed their mother into the UPS Store. As they passed Harriet they made faces and stuck their fingers in their mouths to simulate gagging.

"Hey, just wait a few years, guys," Aiden said and smiled. He turned back to her and leaned in for another, quick kiss. "I'll swing back by here in about twenty minutes, and if you're done, I can give you a ride back down the hill," he said then got back into the truck and drove away.

Harriet went into the UPS Store and, in a matter of minutes, had her e-mail open in front of her. True to her word, Aunt Beth had sent a full-page colored scan of a quilt that was almost identical to Lauren's exhibition piece.

"Wow," Harriet said.

The young woman at the counter looked up from the forms she was studying.

"It's a good picture," Harriet explained sheepishly and looked back at the computer screen. She pressed the print button and, when asked, selected eight copies—she knew the Loose Threads would each want a copy to study.

When the printing began, she forwarded the e-mail to each of them.

She looked at her watch. Aiden would be back by in about five minutes. She shut the computer off and went to the register to pick up and pay for her prints. The rain, which had let up when she'd entered the store, had begun falling in earnest again. She reached into her sweatshirt pocket for her purple hat and realized she'd left it in Aiden's truck, so she stood under the store awning to wait.

Five minutes passed. She felt the crumpled, germ-encrusted five-dollar bill in her pocket and remembered her aspirin mission. She looked at the other stores in the block and spotted a convenience store three doors down. She was back in front of the UPS Store in seven minutes, but there was no sign of Aiden.

If it hadn't been raining, she would have set out, but she waited another fifteen minutes, hoping for either Aiden or a break in the weather. She had just decided she was going to have to walk home in the rain when Darcy pulled into the parking lot in her county car.

She rolled down her window. "You better get in."

Harriet pulled the door open. "I'm glad to see——"

"I'm not here by chance," Darcy interrupted.

"What's wrong," Harriet asked, feeling the blood drain from her face. "Is it Aunt Beth?"

"No, Beth is fine, but there's been an accident."

"Who? What happened?" she said in a rush, instantly feeling guilty at her relief that it wasn't Aunt Beth.

"Aiden," Darcy said, and rested her hand on Harriet's arm. "He's okay. He's bruised and shaken, but he was up walking when I found him. He asked me to find you."

"Take me to him." Ice gripped her heart as memories of Steve's death came flooding back. It must have shown on her face.

"He's going to be fine," Darcy assured her.

"But?" She turned to face her.

"His passenger didn't fare as well."

"His passenger?" Harriet said in a wooden voice.

"Apparently, he picked up an assistant from the animal hospital where he picked up the drugs and was giving her a ride back to the spay-neuter clinic."

"What happened?"

"His truck went off the road and rolled. The passenger side door was down when they hit a rock outcrop. Bad news for the passenger."

"But why did he go off the road?"

"Well, that's where it gets interesting. According to Aiden—and understand, I only spoke to him briefly before they took him to the hospital—he was run off the road. He says someone actually bumped him and forced him over the hillside."

"Why?"

"Everyone would like an answer to that one," Darcy said, and pulled out of the parking lot and pointed the car toward the hospital.

Chapter Fifteen

Darcy filled in the details as she drove. She had gotten a call from the Angel Harbor PD about a preliminary toxicology report, and she was on her way to pick it up when she'd come across Aiden stumbling along on the shoulder of the road. She'd called an ambulance, but he would only agree to treatment if she would go pick up Harriet.

"They were still extracting the girl when I left to go get you," she finished.

"How bad is it?"

"She wasn't conscious, and her leg was pinned. They were cutting the side of the truck apart to free her."

"That's horrible." Harriet wondered if it was the blonde.

Darcy drove up to the walk-in door of the emergency room. "I'll park the car and come find you," she said.

Harriet went to the information desk and was directed to cubicle three. Aiden sat in the bed holding an ice bag against his left temple. His eyes were closed, and he jumped when Harriet gently touched his shoulder. He dropped the ice bag and opened his eyes. The left was surrounded by red, giving his exotic white-blue iris an eerie look. His cheekbone was scarlet, and he was going to have a nasty shiner by morning.

He didn't say anything. Harriet put her arms around him, and he leaned into her. They were still in their silent embrace when the doctor came in.

"You're a lucky man, Dr. Jalbert," he said—he had introduced himself as Dr. King. He was a tall, white-haired man with kind blue eyes and an easy smile. "Your cheekbone isn't broken."

"Good. Can I get out of here now?"

Harriet stepped back as he stood up.

"Not quite so quick there, young man," Dr. King said. "Your cheekbone is okay, but I've called a specialist to come look at your eye." He pulled a small white penlight from his coat pocket and shined it into the injured eye. "Look at the wall over there...It's probably fine, but I'd like the eye guy to look at it and say he agrees.

"You do know that when we release you, we expect you to go home and rest for a few days," Dr. King continued. "I know your patients can't follow that advice, but I expect you to hear me and follow my instructions." He patted Aiden's shoulder and guided him back onto the bed. "Let your young lady here pamper you for a few days. I predict by this time next week this will all be just a memory."

"I don't know if I feel insulted that he spoke to me like I'm a possession or flattered that he called me young," Harriet commented when the doctor was out of earshot.

"I liked the sound of both." Aiden grabbed her hand as he leaned back on the bed. "I'm just going to close my eyes for a minute," he mumbled. "Promise me you won't leave."

She pulled a chair over beside his bed and sat, holding his hand all the while. In a few minutes, his regular breathing told her he had escaped into sleep. She couldn't blame him. She'd had some recent experience with head injuries and knew sleep was the only thing that truly relieved the pain.

A full two hours passed before the specialist declared Aiden fit to be released. He'd taken extra time to convince himself Aiden didn't have any of the common congenital problems that were frequently associated with white-blue eyes. He'd also sent for two of his medical students to observe the rare eye color. Aiden finally offered to come back for a full eye study when his injuries had healed if they would let him go now.

"I need to stop and see how Cammie is on the way out," he told the nurse who was pushing his wheelchair toward the exit.

The triage nurse overheard his request and answered. "She's in surgery. You might as well go get some rest. She's got hours yet to go."

Aiden buried his face in his hands.

"Hey," Harriet said. She put her hand on his shoulder to try and comfort him. "Darcy will be here in a minute. Where are you staying?"

"We're at a bed and breakfast on Eighth Avenue. It's called Helen's House."

"Will you be okay there by yourself?" she asked, and swept a strand of hair out of his face.

"I could stay with you." He looked up with a ghost of his usual impishness crossing his face. "I'm kidding," he said before she could react. "Helen will take good care of me." His face turned serious. "Besides," he continued, "I've got a job for you."

"Sure, what do you need?"

He pulled her closer. "The police talked to me before you got here. I told them someone had hit my truck and sent us over the edge. I don't know if they believe me. They said people don't do stuff like that in broad daylight where anyone could have seen them. I know my truck didn't run off the road because of water on the road like they're saying. I don't care what they think—someone ran me off the road. They rammed me twice."

"What do you want me to do?" Harriet asked, unsure where this was going.

"I saw the vehicle. I couldn't see who was driving, but it was a black Ford Explorer."

She still wasn't connecting the dots.

"Just like the ones I saw parked at your school. I want you to see if any of them have damage or white paint on their front fender or bumper. Don't confront anyone, just look and tell me what you see. Can you do that?"

"Sure. There have to be lots of black Ford Explorers, though. Not just at the school."

"Indulge me," he said.

She would check, but she was already thinking about the car that had taken her to dinner.

Darcy arrived before they could discuss it further. The B&B was less than a mile from the hospital, the house lemon-yellow with lots of the white lacy gingerbread Victorian houses are known for.

The front garden was English and surrounded by a white picket fence. Darcy held the gate open, and Harriet guided Aiden into the yard and then onto the wide porch.

The foyer continued the Victorian theme. A collection of Blue Willow plates were displayed on a lace-edged shelf around the perimeter of the room. A blue floral pitcher and bowl sat on a lace doily on top of a dark cherry bookshelf.

Helen turned out to be a plump woman whose long white hair was twisted into a simple bun on the top of her head. She wore a faded floral shirt-dress topped with a white apron. Her beige shoes were the type nurses and other people who spend a lifetime on their feet sported. She assured Harriet she would treat Aiden as if he were one of her own—he seemed to bring out the mothering gene in women of all ages, even when he didn't have a black eye.

"I expect he'll be just fine, but I'll call you if anything happens," she said. She'd gathered all the relevant phone numbers when they'd arrived.

"We do have a house full of doctors, you know," Aiden reminded them.

"That would be great if you were a dog," Harriet teased. "Oh, wait, you are," she added, and grinned.

"Very funny. I'm supposed to be getting sympathy here."

"Enough," Helen said. "You go get in your jammies, and I'll bring you a nice cup of tea and some toast."

"Hey, I hit my head, not my stomach," Aiden protested as Helen put her arm around his waist and turned him to the stairs.

"He'll be fine," she said, and waved over her shoulder as she followed him up.

Chapter Sixteen

Harriet sat in silence as Darcy drove back to the school.

"Could you stop by the office parking lot before we go back to the Tree House?" she asked when they turned into the main driveway. She quickly explained Aiden's request.

"Sure." Darcy pulled onto the shoulder a few feet before the office lot. "Let me get a couple of things from the trunk. If we find something I'll take a couple of samples, just in case. Even if we do find something, we may not be able to get any kind of evidence that proves anything."

"Thanks for doing this. Aiden seemed pretty sure it was one of the Explorers from here."

They walked up to the row of cars. The lot could hold eight, but only six were currently there: a Volvo station wagon, a small sedan of some sort, and four black Explorers. They stepped carefully to the front of the lot and, one-by-one, examined the cars.

"Make sure you go all the way around," Darcy whispered. "Sometimes the point of contact isn't where you think it will be. And don't touch anything."

She looked at the first car, and Harriet took the second. Both were free of scars. They returned to the front of the row and started toward the next two.

"We just hit the jackpot," Darcy said. "I can see it from here." Harriet came to stand beside her. "Geez, it's not subtle, is it."

Darcy moved closer to the front passenger-side fender. A large dent creased the shiny metal. Or maybe it was shiny plastic; Harriet was never sure these days. Darcy pulled a plastic bag from her pocket, broke it open and removed what looked like a scalpel. She took a small white envelope from her other pocket and scraped the dent, catching the shavings in the envelope. She sealed it and put it back in her pocket.

There wasn't a license plate on the front of the vehicle, so Harriet went around to the back. TOMTOM the vanity plate read. She got a sinking feeling in her stomach.

"I'll get a sample of the remains of the truck Aiden was driving and I can do the lab work when I get back to Foggy Point, but you do realize it won't be official, don't you? I mean, there won't be any chain of custody. And I'm not officially on the job. On the other hand, maybe this will help convince those yahoo's at the police station Aiden didn't just hydroplane off the road."

"I don't want to chance losing the evidence that Aiden was pushed—he thinks the police are pretty willing to write their report and close the books on the whole incident. I'd like to be sure that doesn't happen, whether it's official at this point or not. Besides, I may know who did it, anyway."

"And who would that be, Miss Marple?"

"Look at the vanity license plate."

"It's TomTom. Does that mean something?"

"Selestina's son is Thomas Bainbridge, and I happen to know he drives a black Ford Explorer. It fits, doesn't it?"

"Solving crimes is rarely that neat. You need a few things like means, motive and opportunity."

"I watched one of those reality crime shows with Aunt Beth, and they said you don't have to prove motive. They said juries like to *hear* a motive, but you didn't have to have one."

Darcy led the way back to the car, and they continued the conversation as she drove to the Tree House parking lot.

"Well, the cops I hang out with like to have a theory of the crime. So far, I'm hearing that an upstanding member of the local business community jumps in his car and runs a visiting veterinarian off the road for no apparent reason. Their only connection is that you're friends with one guy and you've—what?—met the other one?"

"I did go to dinner with Tom the other night," Harriet confessed.

"Are you that good?" Darcy asked with a smile. "You want me to believe that after one dinner Mr. Bainbridge tried to kill Aiden?"

"Okay, so there are a few holes in my theory. I'm just saying, on the one hand—black Ford Explorer, vanity plate that says Tom-Tom," She held her hands up as if holding an invisible ball in each hand. "On the other, a man named Tom who drives a black Ford Explorer."

Darcy parked and turned to face her, her pixie's face serious. "I'll do your tests for you, but, Harriet, if someone did run Aiden off the road you need to let the police handle it. And if we show them this evidence, they will. This is nothing to mess around with. And just in case you *are* on to something, stay away from Thomas Bainbridge."

"Okay, okay," Harriet held her hands up in defense. "Aiden asked me to check, and I did. Besides, I've got more than I can handle trying to figure out what's up with Lauren's quilt."

"Speaking of that, did you get the pictures from your aunt?"

Harriet patted the pocket of her sweatshirt. "Right here," she said, and got out of the car. "Let's go look at them with the rest of the group."

"I'll be there in a minute. I've got a few calls to make."

✂ ✂ ✂

"How's Aiden?" Robin asked as soon as Harriet came into the Tree House. She was in the kitchenette arranging lemon-ginger cookie crisps on a blue pottery plate. She was always the first person in line for treats, but somehow the last to show the effects of eating them. It had to be all the yoga, Harriet decided.

"He's pretty banged up, but he's going to be fine. The tech that was with him didn't fare quite as well."

"Did you get the pictures from Beth?" asked Connie from her perch on the sofa in the living room. She was cutting dark-green leaf shapes from a piece of floral fabric and setting them in a pile on the table in front of her.

Mavis was sewing sea-foam green batik triangles to brown squares with the quilting thread she favored for her hand stitching. She had explained to Harriet that quilting thread didn't tangle or fray as quickly as plain cotton sewing thread.

"I did, but I haven't even looked at them yet." She joined them and handed the folded pages to Connie. "I've got to go change into something more comfortable. You guys check them out; I'll be back in a second." With that she turned around and headed up the stairs.

She returned almost immediately, still dressed in her jeans.

"Have you been here all evening?" she asked Mavis and Connie, her voice harder than she intended.

"Yes, why?" asked Mavis.

Connie stood up and came over to her. "Mija, what's wrong? Here, sit down." She tried to lead Harriet to the sofa, but Harriet pulled free of her grasp.

"Someone's trashed my room. My bags were all emptied onto the floor, and the beds are torn apart."

"Can you tell if anything's missing?" Mavis asked.

"It didn't look like it. I mean, my jeans and shirts are there. My sewing things are all over the floor, but I can't imagine anyone would bother to steal that kind of stuff."

Mavis stood up. "Come on, we'll help you set it to rights. If you want, you can move down to our floor. Carla is in the alcove at the end of the hall and the bunk above her is empty. I know she won't mind."

"As long as you don't get between her and that clawfoot tub, she won't care at all," Connie added.

"I'm not leaving my room. I lived in Oakland, for crying out loud. We have one of the highest urban crime rates in the country. I'm not going to be scared off by some backwoods vandal." She paced across the room, running her fingers through her hair. "I have to say, in all my years in Oakland I never had my house robbed, my car prowled and certainly never was assaulted. I've been back in Foggy Point for what—two months? I've been whacked in the head, drugged and now this is the second time my stuff has been tossed." Tears welled up in her eyes, and she swept them angrily away with the back of her hand.

"This isn't Foggy Point," Mavis said gruffly. "Maybe there's a simple explanation." She led the way up the stairs to Harriet's room.

✄ ✄ ✄

"So, do you want us to move you down to Carla's room?" Connie asked when they had picked up Harriet's clothes and sewing equipment. "If you're moving, we don't have to remake the beds up here."

"I'm not moving," Harriet answered emphatically. "Someone was looking for something. If they come back, they can go to Carla's room just as easy as this one."

Connie unfurled the fitted sheet and stretched it onto the mattress. Harriet picked up the flat top sheet and helped her finish making the bed.

"They must have done this while we were in the dining cabin," Mavis decided.

"Wait—I thought you said you'd been here all night," Harriet said.

"I thought you meant here at the Folk Art Center. We went to dinner at six-thirty and got back around seven-thirty."

"Unfortunately, who ever it was had plenty of time to search," Connie said. "You know, now that I recall, when we came in the magazines from the coffee table were on the floor. I didn't think anything of it. It was a little bit windy when we came back from dinner, and I assumed a gust of wind blew in when I opened the front door and blew them off."

"So, someone is looking for something, but what is it?" Mavis wondered.

"I don't know. Where are the others? I wouldn't put it past Lauren to leave my room like that if she was looking for something."

"Oh, honey, Lauren wouldn't do that, and you know it," Mavis scolded.

"I wouldn't put it past her," Harriet repeated. "She's pretty insistent about me owing her."

"Robin and Carla were going to go look at the photography exhibit, and then they were going to see if they could help Lauren. She has to pull together another piece of her work to fill the space her missing quilt occupied. She had done samples of the various techniques she used in her final piece, so they were going to try to mount several of them on a piece of poster board. She said she doesn't have another piece as big as the one that's missing that fits

95

the theme. Sarah met someone at the pottery exhibit the other night, and she went to dinner in town with them." Connie left the room as she continued, "I'll go put the kettle on, and we can have a cup of tea and see if we can make sense out of this."

"Come on, honey," Mavis said, and put her arm abound Harriet's shoulders and gave her a little squeeze. "You've had a rough day. Have you had anything to eat yet? Let me fix you a snack, and then we can put our heads together and figure this thing out."

They followed Connie down the stairs.

"Go ahead," Harriet told Mavis and went to get the phone. "I'm calling the office to report the vandalism in my room."

✂ ✂ ✂

"They didn't seem overly interested," Harriet reported when she'd finished her call. Connie had brought out a tray with a steaming pot of tea and a plate with saltines and small slabs of cheddar cheese on it. She sat the tray on the table then handed Harriet the snack plate.

"I agree with Beth." Mavis picked up her copy of the quilt picture. "It looks a lot like Lauren's."

"What we need is a picture of Lauren's," Harriet said and set her now-empty plate back on the table. She was about to pull her copy of the picture from her pocket when she heard a soft tap followed by the Tree House door opening.

"Hello?" called Patience.

"In here," Connie replied, and got up to meet the new arrival.

"I heard Nancy leaving a message for Tom. She said someone's room in the Tree House was ransacked. I wanted to stop by and make sure everything was okay."

Connie poured her a cup of peppermint tea. "Here," she said, "sit down and we'll fill you in."

Mavis looked at Harriet, and when the younger woman remained silent, she gave Patience a quick account of the event.

Patience was silent for a moment.

"And nothing was missing?" she finally asked.

"I don't have that much here," Harriet said. "I haven't combed through my sewing bag, but my hoop and scissors and ruler and all

96

the big stuff is there. My clothes, my purse and ID are all here. I really don't have anything here worth taking. My cell phone was in my pocket. It makes no sense." She looked at Patience. It was clear the woman was trying to decide whether to say something.

"What? If you know something, say it."

"I don't know if this means anything. I mean, you ladies would know better than I."

"Patience," Mavis said in a firm voice. "Take a deep breath, and then just tell us what you know, or suspect, or whatever."

Patience did as instructed. "Everyone here has heard Lauren say that Harriet owes her. The teachers have been speculating what Harriet could have done to get in debt to Lauren." She pulled her ever-present crumpled tissue from her pocket and dabbed at her nose.

Harriet looked at Mavis with an "I told you so," expression on her face.

"That's not Lauren's style," Mavis protested. "Think about it. When have you ever known Lauren to be sneaky? She's an in-your-face kind of gal. If she thought you had something of hers, she'd demand you give it back." She sat back.

"I hate to say it, but I have to agree," Harriet conceded.

"So, that leaves us back at the beginning," Connie said.

Patience stashed her tissue in her sleeve and drank her tea. She asked polite questions about Connie's applique and Mavis's hand piecing.

"Would you like a refill?" Connie asked and pointed at the green mug.

"No, I need to go back to my cottage and review my class notes. I'll be teaching in Selestina's place. Not that anyone can really take her place, but the students have paid and the material must be presented." She looked like she had the weight of the world on her thin shoulders. "I just wanted to see if you needed anything."

"Thank you," Harriet said. "As you can see, I'm fine."

Patience set her hand on the door latch, and then stopped and looked back at the three women. "I did call the handyman and asked if he could drive around the grounds and watch for any suspicious activity." She left without waiting for any comment.

"So, what's that supposed to do?" Harriet asked. "No one needs to break in around here—nothing's locked. And we know the handyman doesn't live on the property. And everyone knows who he is. It would be pretty easy to avoid detection."

"What'd I miss?" Darcy asked before anyone could respond. She'd come in the door as Patience went out. She looked around. "What did Patience want?"

"She was just checking on us," Mavis said. "We were just about to look at Beth's pictures when she arrived."

Connie and Harriet picked up their copies and resumed their study of the images.

"It's hard to come to any conclusion without having pictures of both, side by side."

"Let me see," Darcy said, and took Mavis's copy. She turned it sideways and then upside down. She held it at arm's length and then propped it on the twig rocker and stepped back to look at it.

"What do you see?" Mavis asked.

"See the curved lines of stitching?"

"The ones that look sort of like topographical lines on a map," Connie asked.

"Yeah, only they're not topo lines. They're the ridge lines of a fingerprint. A thumbprint, to be exact."

"I could have told you that," Lauren said. Everyone turned as she joined the group. Robin and Carla went upstairs without saying anything. Harriet didn't blame them; they'd probably had their fill of Lauren.

"Why didn't you tell us that to begin with?" Harriet demanded.

"What difference would it make? I told you I made my quilt from scratch. What else do you need to know?"

"Now, honey," Mavis said. "If you want Harriet here to restore your reputation and help you find your lost quilt, you're going to need to cooperate just a little."

"What else does she need to know?" Lauren asked. Harriet could see she was truly perplexed. She really did live in another world.

"I'm not sure what else you can tell us, but let me take your fingerprint, and we can get the lady in the office to make an enlargement of it. Then we'll sort-of have proof that your quilt is the original. I mean, if this were a real criminal case, they would say Lauren's fingerprint could have been captured off any number of public surfaces and then used. But that would be bizarre."

"So, let's assume you take the print, we make a copy, we all swear that Lauren's print matches the shape on her quilt, and it's more detailed than what could be accounted for by random chance." Harriet paced as she spoke then turned to face the group. "What difference does it make?"

The cords in Lauren's neck tightened, and Harriet could see her chest rise in preparation for an outburst. She held her hand up, and Mavis put a hand on Lauren's arm.

"Let her finish," she urged in a hushed tone.

"What I'm saying is, as a student of Selestina's it wouldn't be unheard-of for Lauren's work to look like her teacher's. The real question is *why* Selestina would copy Lauren's work. Think about it. She's an acknowledged expert in her field. She's been making art quilts for years. She makes class samples; she's won awards." She looked at Lauren. "I'm not saying your quilt isn't great. It is. But why would an established artist copy the work of a second-year student?"

Lauren's mouth moved, but no words came out. Her anger deflated like a balloon.

"Come on, let's sit and have another cup of tea and think about that," Connie suggested.

"If I drink anymore tea I'm going to be up all night," Mavis announced. "But we do need to talk about this."

Lauren sat down on the couch. She opened her quilted shoulder bag and pulled out a foil-wrapped package.

"Here," she said, and began opening the foil. "My brother made us some brownies."

"Now you're talking," Mavis said. "Bring that pot back, Connie. Maybe I could choke down another dribble of tea with my brownie."

The women sat in near-silence, the only sound the munching of possibly the best brownies ever created.

"These are incredible," Harriet said, and reached for another one. "He's hit just the right balance of chewiness and cakeness."

"Yeah, well, he fancies himself a chef," Lauren said. "I keep

99

telling him he's never going to get anywhere if he won't leave this backwater place. But he says he's learning a lot from that witch in the dining hall."

Carla and Robin rejoined the group, and the quilters brought them up to date on their discovery about Lauren's fingerprint. They all discussed the situation, but no matter how they looked at it, it just didn't make sense. Lauren's piece was nice, but her work still lacked the maturity of a trained artist, so why would a woman whose work sold for thousands of dollars copy it?

Eventually, one by one, they drifted upstairs to their rooms, the problem unsolved.

Chapter Seventeen

Is Lauren Sawyer here?" asked the police officer Mavis found on the front step of the Tree House when she answered the door the next morning. He was a stout, dark-haired man with florid cheeks and a yellow-plastic-handled gun.

Mavis glanced at her watch. "It's a quarter before seven, young man. She's either in bed or taking her shower."

"I need to speak to her. May I come in?"

Connie came up behind Mavis.

"Is there a problem?"

"This officer wants to speak to Lauren."

"*Diós mio!*" Connie put her left hand to her mouth. The officer looked exasperated.

"I guess you better come in, then," Mavis said and stepped back.

"I'll go get Lauren." Connie headed up the staircase.

"I don't care who it is," Lauren could be heard saying from the second-floor landing a moment later. "I'm drying my hair."

Connie returned. "Lauren will be down when she finishes drying her hair."

"Can I get you a cup of coffee?" Mavis offered.

The officer accepted, and was sitting at the dining table with the two older women when Lauren finally came downstairs almost twenty minutes later.

"Lauren Sawyer? I'm Officer Weber. I need to ask you some questions, and I'm afraid you're going to have to come with me to the police station."

"Are you arresting me?" she demanded.

"We can play it however you want to," Weber answered, his voice no longer that of Officer Friendly. "I'd like you to come with me voluntarily to answer some questions. If you don't want to do that, I can arrest you and *then* you can answer our questions. It's your choice."

"Whatever," Lauren said. "Can I at least get my purse and coat?"

"Yeah, but don't try anything cute," Weber said.

Lauren glared at him and went back upstairs, returning moments later wearing a denim jacket and with a leather messenger bag slung crosswise on her body.

"Would you mind opening your bag so I can have a quick look?"

"What's going on?" Harriet said as she came down the stairs and joined the group now standing by the front door.

"What's it look like? Officer Weber here is hauling me to jail."

Weber looked at Harriet. "I'm taking Ms. Sawyer to the station to ask her a few questions, that's all."

"Harriet, come with me," Lauren said in a tone that was somewhere between a plea and a command.

Harriet looked an inquiry at the cop. He looked at Lauren.

"If it means you'll come quietly, sure," he told her

"Take notes in class," Harriet said to Carla, who had now joined the party. She grabbed her coat and wallet and was out the door before Carla could respond.

Weber opened the passenger doors of his Jeep Cherokee, and both women got in. Lauren had climbed into the back seat, so Harriet had no choice but to ride shotgun.

"Can you catch me up, here, Officer Weber? Why are you taking Lauren in for questioning? What is she supposed to have done?"

"She'll be informed when we get to the station."

"Can you at least give us a ball park here? Did she run a red light? Forget to pay her taxes?"

Weber gave Harriet a "you've got to be kidding" look. "She's being questioned by the homicide detectives."

Lauren was so quiet, Harriet had to turn in her seat to look and

102

see if she was okay. Her face was as white as alabaster, and for once she was dead silent.

The threesome rode the rest of the way with no further conversation. Officer Weber pulled to a stop in front of a low brick building then ushered them into a beige-painted lobby trimmed with orange circles inside brown triangles that screamed 1970.

"You can wait here," he said to Harriet, and indicated a row of orange vinyl chairs. Before she could take a full step toward them, Lauren snaked out a cold hand and gripped her arm like a vise.

"I'm not talking to anyone unless Harriet comes along."

Ordinarily, Harriet would welcome the chance to avoid spending time with Lauren, but her curiosity overrode her aversion this time.

"Instead of me," she said, and looked Officer Weber in the eye, "I think I should get Lauren's lawyer to meet us here."

"That won't be necessary. Just let me ask the detective. Wait here."

"Lauren, I wasn't kidding," Harriet said as soon as Weber had gone through a door to the inner office. "You should call a lawyer right now. You don't have to answer any questions without a lawyer present."

"I don't need a lawyer, Harriet." The edge had returned to Lauren's voice. She was nothing if not adaptable. "I haven't done anything wrong. I haven't done anything anyone needs to ask questions about. I'm the victim here. That crone at the school stole my design, and then one of her cohorts stole my quilt. I'm sure that's what they want to ask about."

"They don't use a homicide detective to ask questions about a stolen quilt. Besides, have you even reported it missing? Even if you have, the police don't spend time and money investigating petty theft. When my bike got stolen in Oakland, all I did was file a report."

"He just said that to scare me, and I'll admit, for a minute there, it worked. Do you think they have a homicide department in this backwater town? They probably only have one detective."

"You're wrong there, ma'am," a well-built Hispanic man in a navy suit and red tie said. "Ms. Sawyer, I presume." He held his hand out, but Lauren ignored it. "And you must be her friend

Harriet." Harriet took the proffered hand. "I'm Detective Ruiz."

"Lauren and I are in the same quilt group back in Foggy Point. We're staying in the same lodging at the Folk Art School. She asked me to come with her."

Lauren rolled her eyes skyward.

Harriet wasn't sure why the detective made her so nervous, besides the fact he was incredibly good-looking. She wasn't the one who was being questioned.

"Since this is an informal interview, I don't see any reason you can't join us. Why don't you two follow me back here."

He led them down a short hallway into a windowless beige room with a linoleum-topped steel table that had two chairs on each side of it.

"Have a seat." He pointed to the ones on the far side of the table. "Can I get you some coffee or water?"

They declined, so he sat down opposite them.

"If you don't mind, I'll record our discussion." He pulled a small recorder from his pocket and clicked it on. Harriet was pretty sure it wouldn't have mattered if they *had* minded.

Ruiz spoke a well-practiced identification into the recorder, noting who was present and what the date and time were.

"Ms. Sawyer—may I call you Lauren?" She nodded once, and he continued. "How long have you known Selestina Bainbridge?"

"Uh…" She stopped and cleared her throat. "I've been taking classes at the center for about a year."

Ruiz made a note on a pad he'd pulled from his pocket.

"Umm." Lauren cleared her throat again. "Selestina became my advisor two months ago. Before that, I was taking prerequisites with other people. She gave the introductory talk before each class session, but I didn't speak to her then."

You're talking too much, Harriet thought. She stared at Lauren, but the other woman had her eyes firmly locked on the tabletop as she babbled on.

"It seems you've been quite vocal about Selestina Bainbridge recently," Detective Ruiz commented.

Lauren blushed. Harriet shifted in her seat and kicked her under the table, hoping Ruiz didn't notice. Lauren scowled at her but, for once, she kept her mouth shut. Her compliance could only be an indication of how worried she was.

Detective Ruiz slipped a pair of black plastic-rimmed half-glasses out of his pocket and perched them on his ample nose. He looked over the lenses at Lauren.

"Selestina was my advisor," she went on, "so of course I talked about her to my classmates. We all compared notes about our teachers."

"According to the other students, it was quite a bit more contentious than that."

"We may have expressed our creative differences in front of other people, but that's all there was to it." Lauren looked so sincere Harriet almost believed her.

"Tom Bainbridge has reported to us that someone has been in his mother's office without permission and that many of her files are missing. Can you tell me anything about that?"

Lauren shook her head.

"Perhaps you would like to explain, then, how your fingerprints came to be all over the office of Selestina Bainbridge."

A young blond woman with a mouth full of metal braces opened the door and gestured to Detective Ruiz. He clicked the recorder off and pocketed it before following her out the door.

"*Did* you take the files from Selestina's office?" Harriet demanded as soon as the door was firmly shut.

"Technically, no." Harriet glared at her. "I wasn't in her office when they were taken. That's the truth—I've only been in her office once, and that was when I first signed up for classes. You have to be interviewed by Selestina when you sign up for the two-year program. I had both hands firmly on my notebook the whole two hours while that windbag rattled on."

Harriet pulled her cell phone out of her pocket. "I'm calling Mavis." She dialed the folk art school office and was transferred to the Tree House. "Mavis, thank heaven you're there," she said when the older woman picked up. "Lauren needs an attorney." She glared at Lauren. "They claim they found her fingerprints in Selestina's office, and that there are files missing...Lauren says it's impossible."

Mavis said for her to hold on a minute while she got Robin. She was gone before Harriet could ask why.

"Harriet?" Robin said when she picked up the phone. "I'm coming right over. Tell Lauren to keep her mouth shut. And I mean *shut*. You can tell them she's retained an attorney and that's all."

Robin was known in the Loose Threads for her talent at hand quilting, and anyone who talked to her for more than five minutes knew of her fervent belief that yoga was the answer to most problems one encountered in life. Clearly, she'd had another career before she'd become a yoga teacher and stay-at-home mom.

Harriet wondered briefly what other talents lay hidden within the Loose Threads.

Detective Ruiz returned some time later and sat down again. "Now, Lauren, I believe you were about to explain how your fingerprints ended up in Selestina's office."

"Lauren has been advised by her attorney that she should not answer any more questions at this time."

"What attorney? Are you telling me that all of a sudden you're an attorney?" He glared at Harriet. "Are you trying to pull a fast one? I only let you come in here because Miss Sawyer seemed upset. If this is how you thank me, you can go back out to the waiting room."

"I'm her friend, just like I said. We talked to her attorney, and she said not to say anything else and that she'd be here shortly."

"You do realize this is just an informal chat we're having here. Miss Sawyer isn't under arrest or anything." His voice softened. "We could clear things up and have you out of here before lunch if you could just explain a few things." He looked at Lauren. "I'm sure it's a simple misunderstanding."

The door to the small room opened without warning and Robin charged in.

"Are you arresting my client?" she asked Ruiz.

Harriet held her breath as he remained silent, pondering his options. The muscle in his jaw twitched, but finally, he shook his head.

"Come on, Lauren," Robin said, and almost pulled Lauren out of her chair in her haste to hustle her new client out of the interrogation room. "Here's my card," she said as she pulled an ivory card from her purse and handed it to Detective Ruiz.

"You better give me a dollar," Robin said when they were out of the building. "Call it a retainer. If you do get arrested you can decide then who you want to represent you, but in the meantime, that will make you my client and prevent the police from being able to question me."

"You're an attorney?" Harriet asked, her amazement clear in her voice.

"Yeah, well, we all have our tawdry little secrets. I haven't really practiced since before my first baby was born, but I've kept my license and stayed current on law, just in case..." She looked at Lauren. "...my friends need something." She looked at the black plastic sports watch on her wrist. "It's quarter to ten. If we hustle, we can get back to class before coffee break is over."

"Actually, if you don't mind, could you drop me off on Eighth Street?"

✂ ✂ ✂

Robin pulled to the curb but put her hand on Harriet's arm, stopping her from getting out. She looked at Lauren while she spoke.

"Both of you listen carefully. I only want to say this once." This new Robin was nothing like her carefree, yoga-teaching alter ego, but Harriet found her strangely fascinating. "Number one, this is not over. Until they have someone convicted and on their way to prison, it will not *be* over. Number two, because of number one, keep your mouth shut. Don't complain about anyone or anything. Lauren, I know that means a major personality transplant, but you have no choice. This is a small town. If they can't find the real person who killed Selestina, they could very well make you the scapegoat. People have gone to prison based on less evidence." She looked at Harriet. "And number three, leave this to the professionals. No snooping, no sneaking around, no confronting people. Nothing. This is strictly a defensive game. Let the police catch the killer." She looked at Lauren again. "And let your legal counsel protect you. Understood?"

Lauren grumbled a yes, and Harriet nodded as she opened the car door.

"Okay, I'm going back to class. Call if you want me to pick you up at lunch break."

Robin pulled away from the curb and out into traffic. Since traffic in Angel Harbor consisted of one car and a mail truck, Harriet waited until the car had disappeared down the block before she walked the rest of the way to Helen's House. There was no real reason for her to conceal her destination, but after Robin's warning, she was feeling paranoid.

"Hey," Aiden said, opening the door before Harriet could knock. He pulled her into a crushing embrace. "I cried myself to sleep last night, I missed you so much."

She pushed him away, but not until his hug softened and he'd kissed her. "You're a liar," she said. "I happen to know Helen planned on waking you every two hours all night just to be sure you were okay. She told me before I left last night."

"She was a regular Florence Nightingale." Aiden stretched his left arm in a circle, his right hand on his left shoulder. "My head hurt so much last night, I didn't even notice my shoulder."

"Let me see." She pulled the sleeve of his T-shirt up. "You have a nasty bruise at the top of it. It probably hit the window when your truck rolled."

"A lesser person would be in the hospital, but I think I'll make it. Did you have a chance to check out that thing I asked you about?"

"If you mean the Explorer—"

He put his hand over her mouth.

"Don't say it," he said. "Until we know what's going on, we have to be careful. Don't use names."

"Oookay. I checked out that…thing…and I did find…something, but I'm not sure it tells us much." She didn't plan on mentioning Tom's name until she knew more. The last thing she needed was a wounded Aiden confronting a Tom who had not only run him off the road but quite possibly was a murderer.

"By the way," Aiden said, and grabbed her hand, pulling her to him again. "Why is it that when my mother was killed I was the number-one suspect on everybody's list, but this woman's son you go to the pottery show and dinner with?"

Harriet coughed to conceal the small gasp that had escaped her lips. Had he read her mind?

"If you'll recall," she said, "I went to dinner with Tom before

108

his mother died. And furthermore, if you remember, I went to dinner with you, buddy boy—and more than once—while you were a suspect."

"Well, I don't like the idea of you dating a potential axe murderer." He put his finger under her chin and turned her face to his. "I'm not kidding. Until we know what's going on here, you need to be careful. I can't keep my eye on you all the time, so you need to be cautious. Stay away from Tom Bainbridge and all the other crazies at that school. Stick with Mavis and the Threads."

"Hey, Aiden, you ready to go?" said a slender sandy-haired man dressed in khakis and a blue Angel Harbor Spay and Neuter Clinic T-shirt. He had entered the hall from the staircase, pulling on a navy-blue fleece jacket as he came.

Aiden turned to Harriet. "Jim and I are going to the hospital to check on Cammi and see if we can do anything for Dr. Johnson." He turned back to the other man. "Hang on while I get my coat."

"I'm Jim Park," the sandy-haired man said, extending his hand.

"Harriet Truman," she said, meeting it with her own. His hand was warm and his grip firm but not unpleasantly so.

"That must have been tough growing up," he said. "Are your parents politicians?"

"No, we're relatives. To the former president," she added.

She hated having to explain her parent's naming choice. Her parents were international scientists, currently residing in the Far East, if the latest news magazines were accurate. She'd spent her youth bouncing between boarding schools across Europe and Aunt Beth's house in Foggy Point. Her dad had explained to her when she was six that her name was intended to inspire her to greatness.

"Aiden was really lucky," Jim said, interrupting her journey through self pity. "Or maybe I should say Cammi was *un*lucky. That was a big rock outcrop the truck hit as it rolled down the embankment. It was her bad luck the passenger side was down when they hit bedrock. If they'd made it a few more yards down the road before they skidded off, they would have missed the outcrop completely."

"Do you really think he could have slid off the road? It *was* raining pretty hard yesterday."

"I doubt it. It wasn't that wet at the time. Besides, Aiden told the police someone had sideswiped him. I drove over to the hospital when I heard about the accident, and they were questioning him. When Aiden pushed them, they did say there wasn't anything that would contradict his version of the event. They just didn't think it was the kind of thing that would occur in daylight on a relatively busy road." He shook his head. "It's just hard to say, one way or the other. The police are right that people often don't remember events clearly that happened right before they hit their heads. We'll probably never know."

I know, Harriet thought. And Tom's car had the scrape to prove it.

Aiden came back downstairs, and the two men left. They offered her a ride back to the Folk Art Center, but she declined. She needed to think. Maybe the walk back would help her clear her head. Thankfully, it wasn't raining.

Eighth Street was paved, but Helen's block was the last one with sidewalks. Harriet had to focus her attention on her feet as she walked along the gravel road edge until she reached a pedestrian path that skirted the woods on her right and was a safe thirty feet from the traffic on her left. She picked up her pace, going over the events of the last few days in her mind as she went.

She started with Lauren's situation, trying to list what she knew for sure. She realized quickly that if she questioned everything Lauren had said all she knew for sure was that Lauren's quilt was no longer on display and Lauren had been questioned about the death of Selestina Bainbridge, her advisor and the owner of the Angel Harbor Folk Art School. She had also learned that Lauren's brother was a janitor at the school, and she had seen Lauren going into her brother's apartment building at night. Her brother had been carrying an armload of papers, which may have come from Selestina's office. Harriet wasn't sure if the search of her own room was related or not. She hoped it hadn't been Lauren, but she couldn't be sure.

If she included information she *thought* was true, she could add the fact that Selestina seemed to have made a quilt that was a copy of Lauren's and then hung that quilt at a show in England.

With regard to facts related to Selestina, Harriet knew the woman was dead; everything else was speculation. It appeared

Selestina's son was preparing to sell at least part of the Angel Harbor Folk Art School property. What Harriet didn't know is if he was doing that *for* Selestina or in spite of her. As for enemies, it seemed that to know Selestina was to hate her; the field was wide open. DeAnn had publicly stood up to Selestina, and Carla had cowered under her wrath, and that was just among the Loose Threads. Most of the students Harriet had spoken to during coffee breaks and meals had similar stories about Selestina.

Added to the list of unknowns was Aiden's accident. He clearly believed one of the black Ford Explorers from the school had run him off the road. The damage to the vehicle that sported the "TomTom" vanity plate seemed to support his theory, but why would Tom want to harm Aiden? Could Cammi have been the intended target? Tom hadn't seemed to recognize Cammi at the pottery exhibition. It made no sense.

She looked up, and was surprised to realize she was nearing the drive to the school. She looked at her watch. Good, it was lunchtime.

Chapter Eighteen

The driveway that led into the heart of the Angel Harbor Folk Art School was carved through a stand of tall old-growth timber. The tree trunks were dark and bare, and the gravel on the road bed was barely discernible under the fallen needles, bark and fern leaves. The scent of Douglas fir and pine was released with every step Harriet took, but she was too distracted to notice.

She needed to talk to the Loose Threads and see if there were any new developments, and then she needed to talk to Lauren's brother. During her walk home, she had realized the only common factor among all the facts she knew was the school. Lauren was a student, Selestina and Tom the owner and her son and Aiden believed he'd been run off the road by an AHFAS vehicle.

Harriet's years at boarding school had taught her that if you want to know what's happening in any organization, ask the janitor. They were typically invisible, and yet they had access to everything. She was anxious to find out what Lauren's brother knew.

But first, she needed lunch.

The Loose Threads were seated together at the fiber arts table.

"How's Aiden?" Connie asked. She scooted to her left to make a place for Harriet.

"He's a little banged up, but mostly he's concerned for Cammi Johnson. He's at the hospital checking up on her now."

"Robin told us what happened at the police station," Mavis said. "Do you have anything to add?"

"Not really," she said, looking at Robin for direction. Robin didn't say anything, so she continued. "It doesn't seem like they have anything but gossip against Lauren. What did everyone do in class this morning?" she asked, changing the subject again.

Everyone in turn told what they'd worked on. Sarah and Robin had attended another class in fusibles, learning the technique of tracing their applique image onto paper-lined fusible material then using a sharp pair of scissors to cut the center of the image away leaving a narrow donut of iron-on material. This technique let you avoid the stiff image that most people associated with fusible applique.

Connie had spent the first half of the day covering postcard-sized pieces of foundation material with a variety of machine generated stitch patterns, until all you could see was thread. She had used her usual oranges, reds and yellows. Lauren's half-finished card was predominately purple and brown.

Mavis was still up to her elbows in dye, and Carla was using the half-square rectangle technique she and Harriet had learned to construct star blocks.

Lauren's brother brought out a tray laden with steaming bowls of soup. Today's selection was potato leek, served with dark slabs of Russian rye bread. The group was quiet as they ate their soup and then the fruit cups that followed. Harriet lingered with Mavis as the rest of the group went to either the Tree House or back to their classrooms.

"I've been going over this in my mind," she said.

"And?" Mavis prompted.

"And...none of it makes sense. There is a major piece missing somewhere. I just can't make anything add up to Lauren being the center of things. I get closer when I look at Selestina's son Tom. He seems to be preparing to sell the property. And his car seems to have run Aiden off the road. I can imagine Selestina wouldn't want her property sold out from under her, but we don't know if that's the case. How Aiden ties in is still a mystery."

"Maybe Aiden doesn't fit in. He wasn't in his own vehicle. Who should have been driving that vehicle?"

"Good point, I'll add it to the list."

"I'm going to get out of here so you can get busy getting some of that information." She stood up. "Let me know what you find out."

113

She left, and Harriet picked up their bowls and headed for the kitchen.

"Is Les around?" she asked the cook. The woman was bent over a deep sink, rinsing dishes with a stainless steel goose-necked sprayer then loading them into a rack.

"He's out at the compost pile. Through that door, down the stairs and follow the path—you can't miss it," she said without turning around.

Harriet followed the path and found Les emptying the second of two metal buckets onto the compost heap. A wooden fork was propped up against the end of the chicken wire fence that enclosed three sides of the smoldering organic material.

"Les?" she called. "Do you have a minute?"

He took a long look at her before he spoke. "Yeah, sure. I guess. If it will help you fix things for Lauren." He said it in a flat voice. Harriet found his enthusiasm underwhelming.

"The other night I saw you with an armload of files. Did they come from Selestina's office?"

He looked at her.

"So what if they did?"

"Hey, relax. I'm on your team."

"I doubt that."

"What did you find in the files?"

"A big bunch of nothing. It was shipping records. Angel Harbor has an arrangement with a couple of Folk Art Schools back east. They all give the same certification for their programs, and to be sure they stay calibrated they ship samples of student work to each other and they all evaluate it and see if they all come up with the same assessment.

"There were a couple of slips for shipments to England, but the descriptions weren't detailed enough to know what quilts they were talking about. And there was nothing that told why they were going. Other than that, there was a file of staff insurance forms. I tried to tell Lauren Selestina didn't keep much in that office."

"As janitor you can go into all the offices, right?"

"I have access to the whole school. Mostly, I work in the fiber arts building and its outbuildings."

"What about Tom Bainbridge's office?"

"Yeah, his office is in the ceramic arts building. I work there when we wax the floors or when Brett is on vacation."

"What can you tell me about him?"

"What do you want to know?"

Harriet wanted to smack him. If she were a detective, she'd have been the worst kind. She could see you had to be blessed with a lot of patience, something she didn't possess.

She took a deep breath. "The first day we were here, I saw Tom with some guys who looked like they were surveying the meadow. Is he selling some of the property?"

"I don't know if he's really planning on trying to sell it out from under his mother, but he's been talking to a couple of realtors." He paused. "I guess things are probably different now."

"Is it possible he was just getting the property valued for tax purposes?"

Les set his bucket at his feet and looked her in the eye. "Anything's possible."

"Tell me about the vehicles here. Who has access to the Ford Explorers?"

"Senior staff, Tom. Selestina, of course, although she didn't really drive much. Nancy in the office."

"Did they have assigned vehicles?"

"Not exactly assigned, but people had their favorites."

"But could anyone drive any of the cars? Were the keys kept in a public place?"

"They didn't need to bother. All the keys are the same. You got one, you've got them all."

Harriet clenched her fists at her side. "You must know something that can help me prove your sister didn't kill Selestina," she said. "Come on, throw me a bone."

Les rubbed the fine blond stubble on his chin as he thought.

"I don't know about the murder, but if you're trying to find her missing quilt, I'd check Tom's office and the workshop. He's the one that actually boxes and mails the stuff back and forth."

"Is the workshop in the center of the fiber arts building?"

"No, anyone can get into those rooms. There are some utility buildings in the woods, sort of hidden at the back of the property on the far side of the meadow. I think they were the original barn

115

and outbuildings before they built the school. Selestina has her personal studio there. And Tom does the packing there."

"So, what am I going to find?"

Les spread his hands wide. "I don't know," he said and when Harriet didn't say anything, he continued, "Really. It's the one place I don't have a key for. Selestina wanted her privacy when she was working on her own stuff. It's strictly off-limits."

"Are you sure you don't know anything else?"

"Look, don't you think if I had overheard someone talking about killing Selestina or even about setting Lauren up or stealing her work—don't you think I'd say something?"

"I suppose so. Thanks, anyway. And if you think of anything, let me know."

"You'll be the first," he said in a tone that told Harriet the opposite would be the truth.

Chapter Nineteen

Harriet went back to the Tree House and picked up her bag of tools and fabric. It was hard to think about her half-rectangle project when thoughts of Tom's office kept creeping into her mind.

None of the Loose Threads was in the Tree House, so she went into the kitchenette and helped herself to three chocolate chip cookies; Darcy had picked them up the day before at a little bakery when she was in town. Harriet knew none of the Threads would begrudge her the dose of chocolate, but she also knew Aunt Beth would grill them about her cookie consumption and none of them would stand up well to the pressure. She wiped her face and hands with a damp paper towel to insure she wasn't wearing any evidence and set off for the fiber arts pavilion.

She reached the fork in the path that led to the fiber building, and with thoughts of Robin and Aiden's warning ringing in her head, she went on past it and toward the ceramics pavilion and Tom Bainbridge's office.

When she reached the porch, she stashed her bag under a rattan bench then looked carefully each way before pulling open the large carved-wood door. She strode briskly toward the exhibition area, the one legitimate destination for a person outside the ceramics program. She wandered past a display of mugs without seeing anything; she could hear the grinding of potters' wheels coming from behind her, and a voice delivering a lecture off to her left.

Suddenly, she heard Tom Bainbridge's voice approaching. She stepped into the women's restroom, keeping the door cracked open so she could observe him when he walked past.

His companion turned out to be a cell phone, one with a strong signal, she guessed, given how poor the service was here. He was telling someone he would "be right there." Good, she thought. Wherever *there* was, it should give her enough time to see if Lauren's quilt was in his office. If it wasn't, perhaps there would be some useful shipping information.

She counted to sixty after the door closed behind him—she wanted to be sure he wouldn't come back for forgotten keys or a jacket or anything that would cause him to discover her rifling through his stuff. She went to seventy-five just for good measure then stepped out of the restroom, hurried down the hall and ducked into the room she'd attempted to hide in a few nights earlier.

The octagonal shape of the pavilion made for some unusual interior room shapes, especially since an attempt had been made to create rectangular classrooms wherever possible. Tom's office was one of the rooms that had absorbed a number of oddly angled walls. His desk sat diagonally across a narrow point where two walls came together. The table he'd been sitting at on her previous visit was in the middle of the room. Several sheets of paper were laid out side-by-side on its surface.

Harriet went to the table and picked up two of the papers. They appeared to be real estate documents. She quickly scanned them. They were competing offers for a piece of property that had to be the meadow.

"Find what you were looking for?"

She dropped the documents and turned to the door. Tom stood just behind a handsome gray-haired man carrying a black briefcase.

"If you'll excuse us, Miss Truman?" Tom said, and held the door open.

Harriet felt her cheeks burning. There was nothing she could say. She started out the door, but he grabbed her arm in a none-too-gentle grip.

"I've got a meeting that can't wait, but we aren't through. I will call for you..." He looked at the stainless steel Rolex on his wrist. "...in one and a half hours at the Tree House. Do not disappoint

118

me."

He released her, and she left, not stopping or taking her gaze from the floor until she was back out on the porch. She picked up her bag and headed back to the Tree House.

Mavis was in the kitchenette munching on a cookie when Harriet came in.

"What's wrong, honey," she asked around her mouthful. She reached out, putting the back of her hand on Harriet's forehead. "Your cheeks are pink, are you feeling okay?" she asked. "Do you feel feverish?"

"I'm fine—at least, for now, anyway." She explained her encounter with Tom.

"He can't just barge in here and demand that you go with him," Mavis said indignantly.

"I was trespassing, don't forget, and, actually, apart from my embarrassment, I'd *like* to speak to him. According to Lauren's brother, Tom is the one who ships quilts around from school to school for evaluation. He could have the answers about how a quilt that looks like Lauren's ended up in England."

"Oh, honey, do you think that's wise?"

"If we're going to help Lauren, we need answers." Harriet ticked off the points on her fingers. "One, Selestina copied Lauren's quilt—maybe—and, two, now Lauren is accused of killing Selestina. Three, we know Lauren didn't kill Selestina, but, four, the quilt copying has to be connected. I can just feel it."

She clenched her fists in frustration. "It's just too big a coincidence that as soon as we discover the plagiarism the person most likely to be doing it dies suspiciously. And now we find out that her son was selling her property out from under her, which gives *her* a good reason to want *him* dead, not vice versa."

Mavis took her by both hands, pulled her to a wooden stool and pushed her onto it.

"Take a deep breath, honey, you're turning red again."

Harriet did as instructed.

"All we really know," Mavis said, "is that someone killed Selestina and the police believe it was our Lauren. We know it wasn't, so that means a very dangerous person is still out there, someone willing to kill if you get in his way."

"I'll be careful. I'm telling you, when we figure out what's going on with the quilts, we're going to know who killed Selestina." Harriet picked a Braeburn apple from a bowl of fruit that had appeared on the counter since the last time she was at the house and put it in her pocket. "Besides, killers rarely do in strangers. We're in the most danger when we're with our loved ones."

"Well, that's a happy thought," Mavis said.

Harriet looked at the wall clock. She still had an hour before Tom arrived.

"Les also told me about some studio space Selestina has—it's farther back in the woods. If Selestina was copying student work, maybe the answers will be there. And I've got some time to kill before Tom comes back."

"I don't think going off in the woods by yourself to go snooping in a studio that is obviously private is a good idea," warned Mavis.

"I'll go with," Carla volunteered. She was just coming down the stairs and had apparently heard the last part of the conversation. She laid a sheaf of papers on the counter in front of Harriet.

"Do you even know where I'm talking about?"

"I heard you say it was Selestina's private studio."

"We'll be trespassing," Harriet reminded.

"I think Selestina's beyond caring," Carla replied, surprising Harriet. The girl was starting to show glimpses of a dry wit that might become wicked with the right guidance. "And if we can get things sorted out for Lauren that would be good, right?"

"I'd feel better if you had someone with you, honey," Mavis said as she picked up the tea kettle and started filling it with water.

Harriet looked from Carla's hopeful face to the worry lines on Mavis's wrinkled one.

"Okay," she surrendered with a sigh. "We better go if we're going to do this."

Carla opened the door and found Patience on the porch. She stepped aside to let the teacher in.

"You two look like you're going somewhere."

"We're just going out for a walk around the meadow," Harriet said.

"Yeah, we been sitting all day," Carla added.

Patience looked over the rims of her glasses. "Apparently not in

120

the classroom."

Carla started to say something, but Harriet nudged her and the words died on her lips.

"At least, *one* of you didn't show up. Ray Louise said Harriet wasn't in class today. She asked me to check and make sure nothing was wrong."

"A friend of mine from Foggy Point is here in town, and he was injured yesterday, so I went to visit him this morning. You know, to make sure he was okay."

"Oh, I'm sorry. I didn't mean to imply you were playing hooky. We just…" She stopped and thought a minute, then began again. "Selestina always wanted to make sure students got their money's worth when they were enrolled here, and between our lovely setting and the rigors of our curriculum, students have a tendency to start skipping class as the week wears on. Some of the teachers get overwhelmed with students coming to them at the end wanting notes and materials from the class sessions they missed, and unfortunately, some dealt with the issue by refusing to give notes out except in class."

"So, you're the truant officer," Harriet said with a half smile.

Patience smiled back at her. "I suppose I am."

"I got the handouts for Harriet," Carla said, and then looked at her feet. Harriet realized she hadn't seen her do that lately.

"I guess you won't need these, then," Patience held up a sheaf of papers that was identical to the set Carla had placed on the counter a few minutes earlier.

"Oh, Patience, I'm sorry you went to all the trouble. Thank you," Harriet said.

"It was no trouble. You were doing so well in class yesterday, I didn't want you to miss anything." Patience turned and went back out.

"Seems like people around here are bending over backwards to make sure the students don't leave early because of Selestina," Mavis said. "That woman's visited us at least once a day, hasn't she? Jan said she's been coming by their place, too."

"You can't blame her," Harriet said. "She's still got a business to run. She needs to make sure we all come back."

"I suppose so." Mavis looked at the clock. "You better scoot."

Carla and Harriet left the Tree House and went down the path toward the meadow.

"It's not too late to change your mind," Harriet said as they entered the woods.

"I'm good," Carla said. She tipped her head down. "This is a lot more exciting than diapers and laundry."

Harriet looked at her, and a wave of guilt washed over her as she thought of how much time she spent feeling sorry for herself, sitting with a full stomach on her comfortable couch in her warm parlor with soft music playing on her stereo. Carla was living in a car, raising a baby and probably going to bed hungry, by the looks of it. Yet, here she was at Harriet's side, willing to risk life and limb to help Lauren, who as near as Harriet could tell had never been anything but mean and judgmental toward her.

Chapter Twenty

The path from the Tree House joined the loop trail just beyond the dining cabin. The women followed the trail past the fiber arts building and then the ceramics building. The day was warmer than the previous one, and the damp layer of rotting needles and bark that made up the forest floor gave off a fine cloud of fir-scented steam.

A duck flew across the meadow as they entered the clearing, skidding to an open-winged stop as it reached the water. Carla jumped as it flapped its wings.

"Sorry," she said. "I guess I'm a little jumpy."

Harriet had noticed Carla had the sort of startle reflex one associated with whipped puppies and battered women.

"The studio should be somewhere over there," she said, and pointed across the pond. She raised her hand up to shield her eyes from the sun, but she still couldn't see a building. "Can you see anything?"

Carla squinted and shaded her eyes. "I think I see it." She pointed across the pond and to the left. "See, kind of behind that big spruce tree. It's really dark, but you can see the sun reflecting off the window."

Harriet looked, and could just make out the dark shape of the studio. "Come on," she said and led the way around the water. A flock of mallards skittered away from them and back toward the safety of the pond's center.

"Boy, if Miz Bainbridge was wanting her privacy, she picked a good spot." Carla said.

"I wonder if this was one of the original buildings on this property. Look at how thick the moss is on the roof."

Roof moss in the Pacific Northwest wasn't the pretty lace organism that adorned the graceful old oak trees in the south. The algae and moss that grew on northern roofs appeared in thick, yellowish-green lumps that thrived in the dark and damp weather. It shortened the life of roofs covered in asphalt shingles just as easily as it did wood shakes. In urban areas, you saw a variety of remedies used, from zinc or copper strips to oxygen bleach. In the country, you were more likely to see sagging roofs straining under the load of many years' accumulation.

Selestina's studio was in the latter category. The roof sagged, and the cedar siding was bleached white where the sun reached it and coated in green and black algae where it didn't. The wooden door had three small glass windows at its top. The center pane had a long diagonal crack.

"Now," Harriet said when they had made their way to the front of the building. "I wonder how we're going to get inside."

While she was musing out loud, Carla walked up the rotting wooden steps, grasped the rusty tin doorknob and turned.

"It's open," she called back over her shoulder as she went through the doorway.

"Wait," Harriet called out, but it was too late. Carla was inside, and the door had shut behind her.

Harriet took the steps in two leaps and pulled the door open. She promptly ran into Carla, who was standing just inside, rooted to the spot.

"Wow," said Harriet as she looked around.

They were standing in an entryway facing an open door that led to a large room with a high ceiling. Harriet stepped past Carla to the center of the workspace. A large cutting table was to the left of the door; its surface was made of green self-healing cutting mat material; the mat compound separated when the blade cut into it then closed back up when the blade was past. Selestina could use her rotary cutter—a round, razor-sharp blade in an ergonomic plastic handle that had replaced scissors as the favored cutting tool among quilters—without fear of scarring the table surface. The table looked like it was large enough to lay a double bed-sized quilt on with room to spare.

At one end of the table and a few feet back was a shoulder-high horizontal oak rack that held quilting rulers of all sizes and several shapes. A quilter's ruler is marked in eighth-inch increments both horizontally and vertically. In addition, they often have forty-five-degree and sixty-degree angles marked on their surface. There are several sizes almost every quilter has—six inch by eighteen or twenty-four inch is common. Most people also have a six- or eight-inch square. Beyond that, ruler collections were dictated by the types of quilting the individual did. People who tended toward small, intricately pieced projects usually had smaller rulers; bigger pieced projects dictated larger rulers. Selestina appeared to have one of every size and type ever made.

The long wall behind the table had two large design walls mounted on it. Carla walked around the table and stood in front of the nearest one. A series of fabric squares in varying shades of brown and green were stuck to its surface at eye level.

"These look like the background of Lauren's quilt," she said.

Harriet came around the opposite end of the table to stand beside her.

"Maybe." She pulled one of the squares from the tacky surface.

Traditionally, design walls are a large piece of flannel attached to an empty wall somewhere near a quilter's sewing machine. The one hundred-percent cotton fabric that is used in quilt-making sticks to flannel once the cotton has been cut into pieces, enabling a person to lay out and evaluate segments of their quilt before they stitch the parts together. Selestina had a high-tech version of flannel. Hers had been treated with a sticky material that gripped the cotton more firmly, allowing for more precise layouts.

Harriet felt the fabric then held it up to her nose.

"What are you doing?" Carla asked.

"I was hoping to tell if this was hand-dyed fabric. Lauren dyed her own fabric. This smells faintly of vinegar. Acetic acid is one of the chemicals people use to set dye. There are commercial products that will do the trick, but some people still use vinegar."

Carla walked along the wall past the cutting table area to another table. This one was smaller and lower, with a wheeled armless chair pushed up to it. A light box was built into its surface. She felt along the edge of the table until her finger hit the switch. She flicked it on.

"Wow," she said.

A page that looked like it had been torn from a spiral sketchbook was taped to the center of the lighted portion of the table surface. A larger sheet of tracing paper was taped over the first sheet. It appeared that someone was in the process of copying the image from the sketchbook page to the tracing paper.

"What have you got?"

"Someone is copying a really cool picture from a sketchbook."

"Is it Lauren's?"

Carla bent closer to the page. "It's not the one she's in a flap about. There's some writing at the bottom of the page, but the tape is covering up part of it. I can't tell if it's a name or not."

Harriet crossed to the opposite side of the room. Four sewing machines sat on tables in a row. Selestina had one each of the popular brands, each a high end model for the maker.

"Business must have been good," she said, running her hand across the top of the nearest machine. She opened the partially completed quilt that was folded neatly at its side. "Whoa, look at this." She held it up. "Look familiar?"

"Oh, my gosh, isn't that the quilt that was hanging to the left of the entry door in the exhibition hall? In the group before Lauren's? Or at least most of it?"

"Looks like it's well on its way to being an exact copy." Harriet folded the quilt and put it back on the machine table.

A tall shelving unit filled with folded fabric that was organized by color separated the sewing machine area from what appeared to be a sitting area. Two matching overstuffed chairs with ottomans sat on either side of a multi-headed floor lamp. A woven-wood basket was on the floor beside one of the chairs. A piece of folded fabric lay on top of the basket.

"This just keeps getting better." She unfolded the fabric and held it up.

"Geez," Carla said as she recognized the quilt top. "They copied the applique class, too?"

"So it would seem."

Harriet moved to the final space in the room. Two computers

126

sat on desks, side by side. One had an in-basket next to it on the desktop and a lateral file cabinet standing beside it. The other had an oversized monitor and a *For Dummies* book on a popular quilt design software program lying open beside the keyboard. Clever, thought Harriet. They were using design software to analyze other people's original work.

They still didn't know why the copies were being made, but she and Carla were getting a clear idea of how they were doing it.

"Let's see where the back door leads," she called to Carla.

Two doors were set in the back wall. Harriet turned the knob on the first and pushed, exposing a neat white-tiled bathroom. She leaned her head in and looked around.

"Nothing in here," she said.

Carla turned the knob and opened the remaining door, exposing a large kitchen. A Formica-topped fifties-style table with red vinyl-seated chrome chairs sat in the center of the room. One wall contained typical appliances, including a full-size stove, refrigerator, microwave and an industrial-sized dishwasher. The opposite side of the room had two double utility sinks with wood-topped counter space on either side of the sinks. A bundle of dried flowers and branches lay on the counter to the left. A pair of garden shears was on the counter beside the flowers; a pair of worn leather garden gloves had been abandoned next to them.

"This is quite the set-up," Harriet said as she entered the room. Carla followed her.

"Why didn't they fix up the outside?" Carla wondered. "I mean, the inside is really cool, but the outside looks like it's falling down."

"I don't know, but sometimes when property or zoning laws change, especially if there's an environmental impact, you're only allowed to repair existing structures, not rebuild or replace. People leave old boards to try to prove they haven't really built something new. Maybe something like that happened."

"Seems like it wouldn't be very safe to have that old siding and roof on a building this big."

"Oh, I'd be willing to bet that between in here and the ramshackle outside is a bunch of engineering."

Carla had come to stand beside her. She tilted her head and

looked at the open-beam ceiling. A loud click sounded behind them.

Carla grabbed Harriet's arm. "What was that?" she whispered.

"I don't know." Harriet went back to the connecting door. She twisted and pulled on the knob. "It's locked." she said.

"Are you sure it isn't just stuck?"

Harriet pushed, pulled, twisted and rattled, but the knob didn't budge. She turned around and noticed two doors at the back of the kitchen. The one in the left-hand wall led to a screened porch. She went onto the porch, crossed and tried its door.

"Locked," she reported.

The door in the right wall opened onto a dark stairway that led downward. She shut it again quickly.

"I'm not going down there. We're going to find another way out of here that doesn't involve a dark, damp stairwell into the unknown."

Carla took a thin spatula from the dish rack and went back to the door between the kitchen and the sewing room. She slid the flexible blade between the door and the jamb. It clicked as the blade hit metal.

"Someone's turned the deadbolt," she said, her eyes round.

"Don't panic." Harriet looked around for other possible ways out. She turned a full circle, noting the high clerestory windows. Her eyes came back to the door Carla was standing at.

"Oh, jeez," she said. A thin curl of smoke was seeping under the door. "Get away from the door."

She went to the counter and started pulling drawers open. When she found dishtowels, she pulled a handful out and threw them into the sink. She turned the faucet on and soaked the towels then rolled them lengthwise and carried them back to the door, pressing them along the bottom crack.

"See if you can get anything to open on the porch," she called, but Carla was already there, rattling the storm windows and pulling on the door. Harriet heard a crash. She found Carla banging a ceramic flowerpot she'd found on the floor into the window. A fine pattern of cracks spread across the glass from the point of impact, but the window didn't give.

"There's wire or something in the glass," she cried, panic clear in her voice.

Harriet took a closer look. "It looks like its some kind of safety glass."

She pulled her cell phone from her pocket. She dialed Aiden's number, and his phone went directly into his voicemail.

"We need help," she said, and her phone went dead.

"What happened," Carla asked, her voice rising. "Why did you stop talking?"

"I lost the signal. And his phone went straight to his voicemail anyway."

Carla pulled a drawer open on a hutch standing against the back wall of the building. She found a small common head screwdriver.

"We can unscrew the hinges," she suggested, but Harriet could see the screwdriver wasn't going to be up to the task.

She looked back to the connecting door and could see smoke starting to once again curl into the room, this time around the edges of the rolled towels.

"There has to be another way out of here," she said. "We don't know what's in that basement. What if there's a body?"

"Why would you think that?" Carla's eyes went wide.

"No reason." Harriet tried to mentally take herself to a peaceful place. She imagined a grassy meadow and herself riding bareback on a large white horse.

She'd come home late one night after a movie with her girlfriends and crawled into bed in her dark bedroom beside her cold, dead husband, who had passed away in her absence. It had taken her several years of therapy, during which her counselor had taught her to imagine herself in a safe place, before she could sleep in a bed again. Even though Steve had died five years ago, she still hadn't conquered the dark-room thing.

✂ ✂ ✂

Carla looked at Harriet and straightened her spine. She went over to the cabinet drawers and dug around until she found a small penlight, a couple birthday candles and a book of matches. She clicked the penlight on and was rewarded with a wavering yellow beam that indicated a used-up battery. She flicked it off quickly. It would

129

probably only be good for one quick flash before it died completely.

"Come on." She took Harriet by the hand and led her down the stairs, not mentioning the penlight's condition.

She rhythmically swiped her toe across the next step before putting her weight on it, pulling Harriet along with her. Every two steps she reached up and felt for a low overhead, warning Harriet to duck when they reached one.

Harriet stumbled, jamming her toe on the last step.

"Ouch!" she cried.

"Are you okay?" Carla whispered.

Harriet assured her she was fine but limped when she tried to walk.

"This way, I think," Carla told her and led her slowly to the right, again feeling with her toe and sweeping every now and then with her hand, stopping when they came to a large sheet-metal box.

"I think this is the furnace," she said, and carefully felt her way around it, continuing around the perimeter of the room.

"How is it you're so good at this?"

"I've spent a lot of time in the dark," Carla admitted with a sigh.

They were silent for a few minutes as they continued their exploration.

"My momma was very young when she had me. She's spent a lot of time trying to find a man who would make her troubles go away. My daddy took off when I was born. He said he was too young to be a father.

"Then my momma took up with Danny. She said he beat us; I don't really remember that, though. After that, she was with Bobby Jo, and he liked little girls more than he liked my momma, so she started locking me in the basement or closet or toolshed or wherever she could to keep me away from Bobby Jo until she could get away from there. After that, I guess the closet turned out to be a good babysitter."

✂ ✂ ✂

Harriet was glad for once that it was dark; she knew she had to have a look of horror on her face. Carla was very matter-of-fact in her recitation. A thousand questions came to Harriet's mind, but she didn't want to upset the girl.

"What did you do to pass the time?" she finally asked.

"I pretended I was a princess. My dolly was my attendant. We were in the kingdom of dark and needed to search to find the prince and set him free."

"And did you ever find him?"

"No. I'm still looking. But I've met a lot of interesting creatures along the way."

"You're a stronger woman than I am," Harriet admitted. "I still sleep with a nightlight." She knew if she could see Carla, the young woman would be blushing.

✂ ✂ ✂

Carla sneezed. They had just gone through an open doorway into another space. She sneezed again.

"I have hay fever," she said, apologetic. "There must be something in here." She stepped carefully along the wall of the new room. Something rustled when she swept her hand overhead. She took a half-step and reached up again.

"Feel this," she said, and guided Harriet's hand up to what felt like a clump of dried flowers. She stepped forward and felt again. "I think someone is drying herbs or something in here. It feels like a series of bouquets or something hanging from the ceiling."

✂✂✂

Harriet stepped around Carla and crept forward, moving her hand from one bunch to another.

"I think you're right. Did you notice the dried flower arrangements in our rooms? Someone here seems to be into it. In my room they have dried lavender and eucalyptus in the arrangement. I guess it's a good way to keep the rooms smelling fresh."

"Does eucalyptus grow here?" Carla asked.

"I don't think so. But I bet they harvest wildflower seeds for the meadow. I've tried using those wildflower mixes, and the first year they look great but the second year only the ugly stuff comes back and it goes downhill from there until you have a big patch of weeds. I'd be willing to bet someone seeds that meadow by the pond. It looks too good to be natural."

Carla sneezed again. "Come this way," she said. Harriet moved toward her voice and bumped into her.

"Sorry."

"It's okay. I think I felt a little air coming from across the room. Hold my hand—we're going to take it slow."

Harriet was impressed by how surefooted Carla was. She led them carefully across to the other corner of the room and then along the wall to the right.

"There's a door here," she said.

"Let me see." Harriet found the latch and opened the door. "You're right, there's a definite feel of fresh air in here."

Carla once again led the way.

"Stay close," she said. She started carefully across the room then stopped. "There's a step here. I'm going to go up and see if there are more." She moved, and Harriet heard a thump followed by an "Ouch!"

"There are steps that go up, but the ceiling doesn't."

Harriet stepped onto the first step and reached up. She patted the sloped ceiling. "Do you still have the little light?"

Carla handed her the penlight, and Harriet turned it on, scanning the ceiling.

"Yes," she said, and held her hand up for a high five. Carla slapped it. She swept the small light around the space they were in.

"This is some kind of root cellar, and if we can pry the latch open, it's our path to freedom."

Carla worked her way to a wall shelf revealed by the dim light. Harriet heard the rustle of metal.

"There are some old tools here." She came back with a hammer and some kind of file or chisel. Harriet wedged the chisel under the latch and hit it. The latch popped out of the door on the first try.

It took three tries and all the strength both women possessed, but finally the door swung open with a bang.

"Let's get out of here," Harriet said quietly and limped forward.

They had come out on the west side of the building.

"I think we should go into the woods and circle around the meadow, since we don't know where our tormentor is."

"I like the dark," Carla said quietly.

Harriet shook her head and limped quietly into the woods. A last glance back revealed smoke seeping out of the high windows of the workroom.

"How bad is your foot?" Carla asked. "Do you want me to go get help?"

"It hurts, but I think it's just my toe. It'll be okay. Let's get back to the Tree House and call for help."

Carla positioned herself next to Harriet and pulled Harriet's arm over her thin shoulders.

"Here, lean on me."

They were on the path to the Tree House almost a half-hour before they heard sirens. There wouldn't be much left for the fire-fighters to work with.

Chapter Twenty-one

Mavis pulled the door open as Harriet, leaning heavily on Carla, came onto the Tree House porch. She took over providing support and guided Harriet to the sofa.

"*Diós mio!*" Connie cried, glancing heavenward as she pulled a pillow from the chair and put it on the coffee table. "What have you done?" She gently guided Harriet's foot to the pillow and began undoing her shoelaces.

"What time is it?" Harriet asked, looking at Mavis.

"He hasn't come yet, if that's what you're asking. Are *you* okay?" she asked Carla.

"I'm fine." Carla collapsed onto the sofa beside Harriet.

Connie fetched two glasses of water. "Here, drink this," she commanded.

Harriet took a sip and set her glass down. "Someone tried to kill us," she announced.

"They burned Selestina's studio," Carla said at the same time.

Mavis held her hand up. "One at a time."

Carla's face flushed, and she was silent as Harriet gave a recap of their discovery of the outbuilding, being locked in, trying to call Aiden without luck and then escaping through the root cellar.

"Oh, my gosh—Aiden!" said Mavis. She went to the phone and began dialing. "He called here looking for you. He said he'd gotten a cryptic message. I told him you'd gone to the meadow to look for Selestina's workroom."

She left a brief message stating that Harriet and Carla were back at the Tree House.

"I think we should pack up and go home," Connie announced. "First Aiden's in an accident, and now Harriet and Carla are nearly trapped in a fire."

"What about Lauren?" Harriet asked. "I can't believe I'm saying this, but if we leave now, what's going to happen to her? I'm not saying I owe her or anything, but after the setup we saw, it's pretty clear she's, at the very least, a victim of plagiarism. If we leave, she's the number-one suspect in Selestina's murder with no one to defend her."

"Shouldn't we call the sheriff's office?" Connie asked.

"And tell them Carla and I were locked into a building we'd broken into, and then someone set it on fire? We don't even know for certain we were the target. Maybe whoever was burning the place locked the door out of habit."

"That makes no sense," Mavis argued as she wedged herself between the two younger women. "Why would they bother to lock an interior door if they were going to burn the place down? I do see what you mean about breaking and entering, though."

"The door wasn't locked," Carla offered.

"Well, I guess that's something, honey." Mavis patted her leg.

Harriet closed her eyes and leaned her head back, listening to Connie and Mavis argue the merits of going versus staying. A sudden hammering on the front door interrupted the discussion. Mavis got up, but the door opened before she could reach it.

"Harriet," Tom Bainbridge shouted.

"Tom?" Harriet took her foot off the table and stood up.

"Good afternoon, ladies." He nodded to Connie and Mavis and ignored Carla. "If you don't mind, I'd like to speak to Harriet."

"Go ahead," Mavis sat back down on the sofa.

"Alone, please." Tom remained standing.

"Not a chance," Mavis said.

"It's okay, Mavis. We'll be right out front." Harriet looked at him. His jaw was tight. He nodded once and stalked out onto the porch. She followed and pulled the door shut behind her.

"I'm really sorry," she said as she turned to face him.

"You should be," he snapped. "What did you think you were going to find, going through my files?" He ran his right hand

135

through his hair and began pacing the length of the porch.

"Harriet!" Aiden took the porch steps two at a time, stopping when he reached her side. "Are you okay? Mavis said you and Carla were in a fire." He held her at arm's-length, surveying her intently.

"I'm fine."

"You were at the workshop?" Tom grabbed Harriet's arm and spun her toward him.

"Get your hands off her," Aiden said and shoved him away.

Tom shoved back, and Aiden stumbled down the first two stairs. He leaped back up and hit Tom with a right hook to the jaw. Tom stumbled and fell to sit on the floor.

"Stop it!" Harriet yelled. She pushed Aiden back and crouched down beside Tom.

The door banged open, and Mavis appeared.

"What is going on out here?" she demanded, hands on her hips.

"He grabbed Harriet," Aiden said, sounding more like a spoiled eight-year-old than a grown veterinarian.

Tom stared at Aiden and Mavis but said nothing as he swiped at the trickle of blood leaking from the corner of his mouth.

Mavis turned to Harriet.

"Take Tom into the kitchen and get him cleaned up. And you…" She turned to glare at Aiden. "You go into the living room with Connie, and then we'll get this sorted out."

The men withdrew to their appointed corners, and Mavis put the kettle on the stove. Harriet wet a paper towel and handed it to Tom.

"I should have the lot of you thrown in jail," he muttered.

Harriet rifled through the drawers and found a sandwich bag. She pulled a strange-looking aluminum ice cube tray from the freezer. She tilted it from side to side, trying to figure out how it worked.

"Pull the handle," Mavis said.

Harriet did as instructed, and the cubes loosened. She filled the bag, wrapped it in a towel and handed it to Tom. She could hear Connie's voice from the common room. She couldn't hear the words, but the former teacher's tone said it all. Aiden was getting a thorough tongue-lashing.

Mavis's kettle whistled, and she poured hot water into of mugs she'd prepped with tea bags. She put them on a tolework tray and carried them to the dining table.

"Now, everyone sit down, and we'll see what we've got here," she ordered, and began distributing tea.

Connie brought Aiden in and sat beside him on one side of the table. Harriet and Tom sat opposite them, with Mavis at the head.

"I'll start," Harriet said. "I'm the reason Tom's here." She looked at him. "I'm sorry about this."

Aiden's face reddened, but Connie put her hand on his arm, silencing him.

"Tom found me searching his office this afternoon," Harriet continued. She looked him in the face. "Our friend Lauren is a long-term student here. We went to her exhibition, and my aunt, who was visiting from Foggy Point, joined us. She's just returned from a cruise to Europe, and she noticed that Lauren's quilt was an exact duplicate of one she saw in a gallery over there. Lauren swears she didn't copy anyone else's work and asked me to help her figure out what was going on. We went back to look at her quilt again and discovered it was missing. Someone said you were the one who shipped students' work to the other schools in your system for evaluation."

"You could have asked," he pointed out.

"Yes, I could have, but if you were involved in the copying, why would you tell me the truth?"

"What you're saying makes no sense. You just said your aunt saw a copy in Europe. If I were masterminding a quilt-copying ring, why would I take your friend's quilt *after* the fact? What would I be doing with it? It had already hung in the exhibition."

"Hello! To destroy the evidence?" Connie suggested. "You might have realized we were on to you."

"And just exactly how did I figure that out? I've met Harriet exactly twice. The second time, we went out to dinner when that clown stood her up." The last was accompanied by a smirk at Aiden.

"So, you're saying you don't know anything about Lauren's quilt being copied?" Harriet asked.

137

"That's what I'm telling you. I ship quilts a couple of times a year, but just to the other two folk art schools we work with. They ship students' work to us and we do the same. Everyone evaluates the work independently, and then they all get together to see if they agree."

"Tom, someone is copying quilts. Carla and I saw the evidence. It was in the workshop on the other side of the meadow."

"That's convenient," he scoffed. "That would be the workshop someone tried to burn down? Did you break in there, too?"

"The door was open," Carla said softly from her perch at the end of the sofa in the common room.

"Wait, you said *tried* to burn down?" Harriet said.

"I'm not sure anyone was actually trying to burn anything down. One of the big garbage cans *was* filled with fabric then doused with something flammable and set on fire. The fireman said they would do some tests, but it looked like it was gasoline. It mostly just smoked the place up, though."

"I can imagine what that fabric was," Harriet said. "We saw several copied projects in process."

"It makes no sense," Tom argued. "Why would anyone want to copy *student* work? No offense," he added and glanced at the women sitting around the table.

"That's what we've been trying to figure out," Mavis said.

"Did you ship teachers' work also?" Harriet asked.

"Sometimes, but mostly they did their own thing. We keep acid-free paper and boxes. The teachers came and got packing materials from me once in a while."

"What about your mother?" Harriet persisted.

Tom looked down at the table. It was almost a minute before he spoke. "My mom hasn't shown any of her work in a while," he said quietly.

"Was your mother planning on selling the school?" Harriet asked in an abrupt change of topics. Mavis looked at her and raised her eyebrows.

"No," Tom said. "No." He studied his hands. "I'm sure you saw the property offers on my work table." He looked up at Harriet. "Is that what you were really doing in my office?"

"No," Harriet assured him. "But I have to admit I was curious.

I mean, one day we see you with surveyors, and then a few days later there are property bids."

"It's none of your business what I do or don't do with my mother's property."

Aiden stood. "This isn't getting us anywhere. I've got to go to the hospital to check on Cammi." He looked at Tom. "Sorry," he said and held out his hand. Tom stared at it but made no move to take it. "Whatever," Aiden muttered and left.

"Tom," Harriet said, "I'm sorry I went into your office uninvited, but I spent the morning with Lauren at the police station. They think she killed your mother."

"Maybe she did. Did you ever think of that?"

"Of course, she didn't kill your mother," Mavis snapped. "Why would she?"

"Why would anyone kill my mother? Her students loved her. The teachers respected her. But *someone* killed her."

Harriet wondered if he had ever seen his mother in action.

"The police suspect Lauren because she's been vocal about her work being copied, and your mom is the person who had the most access to Lauren's work," she pointed out. "Maybe your mom was investigating and caught someone in the act."

"Poison is hardly the method you would use if someone caught you in the act of something."

"Well, maybe she saw what we saw in the workroom. She knew someone was copying but didn't know who."

"My mom hadn't been out to her workroom in months," Tom informed her. He rubbed his hands over his face. "You really aren't going to let this go, are you?"

"I can't."

"I guess you're going to find out eventually, so I might as well tell you."

"What?"

"My mom had dementia." He leaned back and sagged in his chair. "She was still in the early stages, but she wasn't doing any new art. And I certainly don't think she could have carried out a scheme to copy student work. This was going to be her last term teaching."

"So, that's why you were selling the property?"

He looked directly at her. "I wish it was that simple."

"I'm sorry," Harriet said.

Tom picked up the cup Mavis had set in front of him earlier and drained it.

"After my mom got diagnosed, I went through a million different scenarios in my mind. The doctors can't predict how long a person will live with dementia, you know. And no one could tell me what the decline would be like. Some people are aware they have it, others aren't. My mom wasn't, so I couldn't talk to her about it.

"In the end, I figured she'd want to be here as long as she could. I had this idea that I could partner with someone who knows the adult foster care business. We could build a couple of homes right on the property, and then people like my mom could continue to do art as long as they are able to." He set his cup on the table and ran his hands through his thick hair again. "Now I don't know what I'm going to do."

"This certainly brings up more questions than it answers," Mavis said with a sigh.

Chapter Twenty-two

I can understand why the police suspect Lauren," said Harriet. "I don't believe she did anything to Selestina, but she *has* been bad-mouthing her to anyone who would listen because she believes Selestina copied her work. What I don't understand is why someone from the school tried to run Aiden off the road, injuring Cammi in the process."

"Don't look at me," Tom protested. "He's the one who hit *me*. All I know about him is that he stood you up for dinner the other night."

"Well, it's too many coincidences to just be random," Connie said.

Harriet looked at Tom and took a deep breath. "Especially since it was a black Ford Explorer that ran him off the road, and one of the school's vehicles is damaged."

"What? Why wasn't I told about this?"

Before anyone could answer, a sharp knock sounded on the Tree House door. Carla jumped at the noise then got up off the sofa and hurried to open it.

"Is Tom Bainbridge here?"

The voice belonged to Detective Ruiz. Tom rose and met him in the entryway.

"I'd like to ask you a few questions about a black Ford Explorer your business owns."

"Sure. I only just heard one of the cars was involved in an accident. Can we go to my office?" He glanced back at the women.

Detective Ruiz agreed, and they left.

141

Mavis gathered the teacups and took them to the kitchenette. Harriet followed her with a handful of used napkins and spent tea bags for the wastebasket under the sink.

"So, Selestina had dementia," she said.

"That kind of puts a new wrinkle in things." Mavis started washing cups with a worn-looking sponge. Harriet took each one in turn, rinsed it and set it in a wooden dish rack on the tile counter.

"I'm not sure it does," she replied. "The effects of early stage dementia could have given Selestina a good reason to be copying student work. Who knows how long it had been affecting her? Maybe she wasn't able to do new work but still was aware enough to know she needed to be putting something out there to keep her reputation."

"And maybe someone else discovered their work had been stolen and took exception?" Mavis suggested.

"I guess it's still pretty weak. I'm sure no one wants their work copied, but there has to be more to it. I know people kill for pocket change, but not quilters."

"Are you sure it was a quilter?"

"I guess we don't have any proof other than the fact that she was teaching a quilting class when she dropped. We need to ask Darcy what's happening regarding the poisoning. Is she still here?"

"I saw her up at the office after lunch. She was talking to a policeman, so I didn't interrupt."

"Anyone home?" Robin sang out as she came into the Tree House.

"In here," Harriet called back.

"Anybody want to go out to eat tonight?" Robin asked. "I could kill for a burger."

Mavis glared at her over the top of her glasses.

"Hey, it's a joke."

"Don't you think it's a bit insensitive, given the circumstances?" Mavis asked.

Robin shrugged. "Chalk it up to lawyer humor."

"No wonder no one likes lawyers," Mavis said. She wiped the area around the edge of the sink.

"Did I hear the word *burger*?" Connie asked. "Sign me up."

"Sarah said to tell everyone she and Lauren are going into

142

town with someone from Lauren's class to buy some mat board," Robin added.

Carla agreed to the plan, and after a round of bathrooming and purse-gathering the group of five got in Robin's van and headed for Angel Harbor.

"Jan Hayes was talking about a place called Big's Burgers," Robin said as she drove up the hill. Harriet could see the yellow tape flapping in the breeze where Aiden's truck had gone over the embankment. "It's supposed to be on the right one block past the UPS Store."

"Up there," Mavis said, and pointed to a red-and-blue sign next to a driveway.

Robin parked, and the group got out and headed for the door. A gray sedan pulled into the parking spot next to her van, and Aiden got out.

"Do you have room for one more?" he asked as they gathered in front of the restaurant.

Mavis looked down her nose over the top of her glasses. "That depends."

"On what?"

"On whether you can behave yourself."

He had the good grace to blush. "I'm sorry. I don't like that guy to begin with, and he was grabbing Harriet."

"I can take care of myself," Harriet said.

Mavis hadn't moved.

"Okay, fine, I'll be good."

"How's Cammi doing?" Connie asked as they went inside to wait for seating.

"Her doctor is hopeful. She can't really move her legs right now, but they think that might change when the swelling in her back goes down. She's got a little bit of feeling in her left foot, so that's a good sign."

"That's just so weird," Robin said. "Do you suppose the other car didn't see you in the rain?"

"Not a chance. I was in front, and the Explorer pulled partway into the other lane and then rammed me so I would go off to the right. Besides, I was in a white full-sized pickup. And it wasn't that stormy."

143

The hostess came and led them to a red leatherette window booth that was big enough for them to sit three on a side. She passed out menus and chatted amiably with them about the burger choices, only leaving when she had everyone's order.

"I've had a little time to think about this," Aiden continued. "I keep going over everything in my mind, trying to figure out why someone would want to run me or Cammi off the road. Between college and my post-graduate work in Uganda, I haven't been around until two months ago. That's hardly enough time to create any enemies. And Cammi's young. She's going to community college. I can't imagine she'd have made someone mad enough to try to kill her.

"Then I got to thinking about Harriet, and how she's in the middle of the trouble at the school, and it made me wonder."

"What?" Harriet asked.

"Did you keep wearing that purple hat I gave you?"

Harriet felt warmth creeping up her neck. "Yes, I did. I kept it on after you gave it to me."

"And then you left it in the truck when I gave you a ride to the copy store."

"Yeah, so?"

"The sun broke through the clouds when Cammi and I were coming back toward town, and she put your hat on."

"Oh, my gosh." Harriet slumped in her seat. "You think someone thought it was *me*?"

"I don't know. I'm just saying there seems to be all kinds of trouble at the folk art school, and the only connection I have to that place is you."

"So it's my fault Cammi got hurt?" Harriet asked, anger and hurt mixing in her voice.

"Now, honey," Mavis protested. "I'm sure Aiden didn't mean it that way."

Aiden looked at Harriet. "It's no one's fault but the person in the Explorer. I'm just saying maybe the driver thought they were eliminating someone who was digging around in things they didn't want dug in."

"Hmmm," said Mavis. "It makes a certain amount of sense."

"I just wish I knew what we were missing," Harriet complained.

"I heard there was a fire at one of the outbuildings," Robin said.

Harriet explained about the discovery of Selestina's workroom and the obvious copying being done there. She ended with their narrow escape from the basement root cellar, Tom's report that the fire was limited to a garbage can, and her supposition the can contained the evidence that had been hanging on the design wall.

"That suggests it was a quilter who did the deed," Aiden said. "I hate to defend Bainbridge, but if he was burning the place for insurance or to conceal evidence, wouldn't he be more likely to burn it to the ground?"

"Good point," Harriet agreed. "And a quilter wouldn't want to see those expensive sewing machines ruined."

"If it was a quilter," Connie said, "that gets us back to the idea of someone killing Selestina because she was copying their work." She shook her head. "It still doesn't seem like enough."

The waitress arrived with their burgers. Aiden and Carla had opted for bacon, and Harriet glanced longingly at the crispy strips of fat that crisscrossed their cheese-dredged patties. In a moment of guilt, she'd ordered a broiled chickenburger with lettuce and tomato after Robin got a veggie-burger. Connie had gone for the jack cheese-and-roasted pepper burger, while Mavis had chosen the basic version with cheddar cheese. The burgers came with heaping plates of Yukon Gold French fried potatoes and a tray of icy sodas.

Aiden finished his burger while Harriet was just picking up the second half of hers. He wiped his hands with his paper napkin and dropped the rumpled remains on his empty plate.

"I know better than to try to tell a determined group of quilters what to do, but I have to say it. Go home. If you hurry, you could still make the last ferry of the night. Let someone else figure out what's going on."

"But, *mijo*, that would leave Lauren on her own. She's been questioned by the police," Connie protested.

"So? You guys don't even like Lauren."

Carla looked from Mavis to Harriet and then to Robin, waiting to see who would refute the statement.

Finally, Mavis spoke. "Lauren doesn't make things easy for herself. And she does seem to take issue with Harriet. But that being

145

said, she's part of our group, and the Loose Threads don't abandon a member who's in trouble."

"So, don't abandon her. Can't you support her from the safety of Foggy Point?"

"I don't think we're going to figure this out if we aren't at the folk art school," Harriet said. "I feel like there's something right in front of us, but we're not seeing it."

"Well, be careful. And don't break into anyone else's office." He slid out from his end position in the booth and stood up. He pulled several bills from his wallet and tossed them on the table. "I've gotta go check on some patients. Can I come by for a cookie later?" he asked Harriet.

Mavis looked at the others. No one changed expression, so she assured him he was welcome as long as he didn't come too late.

"Tell me again how the schedule works tomorrow," Carla said when he was gone.

"In the morning, the teachers will each give a lecture on some aspect of embellishment," Robin said. "Ray Louise is demonstrating dry needle felting. And I think Patience will teach a session on fabric painting with oil sticks. Marla Stevens is going to talk about dyeing thread to match your fabric. There are a few more, but those are the ones I'm interested in. Two sessions will be going on at the same time. We have a complete list back at the Tree House, by the phone."

"After lunch, the teachers will have stations set up in the classroom so you can try the techniques," Mavis added.

"It's kind of nice to have a break from sitting in front of a sewing machine all day," Robin said.

Harriet wished she'd spent a little more time with her machine. Her half-rectangle quilt top was barely started. She was going to have to do some late-night stitching if she wanted to have something for the show-and-tell on the final day of school.

✂ ✂ ✂

There was a fresh bouquet of wildflowers on the table in the entryway when they arrived back at the Tree House. A clear plastic garbage bag full of clean towels sat on the floor.

"I've got to work on my quilt," Harriet said.

"Me, too," Carla chimed in. Harriet felt a small stab of guilt for keeping her from class today.

Harriet had chosen a pale-blue fabric to build her quilt around. She was trying to decide whether to use a pale pink with irregular, multicolored dots on it or a tone-on-tone medium pink that would move the quilt in a brighter direction. If she used the bright pink she would probably add white to the mix. If she went with the pale pink then an off-white or yellow would work better. The trouble was, she liked the lighter pink *and* the white but the two weren't going to work together.

Carla laid her fabrics out on the opposite end of the dining table; she was using a coordinated floral print series and emphasizing the star shape created by the half-rectangles. Harriet's layout would emphasize the curved look of the space between the star images.

Harriet decided she would have to make a sample block with each color combination. She was about to start cutting the two alternatives when the phone rang. Connie answered, and after a brief conversation, she hung up and turned to the group.

"That was Nancy from the front office. She asked if we could empty our wastebaskets into a garbage bag and put it on the front porch for pick-up in the morning."

Mavis and Robin started setting their hand stitching aside.

"Don't get up," Harriet said. "I could use a break. If no one minds me going in their room, I'll gather everyone's garbage."

No one objected, and she took a bag from under the sink and started up the stairs. The work wasn't difficult, as most people had no more than a couple of tissues and a few scraps of fabric in their wastebaskets.

She hadn't seen Lauren downstairs, so she tapped on her door a few times but received no response. She tried the knob, and when it turned easily, she went in without another thought.

The room was dark, but the light from the hall gave enough illumination for her to find the wastebasket and bring it out to her waiting garbage bag. It felt heavy, but a crumpled paper towel obscured whatever was in it.

Harriet gingerly picked up the corner of the paper towel between her thumb and fore finger. The bottom of the container was filled with what looked like a large pile of cooked spinach. She

147

dropped the paper towel and pulled Lauren's door shut, taking the waste container with her downstairs.

"Look what I found in Lauren's room." She lifted the paper towel aside and tilted the basket so Mavis, Connie and Robin could see without getting up. Carla came over and stood beside her.

"What on earth is that?" Connie wondered.

"Looks like Lauren's been cooking her own greens," Robin said.

"Marla talked about dyeing with plant materials the first day of class. I told Lauren about it. Maybe she was experimenting," Mavis suggested.

"That looks like the flowers on the front table," Carla said in a matter-of-fact voice.

"You're right," said Harriet. She lifted the basket closer to her face. "Look, you can see pieces of flower stem."

"Anyone home?" Darcy called from the entryway. "I have to spend another night here, so I thought I'd come by for a cup of tea before I go back to the motel." She set her purse on the coffee table. "What are you doing?"

"Just being snoopy," Harriet answered. "I was taking the garbage out, and I found something weird in Lauren's can."

"Oh, weird garbage, that's right up my alley." Darcy smiled. She had a reputation in the Foggy Point area for her ability to find DNA on discarded objects, a skill that was largely due to her tolerance for picking through noxious garbage.

She looked into the can. Her smile faded, and a ridge formed in her brow.

"Did anyone touch this stuff?" she demanded, looking at each of her friends. Everyone looked at Harriet.

"I just picked up the paper towel. By the corner," she added.

"Did your fingers tingle or anything like that?"

"No, nothing. I barely touched it."

"Set it down, gently," Darcy ordered in a firm voice.

Harriet did as instructed. "What's the matter?"

"Maybe nothing, but I don't like the looks of this stuff." Darcy had her cell phone out but couldn't get enough of a signal to complete her call. Mavis directed her to the phone in the dining room, and Harriet listened as she made a series of calls.

When she finished, she came back to the great room; no one had moved.

"We're still waiting for the final test results," she explained, "but it looks like Selestina was poisoned with aconitum, a plant whose common name is monkshood or wolf's bane."

"I can see where this is headed," Mavis said.

"You're sure no one touched this?" Darcy asked again.

"No," Harriet assured her. "I'm the only one, and I didn't touch the plant stuff."

"Go wash your hands with soap at the kitchen sink, just in case," she directed, and Harriet complied.

"Aconitum is a very potent poison," Darcy continued. "There are stories in the literature about people being killed by casual contact with the plants, but most experts believe it needs to be concentrated, and even then it probably needs to come in contact with broken skin.

"Whoever did this to Selestina almost got away with it—most of her symptoms mimicked coronary artery disease. But she had a few that didn't make sense. She had numbness in her extremities, and her pupils were contracted. Still, if it hadn't been for that moonlighting pathologist I told you about, they might have gotten away with it. He suspected poison. One of the nurses pointed out her thimble finger was irritated. Again, that might not have been noticed in a woman who had arthritis in her fingertips and squeezed her finger into a metal thimble in spite of it. But once they suspected poison, they started looking for a delivery point."

"So, someone cooked poison plants and put the juice in Selestina's thimble?" Connie asked.

"That's the long and short of it."

"But where would someone get the plants? Wouldn't they have to bring them along when they came?" Robin asked. "That would be pretty premeditated."

"No, unfortunately," Darcy said. "Monkshood grows all over the northwest in the hills. In fact..." She walked over to the bouquet of wild flowers. "...this flower right here..." She pointed to a green stem with lavender bluebell-like blossoms on its stalk. "... looks like it might be monkshood."

She removed a latex glove from her pocket, pulled in onto her right hand and carried the vase over to set it on the floor next to the wastebasket.

Everyone was standing in a circle staring at the two containers when the Tree House door opened and Detective Ruiz entered, followed by Officer Weber.

"What have you got?" he asked Darcy.

"I think we've found the source of the poison that killed Selestina Bainbridge." She pointed at the wastebasket. "Don't touch it," she warned. "It looks like someone cooked a batch of plants down to make a concentrated liquid. It's anyone's guess how much of that concentrate might still be in these plants. We'll have to send these to the lab and test them, but I don't think there's much doubt."

"Where did you find this?" Detective Ruiz asked the group.

The women looked at each other. No one wanted to be the one to seal Lauren's fate.

"It's not a difficult question," Ruiz prompted.

"It was in Lauren Sawyer's bedroom," Harriet said in a quiet voice.

Ruiz let his breath out. "And where is Miss Sawyer?"

"I don't know."

"Please, don't play me."

"No, really—we don't know. She didn't come to dinner with us. The last we heard she was going into Angel Harbor with some other students."

Detective Ruiz nodded to the patrolman still standing near the door. "Let's find her," he said.

Weber stepped onto the porch, pulling a radio from his belt as he went. As he went out, Patience came in. She was wearing a faded pair of black cotton knit pants and an oversized lavender T-shirt with the Angel Harbor Folk Art School logo stenciled on the back.

"I'll need to question your client as soon as possible," Detective Ruiz said to Robin. "I trust you'll let me know when she makes contact." He handed Robin a business card. "Officer Weber will stay with the evidence until the lab picks it up."

The ruddy-faced young officer came back in and took up his post in front of the evidence, and Detective Ruiz left.

"Does he really think Lauren would be that stupid?" Robin wondered. "Clearly, someone planted that wastebasket." She curled the first two fingers on each hand in the universal hand symbol for quote marks when she said *planted*.

"The local lab guy will test the basket, and if we're lucky he'll pick up some prints that will tell us something. If there *are* prints, and none of them are Lauren's, that will help."

"What's happened?" Patience asked. "I was in the office when the policemen came."

"It would seem we found the poison that was used on Selestina," Mavis said. She explained the series of events that ended with the appearance of Detective Ruiz.

"My goodness," Patience said. "Why would Lauren want to poison Selestina?"

"Lauren didn't poison anyone," Connie said.

"Someone did," Harriet had to point out.

The local forensic lab people arrived and, using something that looked like Aunt Beth's antique ice tongs, picked up first the wastebasket and then the vase of flowers and stowed them in large plastic boxes. Darcy explained that the boxes weren't ordinary household storage boxes but were made from a hardened low-sodium plastic that wouldn't contaminate the contents.

"I'm going to the lab," she said and picked up the coat, purse and keys she'd dropped on the coffee table earlier. "We probably won't know anything before tomorrow."

Mavis walked her to the door with the usual admonishments to make sure she got enough rest and remembered to eat.

"Shall I put the kettle on?" Connie asked.

"I could do with a cup of tea," Patience said.

Chapter Twenty-three

Mavis went into the kitchenette, pulled a plastic container of homemade lemon sugar cookies from a shelf under the counter and began arranging them on a large plate. Connie set two boxes of mixed tea bags on the table and distributed mugs. Patience, Robin and Harriet took places at the table. Mavis brought the cookies and Connie poured hot water. Carla handed out napkins then perched on a stool at the island.

"Patience," Harriet began, "do you think it's possible that one of Selestina's friends decided to spare her the indignity of dementia?"

"What are you talking about? Selestina didn't have dementia. She was as sharp as you or I. What gave you the idea she had dementia?"

Harriet was confused. Tom had been very clear. "I was talking to her son..." she began.

"Is Tom telling that story again?" Patience asked, a look of righteous indignation on her face. "Last year the school barely broke even, so Tom got this idea he could build assisted living apartments that were geared toward the arts. Someone had talked to him about how much money he could make if he turned the school into a multi-level senior care facility. He's been trying to convince Selestina she had some kind of dementia ever since."

"Wouldn't that be pretty easy to disprove?" Robin asked. "All she'd have to do is have an evaluation. Do you know if she owned the property herself?"

Patience twined her fingers around the handle of her cup. "It's not that simple. Tom is her only child. She herself was an only child, so Tom is it as far as relatives go. Selestina didn't want to risk making Tom mad and being left all alone."

"So, what was she going to do?" Harriet asked.

"She complained about it to anyone who would listen, but she wasn't willing to do anything," Patience said, and sighed. "I told her I would help her, but she wouldn't hear of it. Her plan, if you could call it that, was to try to get more students, so she could put off closing. She figured she couldn't stop him from building the apartments in the meadow by the pond, but she could keep signing students up for long-term programs and keep him at bay." She slipped a crumpled tissue from her pocket and began rolling the edge between her fingers, leaving a small pile of lint on the table.

"That sounds like a disaster in the making," Mavis said.

"It's been a terrible strain on Selestina. I wouldn't be surprised if it turned out her heart gave out in the end."

"That's not likely," Harriet said. "The police are pretty sure she was killed with a plant poison."

"Well, that would be right up Tom's alley," Patience said. "He was a botanist for the forest service before he came home to work at the school."

Harriet leaned back in her chair. It was a lot to take in. Patience sipped her tea and reached for a cookie.

"Is there going to be a memorial service for Selestina?" Mavis asked.

"Every session we have a meeting on the Sunday before everyone goes home. We usually do show-and-tell, and people talk about their classes. We thought this Sunday we would do a tribute to Selestina. Of course, we'll do a proper memorial in town. Selestina was a big part of this community, after all."

✂ ✂ ✂

"I thought she'd never leave," Harriet said fifteen minutes later when Patience had finally finished her cookie and tea and made her exit. "Her little bombshell certainly puts a different spin on things."

"Oh, yeah? What spin is that?" Aiden said as he came in followed by Carla, who had apparently been the only one to hear him knock.

Mavis quickly summarized the information Patience had conveyed.

"I knew there was something off about that guy," he said when she'd finished.

"Being a botanist isn't proof he killed his mother," Harriet protested.

"Yeah, but knowing about an obscure yet plentiful poisonous plant does put him in the running, and at the front of the pack, if you ask me."

"That still doesn't make it okay to hit him," Connie reminded him.

"Yeah, yeah, yeah, I know—use my words not my fists. You've been telling me since I was seven years old."

"And I will *keep* telling you until it sinks in, young man," she retorted in her best teacher voice.

"What did we really learn here tonight?" Robin asked the group.

"Tom thinks Selestina had dementia," Connie said.

"And Tom wants to build some sort of assisted living facility here," Mavis added.

"Someone is working hard to make us think Lauren prepared the poison that killed Selestina," Harriet said.

"Bainbridge has the knowledge to prepare the poison," Aiden said, and sat down next to her.

"Person or persons unknown are running a quilt counterfeiting operation and may or may not be willing to kill people to defend it. That is, if you believe the person who lit the fire knew we were in there," said Harriet.

"Lauren's brother might have set us up," said Carla. Her cheeks immediately reddened.

Harriet looked at her and smiled. "Good point."

"Unfortunately, none of this would stand up in court," Robin pointed out. "None of it except the poison plants in Lauren's room. That would be considered evidence. Let's just hope whoever put it there wiped the container clean of prints, including Lauren's. That would at least be some help."

"The damaged Ford Explorer must be evidence," Aiden said.

"If they match the paint up with the white truck, it proves the two vehicles came in contact. It doesn't tell us who was driving the Ford, or how it connects to anything else. Sorry," she added when she saw disappointment cloud his face.

"We aren't going to solve this tonight," Mavis said. "I say we call it a night and see what tomorrow brings."

"That would be a little easier for me if I knew where Lauren was," said Robin.

"Sarah's not home, either," Connie noted.

"Yeah, it's been kind of nice," Aiden muttered. Harriet bumped him with her shoulder and tried to give him a stern look but grinned instead.

"You want to get up early and go into town for coffee?" he whispered to her. "I'll pick you up in my spiffy gray rental sedan."

"Oh, be still my heart."

"We haven't gotten to go on our date yet," he pleaded.

"Okay," she conceded, "you had me at coffee. What time?"

"That's the tricky part," he said, still keeping his voice low.

"I can tell I'm not going to like this."

Aiden shielded his face with his hands before speaking, peeking from between his spread fingers. "Six-thirty," he said, and ducked.

"Oh, my gosh," Harriet said then turned it into a cough when Connie asked her what was wrong.

"I'm fine. I just swallowed wrong," she gasped, and looked at Aiden.

"You'll be up?"

"With bells on," she said.

Chapter Twenty-four

Harriet gathered her half-rectangle pieces and stowed them in her bag. "I'm going to call it a night," she said, and headed up the stairs. In spite of her intentions, however, it was several hours before she fell into a restless sleep.

She woke with a start at four in the morning. She listened for the telltale sound of a door closing on the floor below her, but drifted back to sleep, awakening for good at five-thirty. Gray light was trying without much success to illuminate her room as she gathered her clothes and went down the hall to the bathroom.

Her shower may not have been a substitute for a good night's sleep, but she had to admit she did feel better. She reached for the doorknob at her room and then froze.

The door was ajar. She'd taken care to shut it without making noise when she'd left for her shower. She stepped back, then reached out and pushed the door open.

"Who's there?" she demanded.

"Oh, please, skip the dramatics and get in here," Lauren snapped.

"Where have you *been*?"

"Not here," Lauren said. "Tell me what you've got."

"Do you realize the police are looking for you?"

"Well, duh." She sat on the other bed, her slender legs crossed, her foot bobbing nervously.

"Where *have* you been?"

"My brother saw the police arrive and heard them mention my name. He came and found me. I stayed at his place. Don't waste

156

any time worrying about ratting me out—I won't be there again—but I need to know. Have you found out who killed Selestina?"

"So far, everything I've found says you did it," Harriet said and sat down on her bed opposite Lauren. "And for what it's worth, I don't think it's a wise move hiding from the police."

"Yeah, that's easy for you to say. You're not the one being framed. Innocent people go to jail all the time."

"So far, all I've found is a lot of contradictory information. Selestina's son at the very least has the knowledge to prepare the poison that killed her, and he freely admits he's trying to change the direction of the business, but it's not obvious he needed to kill his mother to do that. We did find the quilt counterfeiting operation thanks to a tip from your brother, but so far that hasn't gone any-where. I don't know what else to tell you."

"You need to get cracking. I can't stay hidden forever. Someone wanted the old bat dead. You're supposed to be the big crime solver—figure it out."

"Wait a minute! I never claimed to be able to solve crimes."

"You figured out who killed Avanell, and if you can do it for her, you can do it for me. Besides—"

"I know," Harriet cut her off. "I owe you."

Lauren gave her a smug smile. "Yes, you do, so get to work. Now, I've got to go get some clothes and get out of here before someone wakes up and sees me."

She jumped up and swept out of the room. Harriet flopped back on her bed and put her hands on her forehead.

"What am I going to do?" she asked the ceiling.

No answers were forthcoming, so she got up, pulled her gray sweatshirt on over her jeans and green T-shirt, grabbed her wallet and went downstairs.

The kitchenette was dark, and she didn't want to turn on the lights and chance waking one of the early risers, so she went on out to the porch. She never tired of the forest that surrounded the Tree House. The smell of damp earth and pine needles was calming. She took a deep breath and closed her eyes. She was about to sit on the porch swing when she heard a rustle in the bushes.

Harriet quietly stepped down the stairs and around the side of the Tree House toward the restroom building. She could hear

157

voices coming from the trail, and quickly slid behind a large rhododendron.

"That was a really foolish move," a low voice whispered.

"I had to do something, didn't I?" Both people were whispering, and she couldn't identify either one.

"You need to decide whose team you're on, and if it's not mine,
we have a problem. And you know how I feel about problems."

Harriet wiggled around, but the foliage was too thick for her to
see anything. She felt her bush move as someone pushed past it and
went on down the trail. She held her breath and a few seconds
later, heard footsteps crunching the gravel on the trail going in the
opposite direction. She waited what she estimated to be five minutes then crept back to the porch.

Aiden arrived just as she started to sit on the swing for a second
time.

"Did you see anyone on the path or in the parking lot?" she
asked.

"No, should I have?"

She quickly recounted the conversation she'd overheard.

"Oooh, so it's a conspiracy," he said and pulled her into his
arms. "I've missed you." He wrapped his arms around her, pressing
her against his chest.

"You have a funny way of showing it," she complained, but slid
her arms around his waist.

"Hey, I defended your honor, what more do you want?"

"You mean when you clocked some poor guy in the jaw just
because he touched me?"

"Some poor guy who might have killed his own mother."

"Well, there is that," She looked up into his white-blue eyes,
barely suppressing a laugh.

Aiden's face grew serious. "I should have hit him harder. If he
did kill his mother, he's probably the one who ran me off the road
and tried to burn you and Carla alive."

"That's a big if," Harriet said and let go of him. "Come on,
you promised coffee, and it's cold out here."

He leaned in and kissed her lightly, sending shivers all the way
to her toes, then turned and led the way up the path to the parking
area. She sighed and followed. No matter how she fought it, he did

make her heart go pitty-pat.

"Guess who was in my room when I got back from my shower," she said when they were both buckled into their seats in the nondescript rental car.

"Don't even say Tom Bainbridge."

"Lauren," she replied.

"Isn't she staying in the Tree House?" Aiden pulled out of the parking lot and headed for Angel Harbor.

"She was until she went on the lam."

He turned and looked at her.

"Hey, watch the road. One accident this week is enough," she said.

"Are you serious? Lauren is hiding from the police?"

"They're looking for her, and she didn't come home last night. She said she stayed at her brother's, but she won't be there anymore. And before you say anything, yes, I told her she was being foolish and she should turn herself in. She said innocent people go to jail all the time. I have to admit I couldn't argue with that."

"This is getting crazy," he said as he pulled into a parking space in front of a cedar-sided building overlooking the harbor.

"You know what's really crazy?" Harriet said when they had both ordered their drinks, switching to cocoa at the last minute, and were settled on a worn purple sofa that faced a window overlooking the water. "What's crazy is that I've been spending a lot of time with Carla this week."

"If you think that's crazy you need to get out more," Aiden said with a smile.

Harriet gave him a playful punch on his shoulder. "If you would let me finish."

"Please, continue."

"Carla's been working at the quilt store for a couple of months now, and attending the single mothers quilt group for longer than that, but somehow, none of us picked up the fact that she's living with her baby in a borrowed van."

"How can that be? Foggy Point has a homeless shelter—my mom donated a lot of money to it. And I'm pretty sure there's a women's shelter, too."

"She told me herself, so I'm sure it's true. She's not battered, so

159

she probably doesn't qualify for the women's shelter, and frankly, if I were faced with taking a baby to the homeless shelter, I'd probably choose a car myself. She said she takes the baby to a free daycare program. She begged me not to say anything, but I can't stop thinking of her and that baby parked on the street at night."

"That's really harsh."

"I've been toying with the idea of asking her to move into Aunt Beth's place with me. It's certainly big enough."

He put his arm around her shoulders and pulled her to him.

"Has anyone ever told you, you have a really good heart?"

Harriet leaned her head against him. It felt good. "I just feel so bad for her. When we were in the basement of that workshop, she was telling me how her mother used to lock her in closets to keep the mom's boyfriend from hurting her. And she was just so matter-of-fact about it, like it was the most normal thing in the world. And I could hear in her voice that she really believed her mom was protecting her. It wasn't in her reality that her mom had anything to do with the abuser being there in the first place."

"Did you bring home birds that fell out of nests when you were a little girl?" he asked.

"Yeah, right," she said. "I brought home a stray kitten one time, and the head mistress took it from me and made me scrub my hands with a brush."

"That's terrible." He gave her a squeeze.

"It is what it is, and compared to Carla, I had no problems at all."

The waitress brought two mugs of steaming hot cocoa topped with generous dollops of whipped cream and set them on the scarred wooden table in front of the sofa.

"Thanks," Harriet told her with a smile.

"Can we forget all these other people and talk about us?" Aiden asked.

She picked up her cup and sipped.

"I'll take that as a yes," he said. "I'd like to propose that we start over when we get back to Foggy Point."

She started to protest, but he pressed a finger to her lips.

"Let me finish before some other disaster interferes. A couple of weeks ago, I said I wanted to take you out, and then I no-showed. I

160

know that was bad form, but we really were slammed with that contaminated pet food crisis. Then, when we got here, Cammi was fooling with my phone and erased your message. Maybe on purpose, maybe not, but in any case I never got it. Hitting Tom, I still stand by. He's a jerk."

He paused, and Harriet seized her chance.

"I agreed to go out to dinner. We're both adults, you don't owe me anything. You got busy. It happens."

Aiden held her gaze. "You don't believe this is just a casual thing any more than I do," he said.

"I won't deny I find you attractive, but I'm also a lot older than you. A fact I've made very clear was an issue for me."

"If I were ten years older than you, no one would give it a second thought, especially you."

"You don't know that," she objected, but in her heart she knew he was right.

"Let me prove you wrong," he pleaded.

Harriet sipped her cocoa.

"I gave you a chance a few weeks ago, and no matter how good your excuses, you were a no-show, which proves my point that, at your age, you need to concentrate on your career. I understand that."

"Are you trying to tell me that if someone brought you a batch of quilting that had to be done in a short time for some reason, that you wouldn't cancel a date?"

"I would, but the difference is I would call and tell you about it up front."

"Point taken," he said and hung his head. Strands of black hair fell over his eyes. "I'm sorry."

He was right, she thought, she did feel the connection. And if she were truthful with herself, she'd acknowledge that he *had* bruised her fragile ego when he no-showed for their date and then called Jorge instead of her.

She took another sip of her drink. "I suppose we *could* try again when we get back to Foggy Point. This time you have to pick me up at home."

"Wild horses won't be able to stop me," he said with a dazzling smile. He took her cup from her hands and set it on the table and

161

then pulled her onto his lap. He gently took her face in his hands and kissed her. The waitress winked at her, and gave her a thumbs-up.

For once, Harriet didn't care if she was making a spectacle of herself. She ran her fingers through his thick hair, twining them in the long strands.

Aiden broke contact first. "Whew," he said. "We better quit while we still can. Besides, I have an idea."

"You mean you were thinking of something else just now? Way to stroke my ego."

"I didn't say I thought of it just then—believe me, I was only thinking of one thing, and it wasn't Carla's living situation."

"What's your idea for Carla?" She picked up her cup again.

"I've been living in my apartment over the clinic since I've been back in Foggy Point, but I did inherit my mom's house on the hill. I've been toying with the idea of moving back there, but it's a really big house and I'd have to have help to take care of it. My mom's housekeeper was old, and when Mom died, Rose retired."

"So, what does that have to do with Carla and her baby?"

"I was thinking maybe Carla could be my housekeeper. She wouldn't have to do all the work herself—Mom had people that did all the windows and she had a gardener. Carla could make sure the jobs got done. She and her baby could have a couple of rooms, and there would still be space to spare."

"That's a generous idea, but what if she doesn't know how to do the job?"

"How bad could she be? Besides, I'll bet she's pretty resourceful if she's been living on the streets. And she can't be any worse at it than I'd be."

"You can be a sweet guy when you want to be," she said and gave him a quick kiss before standing up. "This has been fun, but we need to get back, don't we?"

"Unfortunately, we do." Aiden drained his cup, picked up hers and carried both to the counter.

"You young men are so evolved," she said with a laugh when he returned.

"What's that supposed to mean?"

"Never mind," she said with a smile.

✂ ✂ ✂

The trip back to the Tree House parking lot was spent planning Carla's move to Aiden's house.

"I'll have to stay in the apartment until the clinic finds another tenant," Aiden explained. "They like to have someone live on-site, since there are often overnight patients. Usually, it's one of the vet techs, but it was available when I came home so it was convenient for me. It'll probably take a couple of months to find someone, which will give Carla some time to settle in at my mom's house."

"This is so great," Harriet said with delight. "Thank you so much for helping her."

"Anything for you." He pulled into the parking lot then leaned over and brushed his lips over hers. "There's more where that came from," he said. "When can I prove it to you?"

"I'm not sure what the dinner plan is tonight, and then there's the whole Lauren thing. Can we talk later?"

"Sure, as long as you promise you're not giving me the brush-off."

She rested her hand on his thigh. "I promise, I'm not brushing you off." She opened the door and got out.

Aiden leaned toward the open door. "I'll talk to you later."

"I'll look forward to it," she said and turned and headed toward the path.

"Harriet?" someone called from the direction of the path. "Is that you?" Nancy from the office appeared around a curve in the path. "I was just coming to find you," she said. "I have a message for you." She held out a pink phone message slip that was folded in half and held shut with a piece of tape. "This note was on my desk when I came in this morning. There was a sticky note attached that asked me to deliver this to you as soon as I got in. So, here."

She thrust the note at Harriet then spun and walked back down the path, disappearing around the curve.

The note tore slightly as Harriet pulled it open. *I've got important information, meet me at my office as soon as you get this*, the note read. It was signed "Tom."

She went back to the parking area then down the road until she came to the next car park. If she had guessed correctly, this one would have a path that led to Pavilion A. She took a longer forested path and eventually came to a clearing that revealed the ceramics

163

building. Perfect, she thought.

The door to the pavilion was unlocked, and she pulled it open. The display pedestals that had held the pottery bowls off to the right on her previous visit had been removed, and a series of narrow shelves sat parallel to each other down the middle of the space. She had to stop and reorient herself. She counted the doorways, but still wasn't sure she choosing the one that led to Tom's office.

The door was slightly ajar, and she pushed it open.

"Tom? Are you here?"

She froze at the scene in front of her. Papers covered every surface. The file cabinet drawers had all been pulled open, and as a result it had tipped forward. The table was on its side. Books had been pulled from the shelves and lay face-down open on the floor. Paper clips and rubber bands were strewn among the papers, and the wastebasket that had held the shredding had been dumped and the contents spread across the carpet.

"Geez Louise," Harriet whispered, but whatever else she might have said was cut off by a strong arm wrapping around her neck from behind.

Pulled backward into someone larger and stronger, she kicked backward hard, connecting with a shin. When the arm loosened slightly, she dropped to the floor and rolled forward, coming to back to her feet in one motion to find herself face-to-face with Tom Bainbridge. At least they would have been face-to-face except that he was hunched over rubbing his shin.

"I think you broke my leg," he gasped.

"Why did you grab me?" she demanded, and stepped forward, righting a chair for him to sit on.

"Stay back," he ordered, and pulled the chair toward him. He sat down and pulled his cell phone from his pocket and started to dial.

"Who are you calling?"

"The police—who do you think?"

"Wait. You don't think I did this, do you?" Her face was hot.

"I've been patient with your snooping. I really have. But this is too much. I don't know who you think you are or what you think you're doing, but you've crossed the line here."

Harriet grabbed for the phone, but he stretched his arm out, holding it as far behind him as he could.

"Look," she said, and pulled the pink note from her pocket. "*You* asked me to meet you here." Anger blazed in her eyes. "I came because you asked me to. The door was open, so I came in and this is what I found." She gestured to indicate the chaos.

"I didn't ask you to meet me here. I got a text message that you had information about my mother and to meet *you* here."

"Let me see the message."

He pulled back his arm and pressed keys to bring up the message screen.

"That's not my phone number," she said. She pulled her own phone out of her pocket and quickly pushed the buttons to display her number. "Look." She held it out. "I've never seen that number."

"Okay, now I really am calling the police." He dialed nine-one-one and quickly described the situation. "They'll be right here."

"Sorry about your shin," she said with a small smile.

He rubbed it. "You have a heck of a kick. Where did you learn that?"

"I used to live in Oakland. With the crime rate there it seemed prudent to take a women's self-defense course."

"You must have been their top student."

Harriet shrugged and smiled again.

✂ ✂ ✂

"Miss Truman," Detective Ruiz said from the doorway a few minutes later. "Why am I not surprised to see you here?" Two uniformed officers stepped past him and into the room.

"I don't know," she said. "Why is a detective responding to a simple break-in?"

"Angel Harbor is a small place," he countered. "We don't have a lot of crime. And when we have an open homicide investigation, well, we tend to take notice of a lot of things. We also tend to notice when an ordinary citizen keeps inserting herself into our investigation. Ordinary citizens don't do that, so that makes us wonder why this one does."

Harriet sighed and looked at the ceiling, silently counting to ten. She handed Detective Ruiz the pink note. "Nancy in the office

165

gave me this note. I thought it was legitimate so I came here. The door was open, and the room looked like this."

"And I got a text message to meet Harriet here," Tom said. "It turns out it wasn't really from her."

"So, what's going on here?" Detective Ruiz asked, looking at Tom and then Harriet.

"I wish I knew," she said.

"I don't understand why anyone would do this to my office," Tom said. "There's nothing of any value here. I mainly have the correspondence between us and our affiliated schools, and the shipping records of materials we send back and forth. The school's tax records and business incorporation papers and that kind of thing are at my home office. And all the financial transactions take place in the school's main office. It doesn't make any sense."

"Someone wanted you two here together," Detective Ruiz speculated. "Perhaps they even timed it so you would think Miss Truman did it."

Tom gave Harriet a guilty glance.

"Maybe it's a smoke screen," Harriet offered.

"Yes," Ruiz concurred. "Your friend Miss Sawyer might be foolish enough to think this would distract us from looking for her."

Harriet raised her eyebrows, her eyes wide. Would Lauren do this?

"You haven't seen your friend, have you?" the detective asked.

"She was in my room this morning when I came back from my shower," Harriet said. Her shoulders sagged. She didn't like giving up a friend, even Lauren, but lying to the police wasn't going to help anyone.

"And you didn't think to let us know?"

"It was six o'clock in the morning, and I was meeting someone for coffee. I didn't really think about it. She told me not to bother trying to find her, and frankly, I put it out of my mind."

"You're so anxious to help us solve this crime. Can't you see that the best way you can help is to tell us everything you know, and when I ask you to let me know if you see someone, call me? Don't go snooping around, don't question people, don't search rooms—just call. Is that clear?"

"Okay," Harriet said, and a very small part of her meant it.

166

Detective Ruiz looked around the office. "At least your coffee-shop story provides an alibi of sorts." He looked back at Harriet. "If it checks out." He waved his hand to encompass the room. "This took some time."

"When can I start cleaning it up?" Tom asked.

"Not yet," Ruiz replied. "We probably aren't going to get anything, but we need to process the scene just in case our perp got careless." He looked at his watch. "Give us a couple of hours."

Chapter Twenty-five

Tom walked her back to the Tree House. "I'm going to the business office and call my attorney," he said. "I'm thinking I need to do something about security here. I don't know what my liability is, but for my own peace of mind I feel like I need to do something. I don't even know where you look for reputable security people—certainly, not anywhere in Angel Harbor."

"Good luck with that. I'm going to go to the lectures today and try to pretend I'm a regular fiber art student." She went up the steps onto the porch.

Mavis pulled the door open. She shivered and pulled the two sides of her plaid wool shirt closed, wrapping her arms across her chest.

"Where have you been, young lady?" she demanded. "You weren't here when we got up, and no one knew where you'd gone."

"I'm sorry. I went to coffee early with Aiden, and when I came back, I got a message to meet Tom at his office. Things went sideways from there." She described the tossing of Tom's office and the false message that led her there, finishing with Detective Ruiz's appearance. "Tom was on his way to the office to try to hire some private security when I left him."

"That's it," Connie said from the kitchenette, where she'd been toasting bagels and eavesdropping. "I think it's time to pack up and go home."

"I'm not leaving early," insisted Sarah from the dining table. "I paid for a whole week, and I'm staying a whole week."

"It's not safe," Connie argued, her voice rising. "Didn't you

168

hear? They're hiring security guards. They don't even think it's safe, and they run the place. For crying out loud, someone's been murdered."

"Get a grip. That doesn't have anything to do with us. I'm going to my first lecture before all the good seats are taken." Sarah went upstairs to get her coat.

"Don't forget, we've still got Lauren to deal with," Mavis reminded Connie. "We can't just leave her here. And Tom is going to hire security. We just need to be extra-careful, not go anywhere alone." She looked at Harriet. "And I mean everyone."

Connie was wearing her thick pink terrycloth robe over brown polyester pants and a salmon-colored tunic style shirt. Harriet's aunt Beth wore her robe over her clothes on chilly mornings, too. A wave of nostalgia swept over Harriet. For a moment, she wished she was still twelve and watching Aunt Beth bustle around her yellow kitchen in Foggy Point.

"I think we should go home, too" she muttered. "Trouble follows Lauren; it doesn't matter what we do."

"Did you eat breakfast?" Mavis asked.

"No, we just had hot chocolate."

Connie picked up a toasted bagel half, smeared it with cream cheese and handed it to her. She spread the second half and handed it to Carla, who had come downstairs during their discussion. Then she poured two glasses of orange juice and handed one to each of them.

Mavis glanced at the clock. "I'm going to go get my notebook. We should leave pretty soon."

Connie put the juice and cream cheese away and followed Mavis upstairs.

"What are you going to do?" Carla asked.

"I'm trying to figure out which lecture to go to. Honestly, I'm so distracted by everything that's been going on I'm not sure I'm going to learn anything."

"I was going to tag along with you." Carla twisted her hands around each other, her eyes downcast. "If that's okay with you, I mean."

"That's fine with me. Mavis did say we were supposed to go in pairs. Did you look at the list of lectures?"

"The one about thread seemed like it might be interesting."

"Thread it is, then," Harriet said. She pulled a paper towel from the dispenser and handed it to Carla, then took one for herself and wiped her hands. "Shall we leave in five minutes?"

✂ ✂ ✂

Robin caught up with Harriet and Carla on the porch of the fiber arts building.

"Have you seen Lauren?" she asked.

Harriet told her about her early-morning visitor.

"I'm getting worried," Robin said. "That detective called me. They're looking for her. They want to know where she was when Tom's office was torn apart. Unfortunately, I couldn't tell him anything."

"I told him what I just told you," Harriet said.

"Lauren is not doing herself any favors. The police automatically suspect people who run. Even if they don't believe you did whatever crime they're investigating, they'll start digging to see what you are guilty of."

"She won't listen," Harriet said. "You can only do so much for her if she won't take your advice."

"If you see her, tell her I'm looking for her," Robin said and pulled the door open. "I'm going to go see what I can learn about painting on fabric."

Harriet and Carla passed the room Robin entered and found places at the back of the classroom where the thread lecture was just starting. Carla crossed her legs and bounced her foot as Ray Louise Hanson started talking about thread weight or thickness. Harriet found herself watching Carla's foot swing and thinking about Lauren's predicament. Carla started picking at a hangnail on her thumb.

After fifteen minutes, Harriet leaned toward Carla and whispered, "Let's get out of here."

"Lead the way," Carla agreed, and then followed as Harriet quietly slid out of her chair and headed for the door.

"I'm sorry, I can't concentrate today," Harriet said once they were out in the hall.

"It's okay. I wasn't thinking about thread, either. I did have an

170

idea about Lauren, though."

"I'm all ears." Harriet said. She was fresh out of ideas herself.

"Why don't we follow her brother?"

"She said she wasn't going back to his place."

"Yeah, but did she say he wasn't going to help her anymore?"

"Good point. And you're right, there are all kinds of places she could be hiding here and who would know better than the janitor? Come on, I think I know where to start."

They went to the dining cabin. Because of the lecture format, the usual breakfast and lunch times had been replaced by a serve-yourself buffet.

"Les seems to have kitchen duties at mealtimes. Let's go in and get a snack and scout it out."

Les was nowhere to be seen when they arrived. Harriet made herself a cup of peppermint tea and Carla followed suit. She picked up a small plate from a stack, grabbed a pair of tongs and selected an assortment of fruits.

"Grab a couple of forks," she said to Carla. "We can share this."

There were two slices of apple left on the plate when Carla stopped eating mid-bite.

"Listen," she whispered. Harriet complied. "I think I hear him in the kitchen."

"Come on." Harriet quickly picked up their dishes and carried them to the gray plastic bus tub. She led the way outside and around the cabin and past the compost pile.

"He's the compost guy. He'll show up out here to empty the compost buckets before lunch," she explained.

The woods around the cabin provided plenty of cover for them to hide in. Harriet was careful to avoid stepping on a trillium flower. She tried to remember what Aunt Beth had told her about trilliums—something about their taking seven years to bloom. If she ever got out of here, she'd have to remember to ask her.

"Here he comes," she said.

They watched as he carried two buckets of orange peels and apple cores and emptied them then went back for a third.

"Bet you didn't think you'd be hanging out at a compost pile when you signed up for classes at the folk art school. I feel guilty for dragging you into all this drama."

"This is so different from my real life. It's been nice even with Lauren's stuff." Carla's cheeks turned red. "No one ever hung out with me before, not even at a compost pile," she said with a shy smile.

"Here he comes again," Harriet said, and motioned toward the dining cabin.

Les was carrying a bucket in one hand and what looked like a cardboard takeout box in the other. He set the box down then emptied the bucket and placed it upside-down on one of the posts that held the chicken wire that enclosed the pile. He turned toward the rhododendron bush they were huddled behind. They hunkered down and held their collective breath.

He turned away and picked up the box. With one last glance around, he started off down a trail that led away from the dining cabin.

The three main pavilions at the folk art school formed a rough triangle in the center of the school property. If you drew a line between the ceramics building and the fiber arts building, the pond and meadow and Selestina's workshop lay directly west. Les was headed in the opposite direction, between the ceramics and photography buildings. Thankfully, that side of the property was heavily wooded, which caused the path to twist and turn around the larger trees and made it easy to follow at a distance.

The path split, and Les chose the narrower, less-traveled branch.

"Is that a building up ahead?" Carla whispered.

Harriet stopped and stepped off the path, pushing the undergrowth aside.

"Looks like some sort of outbuilding," she said.

Unlike Selestina's workshop, this building was clearly of more recent construction. It was at least two stories tall, with dark cedar siding and a moss-free composite roof. It had a white overhead door on the side Harriet could see.

"What's he doing?" Carla asked.

Les had his back to them, so Harriet took the opportunity to move closer. Carla followed.

He rose up onto his toes and looked through the small glass

172

panes on the overhead door. He knocked once, and rattled the door handle. When he got no response, he went around the side of the building. Harriet mirrored his move, maintaining her distance. Les was standing at a white door rattling the doorknob.

"Lauren, come on, open the door." He glanced left and right. "Quit messing around." He pounded on the door, gently at first then harder when he got no response. "Lauren!" he called once again, a whine creeping into his voice. "Don't do this to me."

He turned his back to the door and leaned on it, sliding to the ground, his head in his hands, the take-out box falling to the ground beside him. He sat that way for several minutes then got up and started walking, this time taking another path. Harriet and Carla followed, creeping along the path, listening for his footsteps to be sure he was still moving.

He stopped at a smaller building that looked like the bathroom building behind the dining cabin. There were doors on two sides, presumably to accommodate both men's and women's restrooms. He went into each in turn, calling Lauren's name.

"Where are you?" he cried out when he was outside again.

"Let's go back to the Tree House," Harriet whispered, and quietly stepped onto the path, going in the opposite direction from Les.

"Does this mean what I think it means?" Carla asked when they were out of earshot.

"If you're thinking Les doesn't know where Lauren is, you're right."

"Where could she go?" Carla asked. "She doesn't have a car or anything."

"We can't assume she doesn't have a car until we find out if Les has or had a car. What I don't get is why she would leave the place her brother had her stashed without telling him. She'll have a much more difficult time without his help."

"Maybe someone else is helping her," Carla suggested.

"Who would help her, though? Her charming personality doesn't attract many admirers. No, I think it's something else. Something spooked her."

"What are we going to do now?"

"Let's go back and put in an appearance at our lecture. If we

173

hurry, we can slip back in and maybe no one will know we were gone. At lunchtime, I'd like to go check out Les's apartment."

"I thought she said she wasn't going to be there," Carla said, hurrying to keep up.

"She said she wasn't going to be there, but that doesn't mean she won't be."

Chapter Twenty-six

$\mathcal{R}$ay Louise Hanson finished her lecture and encouraged everyone to come back to her classroom after lunch, when she would have a sample of each of the threads she'd discussed for them to try.

"Oh, and before I let you go," she said, and picked up a piece of paper from the lectern. "It is our custom at the Angel Harbor Folk Art School, and I know at many of your own quilt groups, also, to make a quilt for any member who loses a loved one. This case is special, since it was our founder who died. We are going to make two quilts. One will go to our business manager, Selestina's son Tom, in remembrance of his mother. The second one will be hung in the entry to the fiber arts building and will be a memorial to our founder, Selestina Bainbridge.

"If you would like to make a block for either or both, we will have instruction sheets and pieces of background fabric for you to use available on a table in the entrance hall."

Robin was waiting in the hall when class got out. She was holding three packets of fabric, each with paper folded around it.

"I picked up the fabric and instructions for the memorial quilts," she said, and handed a set to Harriet and another to Carla. "I figured you'd want to do them. I got the background fabric for both of them."

"Thanks," said Carla. "What kind of blocks are we supposed to make?"

"For Tom's quilt, the theme is motherhood. Any way you want to express it. The one to be hung in the entrance is to represent

175

what you've learned here at the school."

Carla looked doubtful.

"Don't worry," Harriet said, "We'll help you figure it out."

"Are you going to another lecture?" Robin asked.

"No, I can't concentrate, I try to listen, but I find my mind wandering to Lauren."

"I'm having the same problem."

"Me, too," Carla said. "I got a real bad feeling about Lauren."

"Has something happened since I talked to you earlier?" Robin asked.

Carla looked at Harriet.

"We ducked out of our lecture and followed Lauren's brother when he left the dining cabin after breakfast cleanup," Harriet said.

"And?"

"It looked like he was carrying a box of food. He went to some kind of garage structure on the other side of the photography building. We were sure he was leading us to Lauren's hideout."

"He was," Carla interrupted. "She just wasn't there."

"It was pretty clear she had been hiding there," Harriet agreed. "He beat on the doors and called to her."

"This just keeps getting better and better. If her brother didn't expect her to have moved, we have to ask ourselves if she moved on her own, or if someone moved her," Robin said. "I don't like this. If we can't find her pretty soon, we may need to get the police involved. From what you're telling me, she may be in real trouble."

"Let's go back to the Tree House," Harriet suggested. "We need to tell the rest of the group and get everyone looking for her."

✂ ✂ ✂

Mavis and Connie were in the kitchenette when Harriet, Carla and Robin got back. Connie was arranging molasses cookies on a green ceramic tray. Mavis was cutting apples into quarters and removing the cores.

"Guess you ladies couldn't sit through another lecture, either, huh?" she said.

"We decided to come back and get started on our blocks," Connie added. "After a little snack."

She pushed the platter of cookies toward Carla, who politely took one.

"By the way," Mavis said, "we found a note taped to the door when we got back. Beth sent a fax to you at the UPS Store, and someone from the school picked it up for you. It's in the front office." She fished the note out the pocket of her plaid shirt and handed it to Harriet.

"Thanks. I guess I'll go see what Aunt Beth's got for us."

Carla put her cookie down.

"You don't have to come. I'm just going to the office, and there are people going back and forth on all the paths."

"I think it'll be okay," Mavis agreed. "Harriet's right. You have your cookie, and when Harriet's back we'll see what Beth's dug up."

Connie poured a glass of milk and handed it to Carla—Harriet wondered if she noticed how the two of them worked at adding nutritious foods to her diet. She had to admit, Carla's skin was clearer for their efforts. If they knew she lived in a car they'd both have strokes, right there on the floor.

"See you in a few," she said, and left.

Tom was in the office when she arrived.

"Hey," he said.

"Hi, I came to pick up a fax from my aunt. Someone brought it here from the UPS Store."

"Yeah, that was me. I was shipping some stuff, and Bill asked if I'd bring you a fax. I left it with Nancy. She stepped out for a minute, but it should be right here."

He started ruffling through the papers on Nancy's desk.

The outside door opened, and two men dressed in jeans and plaid flannel shirts entered the reception area. Harriet moved aside to make room for them. The larger one pulled off his leather work gloves and took a business card from his shirt pocket. He reached across the counter and handed it to Tom.

"We're from Angel's Wing Landscaping. The boss said you have some monkshood you need removed."

"So I've been told," Tom said. "We've found some in a bouquet of cut flowers in one of the residence buildings. We usually get the flowers from our wildflower meadow, so I assume there must be some there. I don't know what it looks like, so I hoped you could

177

check the meadow and, if you find it, remove it. And while you're here, check the rest of the grounds and see if it's growing anywhere else."

"I'm going to be surprised if it turns out you have any here. It's not something that usually grows down this low on its own. Someone would have had to plant it."

"I don't care how it got here," Tom said, a hard edge creeping into his voice. "Someone used it to kill my mother, and I want it gone—now."

The man looked down, avoiding Tom's glare. "I'm sorry for your loss," he said. "Miz Bainbridge was a fine woman." He nudged his partner toward the door. "We'll get right on it."

Tom turned his back to Harriet and continued searching Nancy's desk.

"Here it is," he said and handed it to her. She took the envelope and started for the door. She stopped with her hand on the knob. "Can I ask you something?" she asked.

He looked up. "Sure," he said. "Anything."

"Why do you need to hire guys to identify monkshood for you?"

"Because I don't know what it looks like. Why?"

She turned back to face him. "It just seems a little odd that a guy with a degree in botany would need to hire people to identify a plant."

"What are you talking about?" His voice rose. "Why on earth do you think I have a degree in botany?"

"Patience mentioned it the other day. She said you worked for the forestry department before you came here. I thought she said you had a degree in botany."

"She was right. I did work for the Department of Forestry. As an architect. I still do work for them. I design buildings that are compatible with the forest. Visitor centers, fire lookout structures, that sort of thing."

"I was sure Patience said you were a botanist."

"She probably did. My mom and Patience were obsessed with quilting and this school. I told them a hundred times what I did, and it just went in one ear and out the other. They didn't really listen unless I said something about this school. My own mother

178

couldn't have told you what I did before I came here. I mean, she had a vague knowledge that I graduated from architecture school, but beyond that, not so much."

"Okay, I guess I'll see you later,"

"Wait a minute." He came around the counter and stood toe-to-toe with her. "You think I poisoned my mom, don't you?"

Harriet felt heat creep up her neck to her cheeks. "When Patience said you had a degree in botany, it sort of fit. Who better to condense a poisonous plant than a botanist?" She smiled an embarrassed smile.

"If this weren't so ridiculous I'd be insulted." He clasped her arms just below her shoulders, but before she got to find out what more he was about to say, the door to the office banged open and Aiden appeared.

"Oh, geez, not you again," Tom growled.

"Stop!" Harriet ordered.

"Get your hands off her."

"Aiden, stop—he didn't do anything. We're just talking."

"It doesn't look like 'just talking' from here. Your face is red, and he's got his hands on you again."

Tom dropped his hands and stepped back.

"We just had a misunderstanding," Harriet explained. "Not that it's any of your business. You're not my bodyguard."

"Somebody needs to be."

"Come on, let's not do this again."

He continued to glare at Tom.

"What I need from *both* of you is help," she said. "Lauren's missing."

"Didn't we already know that?" Aiden asked.

"We knew she was dodging the police, but I think she's *really* missing now." She explained her observation of Les, who had obviously expected to find Lauren in the equipment garage, leaving out the part about her and Carla tailing him.

"What do you need from me?" Tom asked.

"I'd like to search the grounds. Not the classrooms but any other outbuildings that might make good hiding spots. I hoped you could identify those places and maybe let us into buildings if they're locked. And if either of you is going into Angel Harbor this

179

afternoon, I'd like to check out Lauren's brother's apartment. She said she'd been staying there but wasn't going to anymore, but I'd still like to check just to be sure."

"You don't ask for much, do you?" Tom said.

"I know, and I'm sorry for what I said earlier, but I'm really starting to worry about Lauren."

Tom looked at his watch. "I have to go meet with a guy about security. The soonest I could look for Lauren would be around one o'clock."

"I have to go, too. I was just stopping by on my way to the hospital. I've got two more hours of surgery when I get back. I can come back after that—probably around two or two-thirty." Aiden took the key to the rental car from his pocket. "Should I meet you back here?"

"Sure, thanks." Lauren could be dead by then, but sure, she thought.

"I can check Les's apartment when I go into Angel Harbor," Tom offered. "I'm not a breaking and entering kind of guy, but I'll knock and see if anyone answers."

"Okay, I guess that's better than nothing."

"We could tell Detective Ruiz our concerns and let *him* search for Lauren," Tom said. "If you really think she's in danger, that might be the best thing to do."

"Detective Ruiz believes Lauren killed your mother. Somehow, I don't think he's going to be concerned about her welfare."

"I just wanted to put it out there," Tom said with a sigh. "I've got to go. I'll see you later." He nodded at Aiden and left the office as Nancy came back in.

Aiden walked Harriet back to the Tree House. "I still don't like that guy, but he does have a point about calling the police."

She stopped in the middle of the path. "Detective Ruiz wants to put Lauren in jail. With her attitude and big mouth, she's liable to resist arrest and end up in jail even though she didn't do anything."

"Okay, I guess I'll be back for the big search, then."

Harriet went up the steps to the Tree House without looking back.

Chapter Twenty-seven

Mavis, **Connie and Carla were seated at the dining table** when Harriet came in. Fat quarters of fabric, the quilters name for a half-yard of material that has been cut in half to make two eighteen-by-twenty-two-inch squares, sat in color-coordinated piles on the table top. Each pile had a swatch of the background fabric they'd been given for the memorial quilts next to it.

"Have you got it figured out?" she asked as she joined them.

"Not quite," Mavis admitted, "but we're getting there. We need a green option. Do you have anything with you that we could try?"

"I have a Kelly green piece with my half-rectangle stuff. Let me go get it." She dropped the envelope with the fax from Aunt Beth on the table and went upstairs, coming back down a few minutes later with her canvas project bag on her arm. She pulled out a handful of green fabric and laid it next to the nearest pile of fabric.

"Hmmm," Mavis said. "This might work."

"Help yourself, I've got plenty."

"What did Beth send?" Connie asked.

"I don't know. I haven't even looked."

Mavis stopped moving piles of fabric and looked at Harriet over the top of her reading glasses.

"You haven't looked?"

Harriet explained about Tom being in the office and Aiden's arrival. Connie picked up the envelope and handed it to her.

"So, let's find out."

There were several pages in the packet. The first was a cover sheet and the second a handwritten note from Beth.

I called the museum and said I was interested in commissioning a quilt that would be similar to the copy of Lauren's. I asked if they could take a couple of pictures, including one of the quilt label. I thought you might find that one useful. I asked for more information about the artist and I've included what they sent me. Let me know if you need anything else. "

It was signed, *Beth.*

Harriet pulled the pictures out and found the one of the label.

"Whoa," she said and began reading. "*Wildwood*, created by Patsy Jackson in September 2007 in Angel Harbor, Washington, USA."

"Who the heck is Patsy Jackson?" Mavis asked.

"Let me see here." Harriet flipped through the papers and pulled one to the top. "'Patsy Jackson is a teacher who comes to England four times a year to do workshops at the guild. She lives in Angel Harbor, Washington, and has been doing fiber arts for twenty-five years.' There's a handwritten addition that says they've been handling her work for five years and have many satisfied customers who would be willing to provide recommendations. It goes on to say that, for the protection of their artists, they don't give out phone numbers or addresses, but would be happy to have Mrs. Jackson contact Aunt Beth if she decided to go forward with her commission."

"I don't remember seeing a Patsy Jackson offering classes here," Mavis said.

"Me, either," Connie agreed. "I wonder what she teaches."

"Maybe she doesn't teach here," Harriet said and flipped through the papers again. "It only says she teaches in England. She *lives* in Angel Harbor, but it says nothing about her teaching here."

"How could she live here and be a quilt teacher and not teach at the Folk Art Center?" Connie asked.

"Politics, maybe," Mavis offered. "The question is, how did she get access to Lauren's quilt in order to copy it?"

"Maybe she's a student here," Carla suggested.

"Good point," Harriet said, and Carla blushed. "Or maybe more than one person is in on it. Maybe she has a partner here. How else could you explain the obvious copying that Carla and I saw? Maybe Patsy and Selestina did it together."

Aunt Beth had included another picture of the quilt, but it didn't reveal anything they didn't already know. It was a really good copy.

"The second round of lectures should be getting out in a few minutes. I think I'll go see if I can borrow a copy of the quilt block encyclopedia from one of the teachers," she decided. "We can look and see if there are any traditional pieced blocks that have the word *mother* in them. And I'll have a chance to ask about Patsy Jackson."

Carla gave her a questioning look.

"Carla, if you want to come with me, while I'm talking to the teachers, you can hang out with the students in the lobby and see if you hear any interesting gossip."

"If you aren't back in a half-hour, we're coming to look for you," Connie warned.

"Let's go," Harriet said.

Students were trickling out of the building when she and Carla arrived. A larger group was clustered around the table in the lobby that had the quilt information on it; Carla sidled up to them. Harriet continued on to the classrooms without saying anything. She found Ray Louise Hanson still in the room she lectured in.

She quickly determined that the school did have several quilt block books that could be loaned to students.

"Come with me back to the teachers' room and you can decide which one you want," Ray Louise said. She gathered her notes and put them in a pink rip-stop nylon bag.

"Do you know a teacher or artist named Patsy Jackson?" Harriet asked as she followed the teacher through the series of doors and short halls. "My aunt is thinking of having her make a wall hanging."

"I don't know anyone by that name." Ray Louise stopped abruptly and turned around. Harriet barely avoided running into her. "I do know your aunt Beth, though, and she could easily make any kind of quilt she could ever want. Whatever you're up to, you need to come up with a better cover story. Too many of us know Beth, and don't try to say it's not Beth. She's been very worried about you the last couple of years."

"Great," Harriet said with a fake smile.

"So, what *are* you up to?"

She explained about Lauren's missing work, Aunt Beth's discovery of the copy and Lauren's comments to anyone who would listen that resulted in her becoming suspect number one in Selestina's death. She finished up with Lauren's disappearance.

"Aunt Beth just faxed us a copy of the label, and it said the quilt was made by Patsy Jackson of Angel Harbor, Washington."

"That has to be an alias," Ray Louise said. "This community is too small for an art quilter of that level to exist here without some of us knowing her." She silently studied her shoe for a moment. "Tell you what," she said when she looked up again. "I'll ask all the teachers at lunch. Inessa Follansbee has been doing a workshop on stash management. She owns Angel Harbor Quilts, the local quilt store. If this Patsy exists, she has to buy fabric. Even if she's one of those people who buy their fabric online she would have to go in there sometime. I'll check with Inessa and let you know. Which residence are you staying in?"

Harriet gave her the particulars and thanked her for her help. Once more, Aunt Beth's big mouth had paid off.

"I have one more question," she said. "Is there a lot of pressure on the staff of the school to keep producing new work?"

"If you're asking if Selestina copied Lauren's work, she wouldn't need to do that as head of the school. Her teachers are a different story. Once most of the students have taken a class on a particular technique, the instructors can't fill a class anymore—there aren't enough new bodies coming in for that. Teachers have to continually come up with new and different projects and techniques to keep our base of repeat students coming back. And I'll tell you, it's hard.

"So, yes, I could see a teacher getting desperate and maybe copying a student's work, but they would have to teach it at a different school. Here people might recognize it. Then again, most teachers teach at multiple locations. Someone could copy work here and teach a class on the technique in a quilt store in Kansas

184

and no one would ever know."

"Thanks," Harriet said.

"Good luck finding your friend's work."

Harriet came back out to the lobby and found a group of women still clustered near the table of instructions. Someone was speaking loudly, and as she got closer she recognized Sarah's voice.

"I don't see why we have to use the theme of motherhood. There aren't any good blocks with *motherhood* in the name. If it's a gift from us to whoever, why can't we make what we think is meaningful? I'd like to make a block that represents the school. I've had such a great time here, I think an applique of the fiber arts building would be a better memorial. This is his mother's school, after all."

"It is hard to think of a motherhood block," a skinny blonde with thin lips said.

"And I don't think we should be limited to techniques we learned here for the other one, either," Sarah continued. "I took a class in Seattle and we made a paste out of flour and cornmeal and ginger ale and spread it on muslin and when it dried we shook it off and then we sprayed dye over the top and when it dries you wash it and the results are very cool."

The blonde asked a question about what, if any, fabric prep Sarah had done. Harriet looked around the entrance hall for Carla, and finally spotted her on a small hand-carved bench near the door to the outside. She crossed the space, and Carla stood up.

"I'm sorry. I couldn't take any more of Sarah. She isn't really letting other people talk anyway."

"Well, it was worth a try."

"It was kinda interesting before she showed up. That blonde in the tight jeans was riling people up about leaving. She said she never liked Selestina and…let me think…she said, 'I merely tolerated her so I could take classes from her teachers.' And then she said she would feel like a hypocrite going to her memorial service on Sunday."

"So, what did the other people say?" Harriet pulled the door open and ushered her out.

"They didn't get a chance to say anything. Patience came up and basically calmed everyone down. She told them that, in spite of Selestina's public persona, she was a real nice lady and only wanted what was best for the students, and after all was said and done, didn't they all have great memories of their time here? And then she said that although the school would continue and they would make many more memories, change was inevitable, and Selestina's passage marked the end of the era and surely that was worth celebrating."

"Did they buy it?"

"Everyone was kind of whispering among themselves, and I couldn't exactly hear what they were saying. I tried to get closer." Her face started to turn pink.

"Hey, you did great."

"I started to go up to the table, but then Sarah showed up and I didn't want her to figure out what I was up to." She held up a handful of paper and fabric. "I had to grab another set of stuff so I'd have a reason to be there. Then I made like I was leaving and found that bench."

Sarah caught up with them as they headed back toward the Tree House.

"I'm going to lunch with a friend," she said, emphasizing the word *friend*. Harriet presumed she was talking about whoever it was keeping her out late the last few nights. She couldn't help but notice that Sarah had abandoned her usual khaki twill pants and blazer for low-rise black slacks with a wide belt and a silky pink T-shirt that hugged her curves and revealed more cleavage than usual for a student at a quilt school.

She brushed past them and hurried on to the Tree House. Carla looked at Harriet and laughed. Harriet just shook her head.

Mavis and Connie were sitting on the sofa in the great room. Mavis had a sketchpad in her lap. Connie was cutting out images she'd drawn on a piece of freezer paper. She had obviously figured out a design, and it was going to involve applique. The waxy side of the freezer paper could be attached to fabric simply by ironing it on. It stuck well enough that you could cut out images drawn on the paper and then sew them to another piece of fabric; and when you were finished, it peeled off without leaving a residue.

"Tell me something good, chiquita."

"No one's heard of our Patsy," Harriet said. "Ray Louise said she'd ask around just to be sure, and she said she'd ask Inessa Follansbee, who owns Angel Harbor Quilts, the local fabric store. Do we have a lunch plan?"

"Are you hungry?" Mavis asked. "There are some of those molasses cookies on the counter in the kitchen."

"Thanks, but I was actually wondering if we could go to town for lunch. Les should be helping with the buffet here, and I'd like to go by his apartment and see if Lauren is there."

"Great minds think alike," Connie said. "Robin went upstairs to get ready while we were waiting for you. She heard about an Italian restaurant that's supposed to be good."

"If it's the one I went to, it's great. And it's perfect. That's where I was when I saw Lauren and Les go up to his apartment."

It was another fifteen minutes before everyone had used the bathroom, gotten her purse and put a coat of some sort on.

"Have *you* heard from Lauren?" Robin asked.

"No, and I take it you haven't either," Harriet said. "I don't like this." She opened the Tree House door. "I'm going to check her brother's apartment while we're at lunch, but I'm not holding out hope."

Chapter Twenty-eight

Tom Bainbridge was sitting at a window table when they entered the restaurant. He nodded at Harriet.

"I guess he likes this place," she said to Mavis.

The hostess led them to a table at the back of the room and handed out menus. The lunch special was a small pork chop with spaghetti marinara and a side salad with a scoop of spumoni ice cream for dessert. The six-dollar price was too good to pass up. The whole group chose the special, making it easy for their waitress.

"Anyone have any idea how I'm going to combine my less than spectacular hand quilting with half-square rectangles for my memorial block?" Harriet asked as they waited for their food.

"I know it isn't your usual style, but maybe you could piece your half-rectangles out of homespun fabrics and then quilt it with a coarse thread and make it look folk-arty," Mavis suggested, and in doing so began a lively discussion that lasted through dessert.

"I'd like to go to Les's apartment with Harriet," Robin said as everyone dug in purse or bag for lunch money. "Angel Harbor Quilts is two streets over and a couple of blocks down. You three can take the car if you want, and Harriet and I can join you there when we're done looking for Lauren." She held up her keys, and Mavis took them.

"We'll give you thirty minutes, and if you aren't at the quilt store we're coming after you." Connie said.

"If we find Lauren, we'll call, so turn your cell phones on."

Mavis and Connie were notorious for faithfully carrying their phones but just as religiously not turning them on. Both women dug in their bags and powered their units.

They split up at the door, and Harriet led Robin around the building and across the alley to where she'd seen Les and Lauren enter the night she'd had dinner with Tom. The door opened into a small entrance hall. Worn gray indoor-outdoor carpeting covered the floor, and dirty gray handprints dulled the beige paint that had probably looked tired when it was new. A row of metal mailboxes was set into the wall at the base of the stairs. Harriet read the names. "Sawyer" was listed as apartment number four.

The doors to the ground floor apartments were set at the back of the tiny vestibule, behind the stairs. A quick glance verified they were units one and two. Robin started up the stairs, and Harriet followed, trying not to touch the grimy handrail.

"I don't like the feel of this place," she said.

Robin stopped when she reached the landing at the top of the stairs. Apartment three was to the right with four on the left.

"Uh-oh," she said.

Harriet looked over her shoulder. The door to apartment four was partially open. She brushed past her and stepped into the doorway. She pulled her sweatshirt sleeve over her hand and pushed on the door.

The apartment had the look that was becoming all too familiar. It had been searched, and none too gently.

"Don't go in," Robin said. "Lauren!" she called out, but both women knew it wasn't likely there would be an answer.

"What's that on the floor?" A line of dark red drops dotted the linoleum just inside the door.

Robin crouched down and took a closer look. She groaned.

"What?"

"It's blood."

✂ ✂ ✂

As was required for an officer of the court, Robin called Detective Ruiz immediately. She might have been wearing a pastel-and-black yoga outfit, but she commanded Harriet stay out of the apartment with the kind of authority Harriet associated with uniforms.

"Lauren might be in the bedroom," Harriet protested. "Someone is obviously hurt, it could be her."

189

"The blood trail is leading from the living room to the door." Robin studied the floor at her feet. "This carpet is so dirty it's hard to tell, but I think the blood continues out here. Look." She pointed to a larger dark stain on the landing.

Harriet stiffened as she heard the downstairs door open.

"Why am I not surprised to find you here?" Detective Ruiz said to her as he ascended the stairs. "It's like I was saying the last time we met at a crime scene—you keep inserting your self into my investigation, and I have to keep asking myself why that would be."

"We came here looking for Lauren," she told him. "She came to Angel Harbor with us. Surely, you can understand why we might be worried about the fact that she's missing."

"We didn't go inside," Robin said in a business-like tone. "Her brother Les works at the Fiber Arts School; this is his apartment."

"Lauren told me she spent the first night she was missing here, but she claimed she was leaving for parts unknown. Knowing Lauren as we do, we figured she might be back here," Harriet added, trying to imitate Robin's tone.

"There's something that looks like blood here in the entry." Robin pointed.

"You two go downstairs and wait outside." Detective Ruiz motioned Officer Weber, who seemed to be his constant companion, inside the apartment. Weber drew his weapon and entered.

Harriet and Robin did as requested and went outside. Robin called Mavis and reported their situation.

"Someone is clearly looking for something more than your friend," Detective Ruiz said when he joined them in the alley. "What do you think that might be?"

"I have no idea," Harriet said immediately. "Lauren's quilt went missing. While we were helping her look for it, we discovered that someone's been making copies of student quilts and selling them. But since she doesn't have her quilt, we've been assuming the copycat was the one who stole it. I don't know why anyone else would be looking for it. Besides, the places that have been torn up aren't the kind of places I'd look for a quilt. We know Lauren doesn't have it, so why would someone look at her brother's place? And Tom's office makes no sense, either."

"We came here to find Lauren and tell her to turn herself in so we can get this cleared up. She didn't do anything to Selestina, even though someone went to some amount of trouble to make it look like she did," Robin said. "I'm getting worried for her safety."

"I'm starting to get worried about your client myself," Ruiz said. "Someone searched that apartment, but it also looks like there was a fight of some kind." He looked away.

"What?" Robin asked.

"Someone lost a lot of blood in the bedroom," he said somberly. "I've called for the forensic folks, and I also asked our crime scene reconstruction guy to come have a look. He'll be able to give us a better idea of what went on here. I'd like to talk to you again when we're done here." He looked at his watch. "It's going to take a couple of hours for my guy to do his thing, so shall we say four o'clock? I'll come by the school."

"Why is he being so nice all of a sudden?" Harriet whispered to Robin as the detective went back upstairs.

"He thinks something bad happened to Lauren, which means she's not the bad guy."

Harriet covered her face with her hands. "I've done my share of complaining about Lauren, but I never wanted anything like this to happen to her." She rubbed her eyes.

Robin called Mavis and Connie again and asked them to come back to the restaurant parking lot to pick them up.

"We might as well go back to the Tree House and try to do our blocks. I'm fresh out of ideas for places to look."

"Tom and Aiden are going to come this afternoon so we can look in the outbuildings at the school."

"I guess it can't hurt. We probably wouldn't be able to concentrate on our blocks anyway. I'll be surprised, though, if it turns out someone who would snatch Lauren would hide her at the school where we might stumble on her."

"I'm learning there are a lot of storage and utility spaces on the grounds, and several of them are hard to find unless you know they're there."

"I guess we can try," Robin said, and led the way back across the alley.

Mavis drove the minivan into the parking lot and opened the door. "You want to drive?" she asked.

"No, you go ahead," Robin told her, and collapsed into a middle row seat. Harriet climbed into the back row and put on her seatbelt.

"You two don't look so good," Connie said. "What happened?"

Harriet explained the details of their attempt to look for Lauren in Les's apartment.

"Tom and Aiden are going to help us search the grounds in a little while. Other than that, we wait and see what the police find out," she finished.

The group drove back to the Tree House, each lost in her own thoughts. The men were waiting on the porch when they trooped single file from the parking lot.

"Put a little oil on her dry food each morning, and it should help that," Aiden was saying to Tom when the women joined them.

"Thanks."

You would never have known Aiden had clubbed Tom in the jaw and Tom had knocked Aiden off this same porch not that long ago. They were smiling and talking like old pals.

"We're here for the big search," Aiden said. "On time, I might add." He checked his watch and then studied Harriet. "What happened?"

Harriet looked at Mavis. "Could you tell him? I need a few minutes." She went on into the house.

Mavis explained the latest news and assured him that nothing had happened to Harriet.

"Maybe I should send everyone home," Tom said.

"That might help," Mavis agreed. "But I doubt you'd get people to leave before the memorial for your mother. And we can't leave here without Lauren."

"I suppose."

✂ ✂ ✂

"Aiden and I talked this over while we were waiting," Tom said when Harriet came back down from her room. She'd washed her face, brushed her teeth and refreshed her deodorant. It didn't help solve the Lauren problem, but she did feel a tiny bit better.

"I brought a couple of maps of the property, and we've divided up the keys," Tom continued.

"Yeah, Harriet and I will be one team, and Robin, Tom and Carla will be the other," Aiden jumped in. He looked at Mavis. "We thought Connie and Mavis could man the phones so if one of us finds something, we can let them know and they'll contact the others."

"The cell phone reception is spotty up here, as I'm sure you've all noticed, but most of the buildings have phones in them, so call on the house phones if you need to," Tom finished.

He handed out the maps. He and Aiden had already divided the keys, obviously assuming the women would agree with their plan.

"As you can see from your maps, the property is roughly a rectangle. I thought we could start in opposite corners and work our way toward each other. The northeast corner is undeveloped, so there's nothing to search. The southwest area is where we are now. We don't really need to search here, and in any case we can do this area last. Aiden has the keys to the buildings on the west half of the property, and I kept the east-side keys. Any questions?"

They had all figured out. Mavis got bottles of water out of the refrigerator and handed one to each of the searchers.

"Good luck," she said. "And call if you find anything."

With a salute to Mavis and Connie, Aiden turned and grabbed Harriet's hand and led her out the door. Harriet shook the map open with her free hand.

"Seems like only yesterday I was in the northwest corner of the property—oh, wait, I was in the northwest corner...trapped in a basement!" she said.

"It will be different this time," Aiden said with a smile. "You'll have me. Maybe we can make a new memory to replace the bad ones."

Harriet rolled her eyes.

He stopped as soon as they were out of sight of the Tree House, pulled her to him and wrapped his arms around her.

"Hey, we're supposed to be looking for Lauren."

"We are," he said, but didn't loosen his hug. "There's no reason we can't do both." He kissed her, but she didn't respond.

"I can't do this right now. Not until we find Lauren. I was worried before, but at Les's apartment, when that detective said he was

193

worried, too, that was more frightening than anything that's happened so far."

"Okay, okay," He let her go and started down the path again. "We will be totally serious." He looked back at her with his best attempt at a serious face, but it was so obviously false, Harriet burst out laughing. "I'm glad you find my efforts to be serious so funny."

"This week hasn't turned out like I expected," Harriet said, catching up with Aiden and walking beside him.

"You mean you didn't expect the head lady to be murdered and one of the Loose Threads to be accused and then to disappear."

"That, and a few other things. And I never even wanted to come here in the first place. I really am more of a homebody. I know my aunt thinks I withdrew from society when Steve died, but she doesn't realize how much I liked spending time in my own home, even when he was alive.

"My parents dragged me all over the world. When I was with them, life happened at an accelerated pace. There were dinners and openings and museums, and if I never see another university science department it will be too soon. I know I was lucky, but I've seen enough. I want to spend time in my studio, with my fabric and my quilting machine. Is that so terrible?"

"Hey, whatever you want to do is fine with me. I'd be happy if you stayed in Foggy Point making quilts all day and sleeping in my arms all night."

"But first we have to find Lauren, and prove she didn't kill Selestina."

"Is that all? No problem."

The two landscapers Harriet had seen in the school office were in the meadow, each carrying a large green plastic bucket. They wore thick gloves and were picking plants that had clusters of purple flowers on thin stems. They carefully put the plants into their buckets, tucking the stems carefully below the rims.

"Those are the guys Tom hired to get rid of the poisonous plants," Harriet said. "It's kind of scary, thinking there were poisonous plants all over the place and any one of us could have accidentally come in contact with them."

"That's the same poison that was used to kill the Pakistani cricket coach at the World Cup a few years ago. At least, an anonymous caller said it was. I thought it grew in the mountains, though."

"I think it does, unless people get plants and put them in their wildflower gardens."

"Tom was telling me about his idea to build a couple of adult foster care homes in this meadow," Aiden said, changing the subject. "He's put a lot of thought into it. His mom could have lived her life out surrounded by art as her memory slipped away. I don't know if she had dementia or not, but he really does believe she did."

"Either that, or he's a good actor." She spotted the studio building in the distance. "We've been assuming someone wrecked his office, making him a victim. What if it was all a set-up? He could have trashed his own office, just like he could have run you off the road. When you think about it, he could be the one counterfeiting the student quilts. There's no reason a man can't be a quilter. And we know he does the shipping. Depending on how many he's selling, it could be a nice little income stream, and no one would be the wiser."

"I suppose he could have hired those landscape guys to reinforce the idea he couldn't recognize the poison plants," Aiden said. "Geez, I was just starting to like the guy, too."

"Do you think Carla and Robin are in danger being with him?"

"No, I don't. He's trying to prove to us that he's an innocent victim in all this. If he's done something to Lauren, he may very well lead them to her. Then again, it may be more effective if he lets *us* find her."

"You think Lauren's dead?"

"I think it's a possibility," Aiden said, his usual smile gone.

When they arrived at Selestina's workshop it was dark.

"Darn it," she said. "I didn't even think about bringing a flashlight. I don't know if the lights in the workshop survived the fire."

Aiden unlocked the workshop door, and she flipped all the switches on the panel to the right of it. Nothing happened. They both looked at the lights, and she flipped them again.

"We should have brought a flashlight," she repeated. "Carla and I searched the kitchen when we were locked in and all we found was a little penlight and a couple of birthday candles."

"There should be enough light from the windows to see if someone is in here," Aiden said and started forward.

"Not in the basement. And if I were going to hide someone, that's where I'd put them."

He sighed. "I've got a flashlight in my bag in the rental car," he said in a flat voice. "Come on, I guess we go back and get it."

"One of us could search the upstairs while the other goes to get the light."

"No, no and no. We do *not* split up for any reason. Let's just hurry back and get the light."

With him leading the way, they made a quick hike back past the Tree House and into the parking lot, where he quickly located the flashlight.

"As long as we're back here, I'm going to the ladies room," Harriet said.

From the parking lot, it was about equal distance to the Tree House or to the restroom behind the dining cabin. She headed for the latter.

"I'll be right here," Aiden said.

Chapter Twenty-nine

The restroom had a two-door set-up. The first one led into a vestibule with the second, which opened into the actual bathroom. The vestibule floor was covered with a piece of synthetic turf that caught the pine needles and debris that were everywhere in the forest. The left wall had a hinged chrome ring set flush to the surface. Harriet assumed it was the pull-out handle to a utility closet.

She pushed open the second door and entered the bathroom.

"Hi," said Jan Hayes. "I wasn't sure you were still here. I haven't seen you around."

"I've been struggling with my half-rectangle project at the Tree House."

Jan gave her a long look. "I thought maybe you were investigating Selestina's death. People were whispering in class yesterday about the police thinking your friend Lauren was involved."

Harriet's impulse was to say *she's not my friend*, but that seemed childish. "The police did question her, but I'm sure they've talked to lots of people. As far as I know, they still don't have a suspect in Selestina's death."

"I heard you solved the murder of Avanell Jalbert a while back. I figured you'd be investigating Selestina's death."

"It was just a coincidence that I was involved in Avanell's murder. I was in the wrong place at the wrong time. Normal people don't really solve murders. That just happens in books."

"Whatever you say," Jan said. "I better get back to the workshops. I'm making a sample using oil paint sticks on black satin.

197

Good luck with your quilt." She went out the door, leaving Harriet alone with her thoughts.

Harriet washed her hands when she had finished her business. She was impressed—the sink was equipped with small bars of French-milled soap and the faucets provided hot water as well as the usual cold most outdoor restrooms were notorious for.

She still had a paper towel in her hand as she opened the door to the vestibule. Later, she would remember the paper towel but not the scraping noise that must have accompanied the opening of the storeroom door. She fell as someone dragged her backward, covering her head with a coarse cloth. She took a breath, and her nostrils filled with dust and chaff, making her sneeze.

A cord tightened around her neck, and she grabbed at her throat, managing to slip the fingers of her right hand under the ligature before it cut her air off completely. She tried to cry out, but any noise she made was muffled by whatever was over her head. All she succeeded in doing was inhaling more moldy dust.

Then something was tied around the outside of the cloth, covering her mouth and effectively gagging her.

She was still being dragged backward, stumbling to keep from falling. She grappled around behind with her left hand, trying to grab whoever was forcing her backward, but she wasn't able to get a grip on anything and was unwilling to move her right hand from the rope at her throat.

She felt the soft surface of the artificial turf change to cement-like hardness as she was dragged through another door. She realized the storeroom must open to the men's room on its opposite side. The cool air when she stumbled through what felt like another door confirmed her suspicion. The storeroom connected the men's room to the ladies room, and she had just been forced through the men's-room door and was being pushed through the forest.

A berry vine slashed her where her jeans leg had ridden up, snagging on her sock and then pulling through her skin as she was half-dragged, half-pushed deeper into the woods. A rivulet of blood trickled down her leg, wetting the top of her sock. The cord around her neck was yanked tighter, and her vision dimmed. The last thing she heard was a grunting voice saying "You can wait here," followed by a laugh.

✂ ✂ ✂

198

When Harriet regained consciousness, the hood had been removed from her head and the rope from around her neck. The painful bruises were still firmly in place.

Wherever she was, it was dark—the sort of dark that prevents you from locating your hands when held in front of your face. She swallowed, and a spasm gripped her throat, making her cough. Which made her head hurt.

She stayed very still and took a couple of deep breaths through her nose. The air was stale, with a slight sour smell.

When she'd regained her equilibrium, she attempted to stand, and was immediately jerked back to the floor, banging her chin painfully on its wooden surface. Her ankles were bound together, her wrists tied behind her back.

A scratching noise interrupted her struggle. It sounded like a large rodent dragging a bag of rocks across the floor.

"Please don't be a rat," she said out loud. "Anything but a rat."

"Always the drama queen," a hoarse voice said from the dark.

"Lauren?"

"Who were you expecting, Brad Pitt? He's busy with Angie and the kids."

"Where are we?"

"How should I know? It's dark. I'm tied up, as I assume you are."

"How did you get here?"

"Stop with the questions already. My head hurts."

Harriet heard her retching, which was followed by a strange swooshing sound.

"Sorry," Lauren rasped. "Whoever put us here hit me in the head. I've been retching ever since I woke up."

"Thanks for sharing that."

"Your sympathy is overwhelming."

"Besides your head, how are you?"

"Oh, I'm just peachy. I'm tied here to my couch, and hey, now I have company. And if my life is going to end here, I can't think of anyone I like to see go down with me more."

"Do you have any other injuries? Assuming I can figure a way out of here, can you walk?" Harriet asked, but she was thinking, She has a couch? I'm here rolling around on the floor, and she has

199

a couch and is still complaining?

"I'm fine," Lauren said with a groan.

Harriet scooted backward until she located the wall behind her. The floorboards were rough, and her knuckles burned as she scraped the skin off of them in the process. She bent her body into a sitting position and, by pressing her back to the wall, was able to worm her way upright.

"Where are you going?" Lauren asked. "You're not leaving me here."

"Of course I'm not. I'm tied up, remember?"

With the wall for balance, and moving her feet in tiny shuffles, Harriet was able to inch along the perimeter of the room. She stopped and listened. She could hear the muffled rustle of wind in trees, but the structure they were in was silent save for the occasional creak of the floorboards.

"What are you doing?" Lauren asked.

Harriet sighed. "If you weren't interrupting me every minute, I'd be exploring my environment and trying to find something useful for getting us out of here. It might help if you would do the same thing."

"There's a smelly couch that I'm lying on and a large dead potted plant I've been retching into. Do you think you're the only clever one here? I searched as soon as I came to."

"Did you get off the couch?"

"Of course not, I'm tied up."

The wall behind Harriet became what felt like a doorway. She slowly turned her face toward the wall and began rubbing her cheek up and down where a switch plate should be. What's a little more lost skin, she thought, and promised herself a facial if she got out of this place alive. She'd even invite Lauren to join her.

She realized she was losing her touch with reality after that last thought. If she got out of this place alive, she was never going anywhere with Lauren Sawyer for the rest of her life.

Her search efforts were rewarded, and with a dull click weak yellow light illuminated the space. She looked around. The ceiling had open beams, and the walls were covered with a mismatched combination of plywood and drywall, with some sections not covered at all. Long wisps of cobweb coated with thick dust drooped in loops overhead while dust bunnies scampered along the floor.

Across the room, Lauren was slumped on a gray sofa with a broken leg that caused it to tilt at a crazy angle. Harriet began the slow shuffle across the plank floor to that corner, the rope around her ankles biting into her skin, sending burning pain up her calves with each step.

The closer she got the worse Lauren looked. The back of her straight blond hair was matted and dark. Her face was streaked with a combination of blood, dirt and tears. Her complexion was pale on a good day, but it now had a gray pallor.

"Tell me what happened to you," Harriet said as she got closer.

She noticed blood on the sofa where Lauren had been resting her head. Her stomach lurched, and she took two slow breaths through her nose. When her stomach steadied, she began again.

"Start with your morning visit to my room."

"What difference does it make? We're here now."

"Please, humor me. Have you got something better to do?"

"I was busy dying until you interrupted."

She was being sarcastic, but a closer look at her face suggested her comments might be closer to the truth than she intended.

"I don't know what good it will do until you tell me. If we can figure out who did this to us, maybe we can figure out where we are. If we know where we are, we can figure out how to get out."

"That's a lot of if-ing and figuring," Lauren said but began anyway. "I left your room and went to my brother's apartment. He had to go back to the school, and he was all worked up about those files he'd taken from Selestina's office. He was afraid the police would find them and think he'd killed her. He wanted to get rid of them, but he doesn't have a shredder, so I sat there with my scissors and cut each and every page into little tiny pieces."

"What was in the files?"

"I don't know. I was cutting, not reading. They were forms of some sort. Probably insurance. There were a few typed pages with signatures on them. It looked like it was employee benefits stuff. It took hours to cut it all up.

"When I was finished, I took the garbage bag full of pieces to the kitchen and put it under the sink, which is where Les keeps his recycling. He had nothing good to eat, so I made a piece of toast, ate it and then I lay down on his bed and took a nap." She laid her head back down on her arm.

"Don't stop. How did you end up here?"

"If I knew that don't you think I'd tell you?"

"What do you mean?"

"Do I have to spell it out? One minute I was sleeping on my brother's bed, the next I'm tied up in this dungeon with a giant headache."

"So, you didn't hear anyone, see anyone, nothing?"

"Hello, didn't I just say that? Now, stop talking, you're making my head hurt."

Harriet reached the sofa and knelt on the seat at the opposite end, facing the wall. A spring poked her knee through the threadbare upholstery. The wall behind the sofa was covered with hinged shutters. If she could pry them open, there just might be a window. A small brass latch held the shutter panels together.

"What are you doing?" Lauren asked.

Harriet looked at her and could see fresh tears streaking her face.

"It looks like this might be a shuttered window. I'm going to see if I can reach the shutters and try to get them open. If I can do that, and then if there's a glass window, I'll break the glass and hopefully get a piece of it and use it to cut your ties and then you can cut mine."

Lauren closed her eyes. "Let me know how that goes."

Moving around when your hands are tied behind your back and your feet tied to each other is a lot more difficult than it seems when you watch people on television do it. Harriet fell down onto the couch several times before she was able to balance on the back and press her face to the shutter. She turned it sideways so her cheekbone took the force of the fall as she propelled herself forward and into contact with the hinged pieces of wood.

Tears filled her eyes, and her nose ran when she hit, but she knew if she stopped she wouldn't start again. She worked her mouth into position and used her tongue to poke at the latch. The brass tasted terrible, and she had to stop and spit before she could continue. The hinge pinched her tongue; and when she slipped, it hit her teeth, sending sharp shards of pain into her skull, but she kept working at it until the hook piece finally flipped off the peg that held the two halves together.

The momentum it took to pull the shutters open knocked her back to the seat of the sofa. Lauren moaned when Harriet accidentally jostled her in the process.

"Sorry, but I got the shutters open."

"Could you see where we are?"

"There's a window, but it's boarded up on the outside, but that's a good thing. When I break the window, the glass will all stay within reach. Hopefully."

As she talked, Harriet worked her way around until she was balanced on the back of the sofa on her side with her feet in position to kick the window glass.

"Here goes nothing," she said, and kicked as hard as she could.

She fell back onto Lauren's legs, causing the prone woman to yelp, but the glass broke with a satisfying tinkle as broken pieces hit the sofa and floor. She spun around and looked at her handiwork. Several large shards remained in the window frame, held in place by the putty.

"I'm going to need your help for this next part," she said to Lauren.

"What do I have to do?" Lauren gave a world-weary sigh.

"I'm getting a piece of glass, and then I'm coming down beside you. You need to sit up, and I'll cut the rope around your wrists and then you can cut mine."

"Oh, no, sister. I'll cut yours first. If anyone's going to slip while they're sawing with a piece of glass, it's going to be me. I'm not having my hand sliced off by your ineptitude."

"Fine, just sit up, turn your back to me and get ready to be handed the glass."

Harriet wiggled around until her bound hands were able to reach the broken window. She pulled out a chunk of glass that was about the size of her fist and dropped back down to the sofa seat beside Lauren. She handed the glass off and with only minor slicing of her wrist, Lauren cut her bonds. Harriet immediately turned around and cut the rope binding Lauren's wrists.

Both women rolled their shoulders and then rubbed their wrists before they reached to their ankles to untie their feet.

"My knot won't move," Lauren whined. "It's hard as a rock."

"Someone was very clever. They saturated the knot with some kind of glue, probably the instant-drying kind." Harriet picked up the piece of glass again and sawed through the ropes on first Lauren's and then her own ankles.

"Can you stand up?" she asked.

"I think so," Lauren said. She rose and fell immediately back to the sofa.

"Take it slow," Harriet advised. She knew from her own experience with head injuries that slow was the only way to take it. She put her arm around Lauren's shoulders and helped her to her feet. They stood still for a moment and let Lauren's head stop spinning.

The door was locked, but the knob assembly was old and loose. Harriet leaned Lauren against the wall then jerked, twisted and rattled the brass knob. When it didn't yield, she went back to the sofa, retrieved the glass shard, wrapped it in the hem of her sweatshirt and used it carefully to pry the knob plate from the wood. The metal pieces fell away, leaving only a hole in the door.

She pulled the door inward and cautiously looked out. There was a landing of some sort that led to a narrow flight of stairs. The air outside their prison was cool and smelled fresh.

The stairway was dark, but the light from the room they were leaving gave enough illumination for them to descend. She retrieved Lauren and, once again putting her arm around her shoulders, guided her to the first step.

"Here, hold the rail," she whispered, and helped Lauren brace herself on the banister. "I'll stay ahead a few steps and make sure it's safe."

"I think I'm going to be sick," Lauren whispered.

"No, you are not. Your stomach is empty. Just stay there while I look ahead." She went down a few steps, crouching to see where they would come out. "Come on," she said, and continued to the bottom.

The stairs ended in a dark hallway. Harriet could see the top of another, wider flight at the opposite end of the hall. The one she and Lauren were on continued down.

"These must be servant's stairs," she whispered. "Tom and Aiden are searching the grounds looking for you, so hopefully we'll run into them once we get outside."

"What makes you think we're on school grounds?" Lauren whispered back. "This place doesn't smell like the forest, and it doesn't smell like dried flowers. Think about it—every room at the school had dried wildflowers in it. The place reeks of dried eucalyptus. And the Tree House smelled like the woods."

"You're right," Harriet said. "It doesn't smell like the school. Maybe this building has been closed up for a long time or something."

She knew as she said it the air smelled too fresh for it to be true, but she didn't want to admit that to Lauren.

The second flight of stairs took them into a narrow, unlit room. Dark stone countertops with pale wood cabinets over them lined the walls. Rows of various styles of wine glasses were lined up on one counter. A flat wooden box with individually wrapped tea bags sat on the opposite side.

"This looks like a butler's pantry," Harriet said. She smelled the faint scent of lemon oil wood cleaner mingled with lavender. This was clearly a place where someone lived, or which was at least cleaned on a regular basis.

She tiptoed to the door and found herself looking into a kitchen. Dim light spread out from the hood over the stove.

There was no evidence of life, so she helped Lauren over to a Formica-topped table in the middle of the room and pulled out a chair.

"I'm getting us some water before we go any farther," she said in a slightly louder whisper. She located two glasses and filled them from the tap. "Here." She pushed one into Lauren's shaking hand. "Don't drink it too fast."

"I'll just wait here," Lauren said when she'd finished, and laid her head down on the table.

"Come on—whoever brought us here could come back at any moment." She took the empty glass from Lauren's hand and pulled her to her feet. Lauren swayed and tried to slump back down to the chair.

"Okay, you can rest for a minute while I call Aiden." Harriet dug in her jeans pocket and pulled out her cell phone. She flipped it open and walked around the kitchen watching the small screen for signs of reception. By the stove, one bar popped to life. She punched Aiden's number in. The call rang but went directly to his voice mail.

"Aiden," she said. "Lauren and I were tied up in a house, but we got loose and are about to go outside, I don't know where we are yet, but—"

The signal went dead.

"Do you see a phone anywhere?" she asked Lauren, but Lauren's eyes were closed so clearly she wasn't seeing anything.

Harriet stepped carefully to a door that looked as if it might lead out of the room. She pushed it open a crack and could see a heavy wood mission-style dining room table surrounded by chairs. Beyond was a living space. Weak light from an outside light illuminated the far room. Night had fallen while they'd been in the attic.

She stepped through the door and quickly scanned the dining and living rooms for a phone. If there was one, it wasn't obvious.

"Come on," she ordered Lauren when she returned. "Naptime's over."

"Huh?"

Harriet put her forearms under Lauren's armpits and hauled her upright. "I know your head hurts, but we have to get out of here."

Lauren tried to shake her off but didn't have the strength to mount much opposition.

"We're going through the dining room and the living room and then outside." She looked at Lauren's pale, tear-streaked face. "Are you ready?"

"Of course I'm not ready," Lauren mumbled but she shuffled forward.

It seemed like an eternity until they reached the door. Lauren had to rest every few steps while Harriet looked behind and ahead of them, listening carefully for any sign they had been discovered.

"When we get outside, we're going to move immediately to the nearest cover. We're not going to stop."

"Whatever you say, Rambo."

Lauren agreeing without a fight worried Harriet more than the bump on her friend's head. She looked at Lauren's face. Her eyes had a dull look she hadn't noticed before. She was no doctor, but anyone could see Lauren was not doing well. She needed medical attention, and she needed it now.

"Let's go."

A narrow porch ran the width of the house. Harriet half-carried Lauren outside and eased the door shut behind them. She took a deep breath and could smell the salty tang of sea air. They definitely weren't on school grounds.

She couldn't think about that right now. She had to focus on Lauren. The four porch steps were a challenge, but Lauren staggered down them and kept moving until they had crossed a small, neat yard and forced their way into a laurel hedge. Lauren collapsed to the ground.

"You can leave me here while you go for help," she moaned.

"Sorry, we don't know whose house this is, but whoever lives here was, at the very least, willing to let us be tied up in their attic. And more than likely, it belongs to the person who put us there. So, get up, we have to keep moving."

If looks could kill, Harriet would have been a goner, but Lauren pulled herself upright again.

The laurel hedge ran along a gravel driveway and soon gave way to dark forest. Lauren was stumbling badly on the rough forest floor. She wasn't going to make it if they stayed in the woods. Harriet didn't like the idea of walking out in the open, but there was no choice. She pulled Lauren onto the driveway and started again.

They had gone no more than a hundred yards when Harriet heard the unmistakable sound of tires on gravel. Someone was coming. She helped Lauren back off the road and propped her against a tree. As the car came into sight, Harriet recognized the boxy shape of a Ford Explorer. And it was black.

She stepped into the road and waved her arms. The car lights blinded her.

"Help!" she cried. "Can you help me?"

The car stopped, and a small form got out.

"Harriet? Is that you?"

"Oh, Patience, thank heaven, it's you. Someone tied me up in an attic, and Lauren was up there, too, and she's badly injured."

"How dreadful," Patience said. "We've all been looking for you.

Here, get in the car." She pulled the door to the back seat open.

"Wait, I've got to get Lauren."

"She's with you?"

"Yes, she's behind that tree." She pointed. "And she's not in very good shape. Whoever kidnapped her hit her on the head, and it looks pretty bad."

"You get in the car, and I'll go fetch her."

Harriet climbed into the warm car and slumped against the seat. She pulled out her cell phone and dialed Aiden again. This time, he picked up on the first ring.

"Thank heaven, you're there," Harriet said. "Lauren and I were trapped in an attic, but it's okay now, Patience just found us. Hang on." At that moment, Patience opened the car door opposite Harriet and pushed Lauren in. Harriet put the phone down and helped get her onto the seat. She reached across Lauren, stretched the seatbelt into position and clicked the buckle. Then she belted herself.

"I think we should take Lauren directly to the hospital," she said.

"The house here is much closer. We can take her inside and then call nine-one-one." Patience got into the car and guided it back to the house.

"No, Patience, it's not safe. This is the house where we were being held hostage."

"Someone must have broken in, then," Patience said. "No one lives in this house, and we're miles from anywhere. This is the closest place to call an ambulance from."

It didn't seem like the best plan to Harriet, but Patience knew Angel Harbor better than she did. Lauren definitely needed to get to the hospital as quickly as possible. All the moving around was taking its toll.

Patience held her on one side and Harriet the other as they wrestled her back up the porch steps and into the house. She flopped down onto the sofa when they let go of her.

"Who's house is this?" Harriet asked. She picked Lauren's feet up off the floor and lifted them onto the sofa. She took a throw pillow from the chair opposite the sofa and gently slid it under Lauren's head.

"It used to be my parents'," Patience replied. "I told Tom I would look for you and Lauren in the woods around here since I had to drive over here to water the house plants anyway." She walked back toward the entrance and opened an interior door set into the wall. A coat closet, Harriet presumed. "My mother died right after Christmas, you see. I've been getting the house ready to sell."

"Where's the phone?" Harriet asked. "We need to call for the ambulance."

"I had it disconnected after the funeral," Patience said in a conversational tone. "Mother had a lot of hospital bills, so there wasn't any money left for extras." She turned around. "And it won't be necessary, anyway," she said.

It took a moment for Harriet to register the shotgun.

"You?" Harriet asked. "You were the one who tied us up in the attic?"

Patience made a slight bow.

"Why?"

"Because you couldn't keep your nose out of other people's business."

"Did you seriously think you could kidnap Lauren and hold her hostage, and that no one would come looking for her?"

"And that one…" Patience waved the barrels of her gun toward Lauren and went on speaking as if Harriet hadn't said anything. "She couldn't keep her mouth shut. She was constantly blabbing about her amazing design and how someone had copied it. Hah! If she only knew. I only got half as much for her design as I did for Jan Hayes's tone-on-tone kaleidoscope."

"Why did you need to take *anyone's* design? You're an accomplished artist. Couldn't you just sell your own work?"

"Couldn't you just sell your own work," she repeated in a nasal sing-song voice. "Do you really think I'm so stupid I didn't think of that? No one wants my traditional calico pieced quilts. They want modern art quilts. But more important, to continue to teach you have to have *fresh* work."

"But surely that doesn't apply to you. You're a partner in the business. Aren't you?"

"I am. Or I would be if your friend here hadn't stolen

Selestina's new will."

"My God." Harriet sank down onto the sofa beside Lauren as the enormity of what Patience was saying sank in. "You killed Selestina? She was your *friend*."

"Exactly—she was my friend. And as her friend, I've spared her the indignity she would have most certainly suffered."

"So, she did have dementia," Harriet said with satisfaction.

"Yes, she did. My old friend was gone. Oh, she could still fool the students, but my old friend was gone."

"If you were so close, why hadn't she made you a partner before this?"

"She *was* my friend, but to her I was always an employee. One she shared her hopes and dreams with, one she shared a good bottle of wine with over an expensive dinner—Dutch treat, of course; but at the end of the day, I was an employee."

"If she rewrote her will making you a partner, why did you need to kill her? Tom was going to make a foster care home in the meadow."

"Don't be so dense, Harriet," Lauren mumbled from the sofa without opening her eyes. "Selestina wasn't ever going to make Patience a partner. Les overheard them talking. Patience tried to talk her into it, but Selestina wasn't the kind of person who would acknowledge the work of others. She may have had dementia, but it hadn't made her any nicer. She laughed at Patience."

"That's not true!" Patience cried.

"If there was a new will, it was forged. Or maybe she tricked Selestina into signing it. But Les says the old bat would have never shared the school with anyone."

"Why didn't you just go somewhere else?" Harriet asked. She slowly eased a second pillow from the chair and held it as if she were going to use it to adjust Lauren's position.

"Are you really that naive?" Patience snapped. "No one wants my work. The schools don't want quilting teachers; they want art teachers who quilt. Besides, I spent the best years of my life building up this school. You met Selestina. Do you think people would have kept coming back if I hadn't been smoothing ruffled feathers and quietly giving students discount coupons if they'd come back again.

"And she was no businesswoman. I redid the catalog every year after she'd okayed it for print. All those years, and once she thought it had gone to print, she never even checked it again."

She was consumed by her righteous anger. Harriet kept her eyes on her but inched slowly to the end of the couch. She just needed Patience to talk for another minute and she'd be clear of the coffee table.

"She was nothing without me," Patience continued, pacing in a small rectangle along the corridor between the dining room and the front door. The shotgun was held loosely in her arms. "It was me who recruited the top teachers, me who called quilt guilds across the country."

It was now or never. When Patience once again turned toward the dining room, Harriet threw the pillow toward the table. As she'd hoped, Patience raised the gun and shot at it. As she did, Harriet dove forward, rolling into her shins. The gun went flying, and Patience hit the floor hard on her back.

Harriet planted a knee in her chest and pressed down, making sure she couldn't catch the breath that had been knocked out of her.

"Here," Lauren said, startling her. She held a thin cord in her hand. Harriet took it and tied Patience's hands behind her.

Lauren sank to the floor. Harriet wouldn't have believed she could have gotten off the couch. She had not only done so but had pulled the lace from her tennis shoe.

"You'll not get away with this," Patience growled. "It will be my word against yours. I'll tell them you came in here and attacked me when I accused you of copying my work."

Harriet looked around the room. Heavy velvet drapes from an earlier era were held back from the front window by a decorative gold tieback cord. She left Patience for a moment and retrieved a cord, letting the drape fall over the window. When she had secured the woman hand and foot, she patted her down, retrieving the car keys.

"Where are you going?" Lauren cried when she saw Harriet move toward the front door.

Harriet paused.

"I was calling Aiden when Patience put you in the car. I put my

211

phone down to help and never picked it up again. Hopefully, it's still there."

She quickly found her phone and returned to the house. She called Aiden but was immediately transferred to his voicemail, which probably meant he had no reception. She tried the Tree House number but got no answer there, either.

"You'll never get away with this," Patience said.

"Funny, I was thinking the same thing about you." Harriet laughed. She dialed nine-one-one. She asked the operator to please notify Detective Ruiz and send an ambulance for Lauren.

Chapter Thirty

Mavis and the rest of the Loose Threads were gathered in the great room of the Tree House when Officer Weber drove Harriet back to the school. He insisted on walking her to the door over her objections, but in reality, she leaned on him more than a little as they walked the path from the parking lot to the porch.

Detective Ruiz had asked her to be available for questioning then after taking a good look at her said, he could come by the Tree House after he was done processing Patience.

"Oh, honey," Mavis said, "come in and tell us what happened."

"*Diós mio,*" Connie said. "Sit down." She motioned to Sarah to move over and make a place for Harriet on the sofa. "Go get a wet wash cloth," she ordered.

Sarah rolled her eyes and sighed but didn't get up. Carla jumped up from her perch on the stone hearth.

"I'll get it."

Connie glared at Sarah and went back to adjusting the pillows behind Harriet and putting her feet up on the coffee table.

"Oh, your poor ankles," she said as Harriet's pant leg rode up and everyone could see the angry gash the bindings had made.

Carla returned with the washcloth, and Connie swabbed Harriet's face and hands. Mavis handed her a mug of peppermint tea with honey in it.

"Enough," she finally said, but did take the proffered chocolate chip cookie.

"Start with your search of the buildings with Aiden," Mavis prompted.

Harriet had just started when Aiden and Tom arrived. They had been searching for her and Lauren, and had just gotten word the women had been found.

"I didn't know who had taken me until Lauren and I had escaped," she concluded after describing her kidnapping from the restroom and escape from the attic. "Has anyone heard how Lauren's doing?" she asked, suddenly aware she'd been so wrapped up in her own rescue she'd forgotten to worry about Lauren.

"I called the hospital a few minutes ago," Robin reported. "She's conscious, but they're running tests. The nurse said she's dehydrated and had lost some blood from her head wounds, so she'll probably be in the hospital a few days. They also suspect she has a concussion."

"I don't get it," Sarah said. "Why on earth would that little mouse kidnap Lauren and Harriet? Didn't she tell us she's a partner in the school? It seems a little counterproductive to kidnap students. Who'd want to come back after that?"

"She wasn't a partner," Tom said, a little louder than was necessary. "I'm sorry, but that witch spread a pack of lies about me and my mother. My mom did have dementia, Patience wasn't a partner and I'm not a botanist." He looked at Harriet when he said the last bit.

"But why did she target Lauren?" Robin asked.

"I think I can answer that," Detective Ruiz said. No one had noticed him come in. "What do I need to do to get a drink around here?"

"We've got tea," Mavis said and got up to get a cup.

"Here, sit down," Connie said and offered him the twig rocker. Mavis brought him tea and a small plate of cookies.

"Thank you." He nodded at Mavis. He sipped his tea and closed his eyes briefly. "My mother always made us tea when we were sick," he said with an embarrassed smile.

Aiden crossed the room and wedged himself in between Sarah and Harriet on the sofa. Tom sat on the floor in front of the river-rock fireplace.

"Lauren was targeted by Patience for two reasons," Detective Ruiz began. "First, it seems that with, to quote Patience, 'that meddling Harriet Truman's help,' Lauren had figured out that her

214

work had been copied and the copy was being sold in Europe. It seems that Patience had been copying and selling student work for years, and no one was the wiser.

"But the main reason she went after Lauren is that Patience had drawn up a new will for Selestina and had tricked her into signing it. After she set the poisoning in motion—that is, she laid out the poisoned thimble and waited for Selestina to use it—she put the new will in a file of employee benefits documents and left it on top of the victim's desk where it could be easily found. The files disappeared, and Patience came to believe that Lauren had them."

"She did," Harriet said. "She just didn't know what she had. Her brother took the files off Selestina's desk. He was in her office and heard someone coming so he just took the whole pile. He and Lauren were searching for evidence of the quilt copying. When Lauren became a suspect, they shredded the files, not realizing they had shredded the fake will."

"I talked to Les," Tom said. "Patience had figured out he must have known something or seen something or at least would have access to something, and she was blackmailing him for reasons I won't go into. When he realized she was targeting Lauren, he tried to get his sister out of here, but Lauren wouldn't stay where he'd put her, and when she went back to his apartment, Patience found her. Les got rid of the files because he didn't want to be implicated in whatever scam Patience was running."

"So, in the end, it was about money and status," Mavis said.

"I'm embarrassed to say I never looked at the teacher payroll until my mother died," Tom said. "I feel partly responsible for all this." He hung his head and took a deep breath. "When I did look at the finances I was shocked to see how little my mother paid Patience. And I guess it's no secret that my mom was difficult to work with. She could have driven anyone over the edge. When I saw what my mom had been doing, I had planned to give Patience a big raise, and then, when my mom no longer was able, I was going to let her run the place." He sighed again.

"I guess she had the same idea," Harriet said. "Only she couldn't wait."

"It's all so senseless," Tom said, and rubbed his hands over his face.

"Oh, honey, you can't blame yourself," Mavis said. "Being difficult is not a reason to kill someone."

"What will happen to her?" Carla asked, and blushed at the sound of her own voice.

"She'll be tried for the murder of Selestina Bainbridge," Detective Ruiz said. "And the attempted murder of Cammi Johnson and Aiden Jalbert.

"We'll investigate the fire in the workshop and see if we've got any evidence to tie her to that. And, of course, the kidnapping and holding of two people against their will. She won't be going anywhere for a long while when we get done with her."

"It's all so senseless," Robin said.

"Crime generally is," Detective Ruiz said. He stood up. "Thank you for the tea and cookies." He looked at Harriet. "If you can come by the station tomorrow we can take your statement then. There's no reason to keep you up tonight." He looked at his watch. "If you hurry, you can get some sleep before then."

"Oh, my goodness, look how late it is," Connie said, looking around the room.

Tom took the hint. "Thank you for everything," he said. He went to Harriet and clasped her hands. "Patience might have gotten away with this if you hadn't put the pressure on her. If you ever want to come back to the school, you've got a lifetime scholarship."

He let go of her hands. Aiden stood up, and a look passed between the two men. What started as a handshake became a bear hug.

"I'll see you next week," Aiden said.

Tom turned away without saying anything, but Harriet could see tears glistening in his eyes. He raised his hand in a wave to the rest of the group and continued out the door.

"You two certainly seem chummy all of a sudden," she said.

"We had a lot of time to talk when we were searching the grounds." He sat back down. "We realized we share a rather exclusive club that no son ever imagines qualifying for."

Harriet rubbed his muscular back with one hand.

The Loose Threads made a show of leaving the great room, with the exception of Sarah, who only left when Connie pulled her to her feet and pushed her toward the stairs. Aiden told Carla he had a business proposition to discuss with her and asked if they could talk the following day during lunch. The young woman looked at Harriet, who nodded encouragement, and then said yes before hurrying away.

"Alone at last," Aiden said, and put his arms around Harriet, pulling her to him. She started to speak, but he kissed her, ending all thoughts of conversation.

END

ABOUT THE AUTHOR

Attempted murder, theft, drug rings, battered women, death threats and more sordid affairs than she could count were the more exciting experiences from ARLENE SACHITANO's nearly thirty years in the high-tech industry.

Prior to writing her first novel, *Chip and Die* (Zumaya 2003), Arlene wrote the story half of the popular Block of the Month quilting patterns "Seams Like Murder," "Seams Like Halloween" and "Nothing's What it Seams" for Storyquilts.com, Inc. *Quilter's Knot* is the second book in the Harriet Truman/Loose Threads quilting mystery series. Arlene also has written a scintillating proprietary tome on electronics assembly.

ABOUT THE ARTIST

APRIL MARTINEZ was born in the Philippines and raised in San Diego, California, daughter to a US Navy chef and a US postal worker, sibling to one younger sister. From as far back as she can remember, she has always doodled and loved art, but her parents never encouraged her to consider it as a career path, suggesting instead that she work for the county. So, she attended the University of California in San Diego, earned a cum laude bachelor's degree in literature/writing and entered the workplace as a regular office worker.

For years, she went from job to job, dissatisfied that she couldn't make use of her creative tendencies, until she started working as an imaging specialist for a big book and magazine publishing house in Irvine and began learning the trade of graphic design. From that point on, she worked as a graphic designer and webmaster at subsequent day jobs while doing freelance art and illustration at night.

In 2003, April discovered the e-publishing industry. She responded to an ad looking for e-book cover artists and was soon in the business of cover art and art direction. Since then, she has created hundreds of book covers, both electronic and print, for several publishing houses, earning awards and recognition in the process. Two years into it, she was able to give up the day job and work from home. April Martinez now lives with her cat in Orange County, California, as a full-time freelance artist/illustrator and graphic designer.

Printed in the United States
1467801V00008B/27/P